PENGUIN BOOKS
Moonraker

Bond paused, almost carried away by the story of
this extraordinary man.

'Yes,' said M. 'Peace in Our Time – This Time. I
remember the headline. A year ago. And now the
rocket's nearly ready. "The Moonraker". And from
all I hear it really should do what he says. It's very
odd.' He relapsed into silence, gazing out of the
window.

He turned back and faced Bond across the desk.

'That's about it,' he said slowly. 'I don't know
much more than you do. A wonderful story.
Extraordinary man.' He paused, reflecting. 'There's
only one thing . . .' M tapped the stem of his pipe
against his teeth.

'What's that, sir?' asked Bond.

M seemed to make up his mind. He looked mildly
across at Bond.

'Sir Hugo Drax cheats at cards.'

Ian Fleming was born in 1908 and educated at Eton. After a brief period at the Royal Military Academy at Sandhurst he went abroad to further his education. In 1931, having failed to get an appointment in the Foreign Office, he joined Reuters News Agency. During the Second World War he was Personal Assistant to the Director of Naval Intelligence at the Admiralty, rising to the rank of Commander. His wartime experiences provided him with a first-hand knowledge of secret operations.

After the war he became Foreign Manager of Kemsley Newspapers. He built his house, Goldeneye, in Jamaica and there at the age of forty-four he wrote *Casino Royale*, the first of the novels featuring Commander James Bond. By the time of his death in 1964, the James Bond adventures had sold more than forty million copies. *Dr No*, the first film featuring James Bond and starring Sean Connery, was released in 1962 and the Bond films continue to be huge international successes. He is also the author of the magical children's book *Chitty Chitty Bang Bang*.

The novels of Ian Fleming were immediately recognized as classic thrillers by his contemporaries Kingsley Amis, Raymond Chandler and John Betjeman. With the invention of James Bond, Ian Fleming created the greatest British fictional icon of the late twentieth century.

THE JAMES BOND BOOKS

Casino Royale

Live and Let Die

Moonraker

Diamonds are Forever

From Russia with Love

Dr No

Goldfinger

For Your Eyes Only

Thunderball

The Spy Who Loved Me

On Her Majesty's Secret Service

You Only Live Twice

The Man with the Golden Gun

Octopussy/The Living Daylights

Moonraker

IAN FLEMING

PENGUIN BOOKS

PENGUIN BOOKS

Published by the Penguin Group
Penguin Books Ltd, 80 Strand, London WC2R 0RL, England
Penguin Putnam Inc., 375 Hudson Street, New York, New York 10014, USA
Penguin Books Australia Ltd, 250 Camberwell Road, Camberwell,
Victoria 3124, Australia
Penguin Books Canada Ltd, 10 Alcorn Avenue, Toronto, Ontario, Canada M4V 3B2
Penguin Books India (P) Ltd, 11 Community Centre,
Panchsheel Park, New Delhi – 110 017, India
Penguin Books (NZ) Ltd, Cnr Rosedale and Airborne Roads,
Albany, Auckland, New Zealand
Penguin Books (South Africa) (Pty) Ltd, 24 Sturdee Avenue,
Rosebank 2196, South Africa

Penguin Books Ltd, Registered Offices: 80 Strand, London WC2R 0RL, England

www.penguin.com

First published in Great Britain by Jonathan Cape Ltd 1955
Published by Hodder and Stoughton 1989
Published simultaneously by Penguin and Viking 2002
2

Set in 9.75/14pt Melior
Typeset by Intype London Ltd
Printed in England by Clays Ltd, St Ives plc

CONTENTS

Part One / *Monday*

The two thirty-eights roared simultaneously.

The walls of the underground room took the crash of sound and batted it to and fro between them until there was silence. James Bond watched the smoke being sucked from each end of the room towards the central Ventaxia fan. The memory in his right hand of how he had drawn and fired with one sweep from the left made him confident. He broke the chamber sideways out of the Colt Detective Special and waited, his gun pointing at the floor, while the Instructor walked the twenty yards towards him through the half-light of the gallery.

Bond saw that the Instructor was grinning. 'I don't believe it,' he said. 'I got you that time.'

The Instructor came up with him. 'I'm in hospital, but you're dead, sir,' he said. In one hand he held the silhouette target of the upper body of a man. In the other a polaroid film, postcard size. He handed this to Bond and they turned to a table behind them on which there was a green-shaded desk-light and a large magnifying glass.

Bond picked up the glass and bent over the photograph. It was a flash-light photograph of him. Around his right hand there was a blurred burst of white flame. He focused the glass carefully on the left side of his dark jacket. In the centre of his heart there was a tiny pinpoint of light.

Without speaking, the Instructor laid the big white man-shaped target under the lamp. Its heart was a black bull's-eye, about three inches across. Just below and half an inch to the right was the rent made by Bond's bullet.

'Through the left wall of the stomach and out at the back,' said the Instructor, with satisfaction. He took out a pencil and scribbled an addition on the side of the target. 'Twenty rounds and I make it you owe me seven-and-six, sir,' he said impassively.

Bond laughed. He counted out some silver. 'Double the stakes next Monday,' he said.

'That's all right with me,' said the Instructor. 'But you can't beat the machine, sir. And if you want to get into the team for the Dewar Trophy we ought to give the thirty-eights a rest and spend some time on the Remington. That new long twenty-two cartridge they've just brought out is going to mean at least 7900 out of a possible 8000 to win. Most of your bullets have got to be in the X-ring and that's only as big as a shilling when it's under your nose. At a hundred yards it isn't there at all.'

'To hell with the Dewar Trophy,' said Bond. 'It's your money I'm after.' He shook the unfired bullets in the chamber of his gun into his cupped hand and laid them and the gun on the table. 'See you Monday. Same time?'

'Ten o'clock'll be fine, sir,' said the Instructor, jerking down the two handles on the iron door. He smiled at Bond's back as it disappeared up the steep concrete stairs leading to the ground floor. He was pleased with Bond's shooting, but he wouldn't have thought of telling him that he was the best shot in the Service. Only M was allowed to know that, and his Chief of Staff, who would be told to enter the scores of that day's shoot on Bond's Confidential Record.

Bond pushed through the green baize door at the top of the basement steps and walked over to the lift that would take him up to the eighth floor of the tall, grey building near Regent's Park that is the headquarters of the Secret Service. He was satisfied with his score but not proud of it. His trigger finger twitched in his pocket as he wondered how to conjure up that little extra flash of speed that would beat the machine, the complicated box of tricks that sprung the target for just three seconds, fired back at him with a blank .38, and shot a pencil of light aimed at him and photographed it as he stood and fired from the circle of chalk on the floor.

The lift doors sighed open and Bond got in. The liftman could smell the cordite on him. They always smelled like that when they came up from the shooting gallery. He liked it. It reminded him of the Army. He pressed the button for the eighth and rested the stump of his left arm against the control handle.

If only the light was better, thought Bond. But M

insisted that all shooting should be done in averagely bad conditions. A dim light and a target that shot back at you was as close as he could get to copying the real thing. 'Shooting hell out of a piece of cardboard doesn't prove anything' was his single-line introduction to the Small-arms Defence Manual.

The lift eased to a stop and as Bond stepped out into the drab Ministry-of-Works-green corridor and into the bustling world of girls carrying files, doors opening and shutting, and muted telephone bells, he emptied his mind of all thoughts of his shoot and prepared himself for the normal business of a routine day at Headquarters.

He walked along to the end door on the right. It was as anonymous as all the others he had passed. No numbers. If you had any business on the eighth floor, and your office was not on that floor, someone would come and fetch you to the room you needed and see you back into the lift when you were through.

Bond knocked and waited. He looked at his watch. Eleven o'clock. Mondays were hell. Two days of dockets and files to plough through. And weekends were generally busy times abroad. Empty flats got burgled. People were photographed in compromising positions. Motorcar 'accidents' looked better, got a more cursory handling, amidst the weekend slaughter on the roads. The weekly bags from Washington, Istanbul, and Tokyo would have come in and been sorted. They might hold something for him.

The door opened and he had his daily moment of pleasure at having a beautiful secretary. 'Morning, Lil,' he said.

The careful warmth of her smile of welcome dropped about ten degrees.

'Give me that coat,' she said. 'It stinks of cordite. And don't call me Lil. You know I hate it.'

Bond took off his coat and handed it to her. 'Anyone who gets christened Loelia Ponsonby ought to get used to pet names.'

He stood beside her desk in the little anteroom which she had somehow made to seem a little more human than an office and watched her hang his coat on the iron frame of the open window.

She was tall and dark with a reserved, unbroken beauty to which the war and five years in the Service had lent a touch of sternness. Unless she married soon, Bond thought for the hundredth time, or had a lover, her cool air of authority might easily become spinsterish and she would join the army of women who had married a career.

Bond had told her as much, often, and he and the two other members of the OO Section had at various times made determined assaults on her virtue. She had handled them all with the same cool motherliness (which, to salve their egos, they privately defined as frigidity) and, the day after, she treated them with small attentions and kindnesses to show that it was really her fault and that she forgave them.

What they didn't know was that she worried herself almost to death when they were in danger and that she loved them equally; but that she had no intention of becoming emotionally involved with any man who might be dead next week. And it was true that an appointment in the Secret Service was a form of peonage. If you were a woman there wasn't much of you left for other relationships. It was easier for the men. They had an excuse for fragmentary affairs. For them marriage and children and a home were out of the question if they were to be of any use 'in the field' as it was cosily termed. But, for the women, an affair outside the Service automatically made you a 'security risk' and in the last analysis you had a choice of resignation from the Service and a normal life, or of perpetual concubinage to your King and Country.

Loelia Ponsonby knew that she had almost reached the time for decision and all her instincts told her to get out. But every day the drama and romance of her Cavell-Nightingale world locked her more securely into the company of the other girls at Headquarters and every day it seemed more difficult to betray by resignation the father-figure which the Service had become.

Meanwhile she was one of the most envied girls in the building, and a member of the small company of Principal Secretaries who had access to the innermost secrets of the Service – 'The Pearls and Twin-set' as they were called behind their backs by the other girls, with ironical reference to their supposedly 'County' and 'Kensington' backgrounds – and, so far as the Personnel Branch was concerned, her destiny in twenty years' time would be that single golden line right at the end of a New Year's Honours List, among the medals for officials of the Fishery Board, of the Post Office, of the Women's Institute, towards the bottom of the OBEs: 'Miss Loelia Ponsonby, Principal Secretary in the Ministry of Defence.'

She turned away from the window. She was dressed in a sugar-pink and white striped shirt and a plain dark blue skirt.

Bond smiled into her grey eyes. 'I only call you Lil on Mondays,' he said. 'Miss Ponsonby the rest of the week. But I'll never call you Loelia. It sounds like somebody in an indecent limerick. Any messages?'

'No,' she said shortly. She relented. 'But there's piles of stuff on your desk. Nothing urgent. But there's an awful lot of it. Oh, and the powder-vine says that 008's got out. He's in Berlin, resting. Isn't it wonderful!'

Bond looked quickly at her. 'When did you hear that?'

'About half an hour ago,' she said.

Bond opened the inner door to the big office with the three desks and shut it behind him. He went and stood by the window, looking out at the late spring green of the trees in Regent's Park. So Bill had made it after all. Peenemunde and back. Resting in Berlin sounded bad. Must be in pretty poor shape. Well, he'd just have to wait for news from the only leak in the building – the girls' rest-room, known to the impotent fury of the Security staff as 'The powder-vine'.

Bond sighed and sat down at his desk, pulling towards him the tray of brown folders bearing the top-secret red star. And what about 0011? It was two months since he had vanished into the 'Dirty Half-mile' in Singapore. Not a word since. While he, Bond, No. 007, the senior of the three men in the Service who had earned the double O number, sat at his comfortable desk doing paper-work and flirting with their secretary.

He shrugged his shoulders and resolutely opened the top folder. Inside there was a detailed map of southern Poland and north-eastern Germany. Its feature was a straggling red line connecting Warsaw and Berlin. There was also a long typewritten memorandum headed *Mainline: A well-established Escape Route from East to West.*

Bond took out his black gunmetal cigarette-box and his black-oxidized Ronson lighter and put them on the desk beside him. He lit a cigarette, one of the Macedonian blend with the three gold rings round the butt that Morlands of Grosvenor Street made for him, then he settled himself forward in the padded swivel chair and began to read.

It was the beginning of a typical routine day for Bond. It was only two or three times a year that an assignment came along requiring his particular abilities. For the rest of the year he had the duties of an easy-going senior civil servant – elastic office hours from around ten to six; lunch, generally in the canteen; evenings spent playing cards in the company of a few close friends, or at Crockford's; or making love, with rather cold passion, to one of three similarly disposed married women; weekends playing golf for high stakes at one of the clubs near London.

He took no holidays, but was generally given a fortnight's leave at the end of each assignment – in addition to any sick-leave that might be necessary. He earned £1500 a year, the salary of a Principal Officer in the Civil Service, and he had a thousand a year free of tax of his own. When he was on a job he could spend as much as he liked, so for the other months of the year he could live very well on his £2000 a year net.

He had a small but comfortable flat off the King's Road, an elderly Scottish housekeeper – a treasure called May – and a 1930 4½-litre Bentley coupé, supercharged, which he kept expertly tuned so that he could do a hundred when he wanted to.

On these things he spent all his money and it was his ambition to have as little as possible in his banking account when he was killed, as, when he was depressed, he knew he would be, before the statutory age of forty-five.

Eight years to go before he was automatically taken off the OO list and given a staff job at Headquarters. At least eight tough assignments. Probably sixteen. Perhaps twenty-four. Too many.

There were five cigarette-ends in the big glass ashtray

by the time Bond had finished memorizing the details of 'Mainline'. He picked up a red pencil and ran his eye down the distribution list on the cover. The list started with 'M', then 'CoS.', then a dozen or so letters and numbers and then, at the end 'oo'. Against this he put a neat tick, signed it with the figure 7, and tossed the file into his OUT tray.

It was twelve o'clock. Bond took the next folder off the pile and opened it. It was from the Radio Intelligence Division of NATO, 'For Information Only' and it was headed 'Radio Signatures'.

Bond pulled the rest of the pile towards him and glanced at the first page of each. These were their titles:

The Inspectoscope – a machine for the detection of contraband.

Philopon – A Japanese murder-drug.

Possible points of concealment on trains. No. II. Germany.

The methods of Smersh. No. 6. Kidnapping.

Route five to Pekin.

Vladivostock. A photographic Reconnaissance by U.S. Thunderjet.

Bond was not surprised by the curious mixture he was supposed to digest. The OO Section of the Secret Service was not concerned with the current operations of other sections and stations, only with background information which might be useful or instructive to the only three men in the Service whose duties included assassination – who might be ordered to kill. There was no urgency about these files. No action was required by him or his two colleagues except that each of them jotted down the numbers of dockets which he considered the other two should also read when they were next attached to Headquarters. When the OO Section had finished with this lot they would go down to their final destination in 'Records'.

Bond turned back to the NATO paper.

'The almost inevitable manner', he read, 'in which individuality is revealed by minute patterns of behaviour, is demonstrated by the indelible characteristics of the "fist" of each radio operator. This "fist", or manner of tapping out messages, is distinctive and recognizable by those who are practised in receiving messages. It can also be measured by very sensitive mechanisms. To illustrate, in 1943 the United States Radio Intelligence Bureau made use of this fact in tracing an enemy station in Chile operated by "Pedro", a young German. When the Chilean police closed in on the station, "Pedro" escaped. A year later, expert listeners spotted a new illegal transmitter and were able to recognize "Pedro" as the operator. In order to disguise his "fist" he was transmitting left-handed, but the disguise was not effective and he was captured.

'NATO Radio Research has recently been experimenting with a form of "scrambler" which can be attached to the wrist of operators with the object of interfering minutely with the nerve centres which control the muscles of the hand. However . . .'

There were three telephones on Bond's desk. A black one for outside calls, a green office telephone, and a red one which went only to M and his Chief of Staff. It was the familiar burr of the red one that broke the silence of the room.

It was M's Chief of Staff.

'Can you come up?' asked the pleasant voice.

'M?' asked Bond.

'Yes.'

'Any clue?'

'Simply said if you were about he'd like to see you.'

'Right,' said Bond, and put down the receiver.

He collected his coat, told his secretary he would be with M and not to wait for him, left his office and walked along the corridor to the lift.

While he waited for it, he thought of those other times, when, in the middle of an empty day, the red telephone had suddenly broken the silence and taken him out of one world and set him down in another. He shrugged his shoulders – Monday! He might have expected trouble.

The lift came. 'Ninth,' said Bond, and stepped in.

The ninth was the top floor of the building. Most of it was occupied by Communications, the hand-picked inter-services team of operators whose only interest was the world of microwaves, sunspots, and the 'heaviside layer'. Above them, on the flat roof, were the three squat masts of one of the most powerful transmitters in England, explained on the bold bronze list of occupants in the entrance hall of the building by the words 'Radio Tests Ltd'. The other tenants were declared to be 'Universal Export Co.', 'Delaney Bros. (1940) Ltd.', 'The Omnium Corporation', and 'Enquiries (Miss E. Twining, OBE)'.

Miss Twining was a real person. Forty years earlier she had been a Loelia Ponsonby. Now, in retirement, she sat in a small office on the ground floor and spent her days tearing up circulars, paying the rates and taxes of her ghostly tenants, and politely brushing off salesmen and people who wanted to export something or have their radios mended.

It was always very quiet on the ninth floor. As Bond turned to the left outside the lift and walked along the softly carpeted corridor to the green baize door that led to the offices of M and his personal staff, the only sound he heard was a thin high-pitched whine that was so faint that you almost had to listen for it.

Without knocking he pushed through the green door and walked into the last room but one along the passage.

Miss Moneypenny, M's private secretary, looked up from her typewriter and smiled at him. They liked each other and she knew that Bond admired her looks. She was wearing the same model shirt as his own secretary, but with blue stripes.

'New uniform, Penny?' said Bond.

She laughed. 'Loelia and I share the same little woman,' she said. 'We tossed and I got blue.'

A snort came through the open door of the adjoining room. The Chief of Staff, a man of about Bond's age, came out, a sardonic grin on his pale, overworked face.

'Break it up,' he said. 'M's waiting. Lunch afterwards?'

'Fine,' said Bond. He turned to the door beside Miss Moneypenny, walked through and shut it after him. Above it, a green light went on. Miss Moneypenny raised her eyebrows at the Chief of Staff. He shook his head.

'I don't think it's business, Penny,' he said. 'Just sent for him out of the blue.' He went back into his own room and got on with the day's work.

When Bond came through the door, M was sitting at his broad desk, lighting a pipe. He made a vague gesture with the lighted match towards the chair on the other side of the desk and Bond walked over and sat down. M glanced at him sharply through the smoke and then threw the box of matches on to the empty expanse of red leather in front of him.

'Have a good leave?' he asked abruptly.

'Yes, thank you, sir,' said Bond.

'Still sunburned, I see.' M looked his disapproval. He didn't really begrudge Bond a holiday which had been partly convalescence. The hint of criticism came from the Puritan and the Jesuit who live in all leaders of men.

'Yes, sir,' said Bond noncommittally. 'It's very hot near the equator.'

'Quite,' said M. 'Well-deserved rest.' He screwed up his eyes without humour. 'Hope the colour won't last too long. Always suspicious of sunburned men in England. Either they've not got a job of work to do or they put it on with a sun-lamp.' He dismissed the subject with a short sideways jerk of his pipe.

He put the pipe back in his mouth and pulled at it absent-mindedly. It had gone out. He reached for the matches and wasted some time getting it going again.

'Looks as if we'll get that gold after all,' he said finally. 'There's been some talk of the Hague Court, but Ashenheim's a fine lawyer.'[1]

'Good,' said Bond.

[1] This refers to Bond's previous assignment, described in *Live and Let Die*, by the same author.

There was silence for a moment. M gazed into the bowl of his pipe. Through the open windows came the distant roar of London's traffic. A pigeon landed on one of the window-sills with a clatter of wings and quickly took off again.

Bond tried to read something in the weatherbeaten face he knew so well and which held so much of his loyalty. But the grey eyes were quiet and the little pulse that always beat high up on the right temple when M was tense showed no sign of life.

Suddenly Bond suspected that M was embarrassed. He had the feeling that M didn't know where to begin. Bond wanted to help. He shifted in his chair and took his eyes off M. He looked down at his hands and idly picked at a rough nail.

M lifted his eyes from his pipe and cleared his throat.

'Got anything particular on at the moment, James?' he asked in a neutral voice.

'James.' That was unusual. It was rare for M to use a Christian name in this room.

'Only paper-work and the usual courses,' said Bond. 'Anything you want me for, sir?'

'As a matter of fact there is,' said M. He frowned at Bond. 'But it's really got nothing to do with the Service. Almost a personal matter. Thought you might give me a hand.'

'Of course, sir,' said Bond. He was relieved for M's sake that the ice had been broken. Probably one of the old man's relations had got into trouble and M didn't want to ask a favour of Scotland Yard. Blackmail, perhaps. Or drugs. He was pleased that M should have chosen him. Of course he would take care of it. M was such a desperate stickler about Government property and personnel. Using Bond on a personal matter must have seemed to him like stealing the Government's money.

'Thought you'd say so,' said M, gruffly. 'Won't take up much of your time. An evening ought to be enough.' He paused. 'Well now, you've heard of this man Sir Hugo Drax?'

'Of course, sir,' said Bond, surprised at the name. 'You can't open a paper without reading something about him. *Sunday Express* is running his life. Extraordinary story.'

'I know,' said M shortly. 'Just give me the facts as you see them. I'd like to know if your version tallies with mine.'

Bond gazed out of the window for a moment to marshal his thoughts. M didn't like haphazard talk. He liked a fully detailed story with no um-ing and er-ing. No afterthoughts or hedging.

'Well, sir,' said Bond finally. 'For one thing the man's a national hero. The public have taken to him. I suppose he's in much the same class as Jack Hobbs or Gordon Richards. They've got a real feeling for him. They consider he's one of them, but a glorified version. A sort of superman. He's not much to look at, with all those scars from his war injuries, and he's a bit loud-mouthed and ostentatious. But they rather like that. Makes him a sort of Lonsdale figure, but more in their class. They like his friends calling him "Hugger" Drax. It makes him a bit of a card and I expect it gives the women a thrill. And then when you think what he's doing for the country, out of his own pocket and far beyond what any government seems to be able to do, it's really extraordinary that they don't insist on making him Prime Minister.'

Bond saw the cold eyes getting chillier, but he was determined not to let his admiration for Drax's achievements be dampened by the older man. 'After all, sir,' he continued reasonably, 'it looks as if he's made this country safe from war for years. And he can't be much over forty. I feel the same as most people about him. And then there's all this mystery about his real identity. I'm not surprised people feel rather sorry for him, although he is a multimillionaire. He seems to be a lonely sort of man in spite of his gay life.'

M smiled drily. 'All that sounds rather like a trailer for the *Express* story. He's certainly an extrordinary man. But what's your version of the facts? I don't expect I know much more than you do. Probably less. Don't read the papers very carefully, and there are no files on him except at the War Office and they're not very illuminating. Now then. What's the gist of the *Express* story?'

'Sorry, sir,' said Bond. 'But the facts are pretty slim. Well,' he looked out of the window again and concentrated, 'in the German breakthrough in the Ardennes in the winter of '44, the Germans made a lot of use of guerrillas and saboteurs. Gave them the rather spooky name of Werewolves. They did quite a lot of damage of one sort or another. Very good at camouflage and stay-behind tricks of all sorts and some of them went on operating long after Ardennes had failed and we had crossed the Rhine. They were supposed to carry on even when we had overrun the country. But they packed up pretty quickly when things got really bad.

'One of their best coups was to blow up one of the rear liaison HQs between the American and British armies. Reinforcement Holding Units I think they're called. It was a mixed affair, all kinds of Allied personnel – American signals, British ambulance drivers – a rather shifting group from every sort of unit. The Werewolves somehow managed to mine the mess-hall and, when it blew, it took with it quite a lot of the field hospital as well. Killed or wounded over a hundred. Sorting out all the bodies was the hell of a business. One of the English bodies was Drax. Half his face was blown away. Total amnesia that lasted a year and at the end of that time they didn't know who he was and nor did he. There were about twenty-five other unidentified bodies that neither we nor the Americans could sort out. Either not enough bits, or perhaps people in transit, or there without authorization. It was that sort of a unit. Two commanding officers, of course. Sloppy staff work. Lousy records. So after a year in various hospitals they took Drax through the War Office file of Missing Men. When they came to the papers of a no-next-of-kin called Hugo Drax, an orphan who had been working in the Liverpool docks before the war, he showed signs of interest, and the photograph and physical description seemed to tally more or less with what our man must have looked like before he was blown up. From that time he began to mend. He started to talk a bit about simple things he remembered, and the doctors got very proud of him. The War Office found a man who had served in the same Pioneer unit as this Hugo Drax and he came along to the hospital and said he was sure the man was Drax. That settled it. Advertising didn't produce another Hugo Drax and he was finally discharged late in 1945 in that name with back pay and a full disability pension.'

'But he still says he doesn't really know who he is,' interrupted M. 'He's a member of Blades. I've often played cards with him and talked to him afterwards at dinner. He says he sometimes gets a strong feeling of "having been there before". Often goes to Liverpool to try and hunt up his past. Anyway, what else?'

Bond's eyes were turned inwards, remembering. 'He seems to have disappeared for about three years after the war,' he said. 'Then the City started to hear about him from all over the world. The Metal Market heard about him first. Seems he'd cornered a very valuable ore called Columbite. Everybody was wanting the stuff. It's got an extraordinarily high melting point. Jet engines can't be made without it. There's very little of it in the world, only a few thousand tons are produced every year, mostly as a by-product of the Nigerian tin mines. Drax must have looked at the Jet Age and somehow put his finger on its main scarcity. He must have got hold of about £10,000 from somewhere because the *Express* says that in 1946 he'd bought three tons of Columbite, which cost him around £3000 a ton. He got a £5000 premium on this lot from an American aircraft firm who wanted it in a hurry. Then he started buying futures in the stuff, six months, nine months, a year forward. In three years he'd made a corner. Anyone who wanted Columbite went to Drax Metals for it. All this time he'd been playing about with futures in other small commodities – Shellac, Sisal, Black Pepper – anything where you could build up a big position on margin. Of course he gambled on a rising commodity market but he had the guts to keep his foot right down on the pedal even when the pace got hot as hell. And whenever he took a profit he ploughed the money back again. For instance, he was one of the first men to buy up used ore-dumps in South Africa. Now they're being re-mined for their uranium content. Another fortune there.'

M's quiet eyes were fixed on Bond. He puffed at his pipe, listening.

'Of course,' continued Bond, lost in his story, 'all this made the City wonder what the hell was going on. The commodity brokers kept on coming across the name of Drax. Whatever they wanted Drax had got it and was holding out for a much higher price than they were prepared to pay. He operated from Tangier – free port, no taxes, no currency restrictions. By 1950 he was a multimillionaire. Then he came back to England and started spending it. He simply threw it about. Best houses, best cars, best women. Boxes at the Opera, at Goodwood. Prize-winning Jersey herds. Prize-winning carnations. Prize-winning two-year-olds. Two yachts; money for the Walker Cup team; £100,000 for the Flood Disaster Fund; Coronation Ball for Nurses at the Albert Hall – there wasn't a week when he wasn't hitting the headlines with some splash or other. And all the time he went on getting richer and the people simply loved it. It was the Arabian Nights. It lit up their lives. If a wounded soldier from Liverpool could get there in five years, why shouldn't they or their sons? It sounded almost as easy as winning a gigantic football pool.

'And then came his astonishing letter to the Queen: "Your Majesty, may I have the temerity . . ." and the typical genius of the single banner-line across the *Express* next day: TEMERITY DRAX, and the story of how he had given to Britain his entire holding in Columbite to build a super atomic rocket with a range that would cover nearly every capital in Europe – the immediate answer to anyone who tried to atom-bomb London. £10,000,000 he was going to put up out of his own pocket, and he had the design of the thing and was prepared to find the staff to build it.

'And then there were months of delay and everyone got impatient. Questions in the House. The Opposition nearly forced a vote of Confidence. And then the announcement by the Prime Minister that the design had been approved by the Woomera Range experts of the Ministry of Supply, and that the Queen had been graciously pleased to accept the gift on behalf of the people of Britain and had conferred a knighthood on the donor.'

Bond paused, almost carried away by the story of this extraordinary man.

'Yes,' said M 'Peace in Our Time – This Time. I remember the headline. A year ago. And now the rocket's nearly ready. "The Moonraker". And from all I hear it really should do what he says. It's very odd.' He relapsed into silence, gazing out of the window.

He turned back and faced Bond across the desk.

'That's about it,' he said slowly. 'I don't know much more than you do. A wonderful story. Extraordinary man.' He paused, reflecting. 'There's only one thing . . .' M tapped the stem of his pipe against his teeth.

'What's that, sir?' asked Bond.

M seemed to make up his mind. He looked mildly across at Bond.

'Sir Hugo Drax cheats at cards.'

3 / 'BELLY STRIPPERS', ETC.

'Cheats at cards?'

M frowned. 'That's what I said,' he commented drily. 'It doesn't seem to you odd that a multimillionaire should cheat at cards?'

Bond grinned apologetically. 'Not as odd as all that, sir,' he said. 'I've known very rich people cheat themselves at Patience. But it just didn't fit in with my picture of Drax. Bit of an anticlimax.'

'That's the point,' said M. 'Why does he do it? And don't forget that cheating at cards can still smash a man. In so-called Society, it's about the only crime that can still finish you, whoever you are. Drax does it so well that nobody's caught him yet. As a matter of fact I doubt if anyone has begun to suspect him except Basildon. He's the Chairman of Blades. He came to me. He's got a vague idea I've got something to do with Intelligence and I've given him a hand over one or two little troubles in the past. Asked my advice. Said he didn't want a fuss at the club, of course, but above all he wants to save Drax from making a fool of himself. He admires him as much as we all do and he's terrified of an incident. You couldn't stop a scandal like that getting out. A lot of MPs are members and it would soon get talked about in the Lobby. Then the gossip-writers would get hold of it. Drax would have to resign from Blades and the next thing there'd be a libel action brought in his defence by one of his friends. Tranby Croft all over again. At least, that's how Basildon's mind is working and I must say I can see it that way too. Anyway,' said M with finality, 'I've agreed to help and', he looked levelly at Bond, 'that's where you come in. You're the best card-player in the Service, or,' he smiled ironically, 'you should be after the casino jobs you've been on, and I remembered that we'd spent quite a lot of money putting you through a course in card-sharping before you went after those Roumanians in Monte Carlo before the war.'

Bond smiled grimly. 'Steffi Esposito,' he said softly. 'That was the chap. American. Made me work ten hours a day for a week learning a thing called the Riffle Stack and how to deal Seconds and Bottoms and Middles. I wrote a long report about it at the time. Must be buried in Records. He knew every trick in the game. How to wax the aces so that the pack will break at them; Edge Work and Line Work with a razor on the backs of the high cards; Trimming; Arm Pressure Hold-outs – mechanical gadgets up your sleeve that feed you cards. Belly Strippers – trimming a whole pack less than a millimetre down both sides, but leaving a slight belly on the cards you're interested in – the aces, for instance. Shiners, tiny mirrors built into rings, or fitted into the bottom of a pipe-bowl. Actually,' Bond admitted, 'it was his tip about Luminous Readers that helped me on that Monte Carlo job. A croupier was using an invisible ink the team could pick out with special glasses. But Steffi was a wonderful chap. Scotland Yard found him for us. He could shuffle the pack once and then cut the four aces out of it. Absolute magic.'

'Sounds a bit too professional for our man,' commented M. 'That sort of work needs hours of practice every day, or an accomplice, and I can't believe he'd find that at Blades. No, there's nothing sensational about his cheating and for all I know it might be a fantastic run of luck. It's odd. He's not a particularly good player – he only plays bridge by the way – but quite often he brings off bids or doubles or finesses that are absolutely phenomenal – quite against the odds. Or the conventions. But they come off. He's always a big winner and they play high at Blades. He hasn't lost on a weekly settlement since he joined a year ago. We've got two or three of the finest players in the world in the Club and none of them has ever had a record like that over twelve months. It's getting talked about in a sort of joking way and I think Basildon's right to do something about it. What system do you suppose Drax has got?'

Bond was longing for his lunch. The Chief of Staff must have given him up half an hour ago. He could have talked to M about cheating for hours, and M, who never seemed to be interested in food or sleep, would have listened to everything and remembered it afterwards. But Bond was hungry.

'Assuming he's not a professional, sir, and can't doctor the cards in any way, there are only two answers. He's either looking, or else he's got a system of signals with his partner. Does he often play with the same man?'

'We always cut for partners after each rubber,' said M. 'Unless there's a challenge. And on guest nights, Mondays and Thursdays, you stick to your guest. Drax nearly always brings a man called Meyer, his metal broker. Nice chap. Jew. Very fine player.'

'I might be able to tell if I watched,' said Bond.

'That's what I was going to say,' said M. 'How about coming along tonight? At any rate you'll get a good dinner. Meet you there about six. I'll take some money off you at piquet and we'll watch the bridge for a little. After dinner we'll have a rubber or two with Drax and his friend. They're always there on Monday. All right? Sure I'm not taking you away from your work?'

'No, sir,' said Bond with a grin. 'And I'd like to come very much. Bit of a busman's holiday. And if Drax is cheating, I'll show him I've spotted it and that should be enough to warn him off. I wouldn't like to see him get into a mess. That all, sir?'

'Yes, James,' said M. 'And thank you for your help. Drax must be a bloody fool. Obviously a bit of a crank. But it isn't the man I'm worried about. I wouldn't like to chance anything going wrong with this rocket of his.

And Drax more or less *is* the Moonraker. Well, see you at six. Don't bother about dressing. Some of us do for dinner and some of us don't. Tonight we won't. Better go along now and sandpaper your fingertips or whatever you sharpers do.'

Bond smiled back at M and got to his feet. It sounded a promising evening. As he walked over to the door and let himself out he reflected that here at last was an interview with M that didn't cast a shadow.

M's secretary was still at her desk. There was a plate of sandwiches and a glass of milk beside her typewriter. She looked sharply at Bond, but there was nothing to be read in his expression.

'I suppose he gave up,' said Bond.

'Nearly an hour ago,' said Miss Moneypenny reproachfully. 'It's half-past two. He'll be back any minute now.'

'I'll go down to the canteen before it closes,' he said. 'Tell him I'll pay for his lunch next time.' He smiled at her and walked out into the corridor and along to the lift.

There were only a few people left in the officers' canteen. Bond sat by himself and ate a grilled sole, a large mixed salad with his own dressing laced with mustard, some Brie cheese and toast, and half a carafe of white Bordeaux. He had two cups of black coffee and was back in his office by three. With half his mind preoccupied with M's problem, he hurried through the rest of the NATO file, said goodbye to his secretary after telling her where he would be that evening, and at four-thirty was collecting his car from the staff garage at the back of the building.

'Supercharger's whining a bit, sir,' said the ex-RAF mechanic who regarded Bond's Bentley as his own property. 'Take it down tomorrow if you won't be needing her at lunch-time.'

'Thanks,' said Bond, 'that'll be fine.' He took the car quietly out into the park and over to Baker Street, the two-inch exhaust bubbling fatly in his wake.

He was home in fifteen minutes. He left the car under the plane trees in the little square and let himself into the ground floor of the converted Regency house, went into the book-lined sitting-room and, after a moment's search, pulled *Scarne on Cards* out of its shelf and dropped it on the ornate Empire desk near the broad window.

He walked through into the smallish bedroom with the white and gold Cole wallpaper and the deep red curtains, undressed and threw his clothes, more or less tidily, on the dark blue counterpane of the double bed. Then he went into the bathroom and had a quick shower. Before leaving the bathroom he examined his face in the glass and decided that he had no intention of sacrificing a lifetime prejudice by shaving twice in one day.

In the glass, the grey-blue eyes looked back at him with the extra light they held when his mind was focused on a problem that interested him. The lean, hard face had a hungry, competitive edge to it. There was something swift and intent in the way he ran his fingers along his jaw and in the impatient stroke of the hairbrush to put back the comma of black hair that fell down an inch above his right eyebrow. It crossed his mind that, with the fading of his sunburn, the scar down the right cheek that had shown so white was beginning to be less prominent, and automatically he glanced down his naked body and registered that the almost indecent white area left by his bathing trunks was less sharply defined. He smiled at some memory and went through into the bedroom.

Ten minutes later, in a heavy white silk shirt, dark blue trousers of Navy serge, dark blue socks, and well-polished black moccasin shoes, he was sitting at his desk with a pack of cards in one hand and Scarne's wonderful guide to cheating open in front of him.

For half an hour, as he ran quickly through the section on Methods, he practised the vital Mechanic's Grip (three fingers curled round the long edge of the cards, and the index finger at the short upper edge away from him), Palming and Nullifying the Cut. His hands worked automatically at these basic manoeuvres, while his eyes read, and he was glad to find that his fingers were supple and assured and that there was no noise from the cards even with the very difficult single-handed Annulment.

At five-thirty he slapped the cards on the table and shut the book.

He went into his bedroom, filled the wide black case with cigarettes and slipped it into his hip pocket, put on a black knitted silk tie and his coat and verified that his cheque book was in his notecase.

He stood for a moment, thinking. Then he selected two white silk handkerchiefs, carefully rumpled them, and put one into each side-pocket of his coat.

He lit a cigarette and walked back into the sitting-room and sat down at his desk again and relaxed for ten minutes, gazing out of the window at the empty square and thinking about the evening that was just going to begin and about Blades, probably the most famous private card club in the world.

The exact date of the foundation of Blades is uncertain. The second half of the eighteenth century saw the opening of many coffee houses and gaming rooms, and premises and proprietors shifted often with changing fashions and fortunes. White's was founded in 1755, Almack's in 1764, and Brooks's in 1774, and it was in that year that the Scavoir Vivre, which was to be the cradle of Blades, opened its doors on to Park Street, a quiet backwater off St James's.

The Scavoir Vivre was too exclusive to live and it blackballed itself to death within a year. Then, in 1776, Horace Walpole wrote: 'A new club is opened off St James's Street that piques itself in surpassing all its predecessors' and in 1778 'Blades' first occurs in a letter from Gibbon, the historian, who coupled it with the name of its founder, a German called Longchamp at that time conducting the Jockey Club at Newmarket.

From the outset Blades seems to have been a success, and in 1782 we find the Duke of Wirtemberg writing excitedly home to his younger brother: 'This is indeed the "Ace of Clubs"! There have been four or five quinze tables going in the room at the same time, with whist and piquet, after which a full Hazard table. I have known two at the same time. Two chests each containing 4000 guinea rouleaus were scarce sufficient for the night's circulation.'

Mention of Hazard perhaps provides a clue to the club's prosperity. Permission to play this dangerous but popular game must have been given by the Committee in contravention of its own rules which laid down that 'No game is to be admitted to the House of the Society but Chess, Whist, Picket, Cribbage, Quadrille, Ombre and Tredville'.

In any event the club continued to flourish and remains to this day the home of some of the highest 'polite' gambling in the world. It is not as aristocratic as it was, the redistribution of wealth has seen to that, but it is still the most exclusive club in London. The membership is restricted to two hundred and each candidate must have two qualifications for election; he must behave like a gentleman and he must be able to 'show' £100,000 in cash or gilt-edged securities.

The amenities of Blades, apart from the gambling, are so desirable that the Committee has had to rule that every member is required to win or lose £500 a year on the club premises, or pay an annual fine of £250. The food and wine are the best in London and no bills are presented, the cost of all meals being deducted at the end of each week *pro rata* from the profits of the winners. Seeing that about £5000 changes hands each week at the tables the impost is not too painful and the losers have the satisfaction of saving something from the wreck; and the custom explains the fairness of the levy on infrequent gamblers.

Club servants are the making or breaking of any club and the servants of Blades have no equal. The half-dozen waitresses in the dining-room are of such a high standard of beauty that some of the younger members have been known to smuggle them undetected into débutante balls, and if, at night, one or other of the girls is persuaded to stray into one of the twelve members' bedrooms at the back of the club, that is regarded as the members' private concern.

There are one or two other small refinements which contribute to the luxury of the place. Only brand-new currency notes and silver are paid out on the premises and, if a member is staying overnight, his notes and small change are taken away by the valet who brings the early morning tea and *The Times* and are replaced with new money. No newspaper comes to the reading room before it has been ironed. Floris provides the soaps and lotions in the lavatories and bedrooms; there is a direct wire to Ladbroke's from the porter's lodge; the club has the finest tents and boxes at the principal race-meetings, at Lord's, Henley, and Wimbledon, and members travelling abroad have automatic membership of the leading club in every foreign capital.

In short, membership of Blades, in return for the £100 entrance fee and the £50 a year subscription, provides the standard of luxury of the Victorian age together with the opportunity to win or lose, in great comfort, anything up to £20,000 a year.

Bond, reflecting on all this, decided that he was going to enjoy his evening. He had only played at Blades a dozen times in his life, and on the last occasion he had burnt his fingers badly in a high poker game, but the prospect of some expensive bridge and of the swing of a few, to him, not unimportant hundred pounds made his muscles taut with anticipation.

And then, of course, there was the little business of Sir Hugo Drax, which might bring an additional touch of drama to the evening.

He was not even disturbed by a curious portent he encountered while he was driving along King's Road into Sloane Square with half his mind on the traffic and the other half exploring the evening ahead.

It was a few minutes to six and there was thunder about. The sky threatened rain and it had become suddenly dark. Across the square from him, high up in the air, a bold electric sign started to flash on and off. The fading light-waves had caused the cathode tube to start the mechanism which would keep the sign flashing through the dark hours until, around six in the morning, the early light of day would again sensitize the tube and cause the circuit to close.

Startled at the great crimson words. Bond pulled in to the curb, got out of the car and crossed to the other side of the street to get a better view of the big skysign.

Ah! That was it. Some of the letters had been hidden by a neighbouring building. It was only one of those Shell advertisements. 'SUMMER SHELL IS HERE' was what it said.

Bond smiled to himself and walked back to his car and drove on.

When he had first seen the sign, half-hidden by the building, great crimson letters across the evening sky had flashed a different message.

They had said: 'HELL IS HERE . . . HELL IS HERE . . . HELL IS HERE.'

Bond left the Bentley outside Brooks's and walked round the corner into Park Street.

The Adam frontage of Blades, recessed a yard or so back from its neighbours, was elegant in the soft dusk. The dark red curtains had been drawn across the ground-floor bow-windows on either side of the entrance and a uniformed servant showed for a moment as he drew them across the three windows of the floor above. In the centre of the three, Bond could see the heads and shoulders of two men bent over a game, probably backgammon he thought, and he caught a glimpse of the spangled fire of one of the three great chandeliers that illuminate the famous gambling room.

Bond pushed through the swing doors and walked up to the old-fashioned porter's lodge ruled over by Brevett, the guardian of Blades and the counsellor and family friend of half the members.

'Evening, Brevett. Is the Admiral in?'

'Good evening, sir,' said Brevett, who knew Bond as an occasional guest at the club. 'The Admiral's waiting for you in the card room. Page, take Commander Bond up to the Admiral. Lively now!'

As Bond followed the uniformed page-boy across

the worn black and white marble floor of the hall and up the wide staircase with its fine mahogany balustrade, he remembered the story of how, at one election, nine blackballs had been found in the box when there were only eight members of the committee present. Brevett, who had handed the box from member to member, was said to have confessed to the Chairman that he was so afraid the candidate would be elected that he had put in a blackball himself. No one had objected. The committee would rather have lost its chairman than the porter whose family had held the same post at Blades for a hundred years.

The page pushed open one wing of the tall doors at the top of the stairs and held it for Bond to go through. The long room was not crowded and Bond saw M sitting by himself playing patience in the alcove formed by the left hand of the three bow windows. He dismissed the page and walked across the heavy carpet, noticing the rich background smell of cigar-smoke, the quiet voices that came from the three tables of bridge, and the sharp rattle of dice across an unseen backgammon board.

'There you are,' said M as Bond came up. He waved to the chair that faced him across the card table. 'Just let me finish this. I haven't cracked this man Canfield for months. Drink?'

'No, thanks,' said Bond. He sat down and lit a cigarette and watched with amusement the concentration M was putting into his game.

'Admiral Sir M – M – : something at the Ministry of Defence.' M looked like any member of any of the clubs in St James's Street. Dark grey suit, stiff white collar, the favourite dark blue bow-tie with spots, rather loosely tied, the thin black cord of the rimless eyeglass that M seemed only to use to read menus, the keen sailor's face, with the clear, sharp sailor's eyes. It was difficult to believe that an hour before he had been playing with a thousand live chessmen against the enemies of England; that there might be, this evening, fresh blood on his hands, or a successful burglary, or the hideous knowledge of a disgusting blackmail case.

And what could the casual observer think of him, 'Commander James Bond, GMG, RNVSR', also 'something at the Ministry of Defence', the rather saturnine young man in his middle thirties sitting opposite the Admiral? Something a bit cold and dangerous in that face. Looks pretty fit. May have been attached to Templer in Malaya. Or Nairobi. Mau Mau work. Tough-looking customer. Doesn't look the sort of chap one usually sees in Blades.

Bond knew that there was something alien and un-English about himself. He knew that he was a difficult man to cover up. Particularly in England. He shrugged his shoulders. Abroad was what mattered. He would never have a job to do in England. Outside the jurisdiction of the Service. Anyway, he didn't need a cover this evening. This was recreation.

M snorted and threw his cards down. Bond automatically gathered in the pack and as automatically gave it the Scarne shuffle, marrying the two halves with the quick downward riffle that never brings the cards off the table. He squared off the pack and pushed it away.

M beckoned to a passing waiter. 'Piquet cards, please, Tanner,' he said.

The waiter went away and came back a moment later with the two thin packs. He stripped off the wrapping and placed them, with two markers, on the table. He stood waiting.

'Bring me a whisky and soda,' said M. 'Sure you won't have anything?'

Bond looked at his watch. It was half past six. 'Could I have a dry Martini?' he said. 'Made with Vodka. Large slice of lemon peel.'

'Rot-gut,' commented M briefly as the waiter went away. 'Now I'll just take a pound or two off you and then we'll go and have a look at the bridge. Our friend hasn't turned up yet.'

For half an hour they played the game at which the expert player can nearly always win even with the cards running slightly against him. At the end of the game Bond laughed and counted out three pound-notes.

'One of these days I'm going to take some trouble and really learn piquet,' he said. 'I've never won against you yet.'

'It's all memory and knowing the odds,' said M with satisfaction. He finished his whisky and soda. 'Let's go over and see what's going on at the bridge. Our man's playing at Basildon's table. Came in about ten minutes ago. If you notice anything, just give me a nod and we'll go downstairs and talk about it.'

He stood up and Bond followed suit.

The far end of the room had begun to fill up and half a dozen tables of bridge were going. At the round poker table under the centre chandelier three players were counting out chips into five stacks, waiting for two more players to come in. The kidney-shaped baccarat table was still shrouded and would probably remain so until after dinner, when it would be used for chemin-de-fer.

Bond followed M out of their alcove, relishing the scene down the long room, the oases of green, the tinkle of glasses as the waiters moved amongst the tables, the hum of talk punctuated by sudden exclamations and warm laughter, the haze of blue smoke rising up through the dark red lamp shades that hung over the centre of each table. His pulses quickened with the smell of it all and his nostrils flared slightly as the two men came down the long room and joined the company.

M, with Bond beside him, wandered casually from table to table, exchanging greetings with the players until they reached the last table beneath the fine Lawrence of Beau Brummel over the wide Adam fireplace.

'Double, damn you,' said the loud, cheerful voice of the player with his back to Bond. Bond thoughtfully noted the head of tight reddish hair that was all he could see of the speaker, then he looked to the left at the rather studious profile of Lord Basildon. The Chairman of Blades was leaning back, looking critically down his nose at the hand of cards which he held out and away from him as if it were a rare object.

'My hand is so exquisite that I am forced to redouble, my dear Drax,' he said. He looked across at his partner. 'Tommy,' he said. 'Charge this to me if it goes wrong.'

'Rot,' said his partner. 'Meyer? Better take Drax out.'

'Too frightened,' said the middle-aged florid man who was playing with Drax. 'No bid.' He picked up his cigar from the brass ashtray and put it carefully into the middle of his mouth.

'No bid here,' said Basildon's partner.

'And nothing here,' came Drax's voice.

'Five clubs redoubled,' said Basildon. 'Your lead, Meyer.'

Bond looked over Drax's shoulder. Drax had the ace of spades and the ace of hearts. He promptly made them both and led another heart which Basildon took on the table with the king.

'Well,' said Basildon. 'There are four trumps against me including the queen. I shall play Drax to have her.' He finessed against Drax. Meyer took the trick with the queen.

'Hell and damnation,' said Basildon. 'What's the queen doing in Meyer's hand? Well, I'm damned. Anyway the rest are mine.' He fanned his cards down on the table. He looked defensively at his partner. 'Can you beat it, Tommy? Drax doubles and Meyer has the queen.' There was not more than a natural exasperation in his voice.

Drax chuckled. 'Didn't expect my partner to have a Yarborough did you?' he said cheerfully to Basildon. 'Well, that's just the four hundred above the line. Your deal.' He cut the cards to Basildon and the game went on.

So it had been Drax's deal the hand before. That might be important. Bond lit a cigarette and reflectively examined the back of Drax's head.

M's voice cut in on Bond's thoughts. 'You remember my friend Commander Bond, Basil? Thought we'd come along and play some bridge this evening.'

Basildon smiled up at Bond. 'Evening,' he said. He waved a hand round the table from the left to right. 'Meyer, Dangerfield, Drax.' The three men looked up briefly and Bond nodded a greeting to the table in general. 'You all know the Admiral,' added the Chairman, starting to deal.

Drax half turned in his chair. 'Ah, the Admiral,' he said boisterously. 'Glad to have you aboard, Admiral. Drink?'

'No, thanks,' said M with a thin smile. 'Just had one.'

Drax turned and glanced up at Bond, who caught a glimpse of a tuft of reddish moustache and a rather chilly blue eye. 'What about you?' asked Drax perfunctorily.

'No, thanks,' said Bond.

Drax swivelled back to the table and picked up his

cards. Bond watched the big blunt hands sort them.

Then he moved round the table with a second clue to ponder.

Drax didn't sort his cards into suits as most players do, but only into reds and blacks, ungraded, making his hand very difficult to kibitz and almost impossible for one of his neighbours, if they were so inclined to decipher.

Bond knew it for the way people hold their hands who are very careful card-players indeed.

Bond went and stood beside the chimneypiece. He took out a cigarette and lit it at the flame from a small gas-jet enclosed in a silver grille – a relic of the days before the use of matches – that protruded from the wall beside him.

From where he stood he could see the hand of Meyer, and by moving a pace to the right, of Basildon. His view of Sir Hugo Drax was uninterrupted and he inspected him carefully while appearing to interest himself only in the game.

Drax gave the impression of being a little larger than life. He was physically big – about six foot tall, Bond guessed – and his shoulders were exceptionally broad. He had a big square head and the tight reddish hair was parted in the middle. On either side of the parting the hair dipped down in a curve towards the temples with the object, Bond assumed, of hiding as much as possible of the tissue of shining puckered skin that covered most of the right half of his face. Other relics of plastic surgery could be detected in the man's right ear, which was not a perfect match with its companion on the left, and the right eye, which had been a surgical failure. It was considerably larger than the left eye, because of a contraction of the borrowed skin used to rebuild the upper and lower eyelids, and it looked painfully bloodshot. Bond doubted if it was capable of closing completely and he guessed that Drax covered it with a patch at night.

To conceal as much as possible of the unsightly taut skin that covered half his face, Drax had grown a bushy reddish moustache and had allowed his whiskers to grow down to the level of the lobes of his ears. He also had patches of hair on his cheek-bones.

The heavy moustache served another purpose. It helped to hide a naturally prognathous upper jaw and a marked protrusion of the upper row of teeth. Bond reflected that this was probably due to sucking his thumb as a child, and it had resulted in an ugly splaying, or diastema, of what Bond had heard his dentist call 'the centrals'. The moustache helped to hide these 'ogre's teeth' and it was only when Drax uttered, as he frequently did, his short braying laugh that the splay could be seen.

The general effect of the face – the riot of red-brown hair, the powerful nose and jaw, the florid skin – was flamboyant. It put Bond in mind of a ring-master at a circus. The contrasting sharpness and coldness of the left eye supported the likeness.

A bullying, boorish, loud-mouthed vulgarian. That would have been Bond's verdict if he had not known something of Drax's abilities. As it was, it crossed his mind that much of the effect might be Drax's idea of a latter-day Regency buck — the harmless disguise of a man with a smashed face who was also a snob.

Looking for further clues, Bond noticed that Drax was sweating rather freely. Despite the occasional growl of thunder outside it was a cool evening, and yet Drax was constantly mopping his face and neck with a huge bandana handkerchief. He smoked incessantly, stubbing out the cork-tipped Virginia cigarettes after a dozen lungfuls of smoke and almost immediately lighting another from a box of fifty in his coat pocket. His big hands, their backs thickly covered with reddish hair, were always on the move, fiddling with his cards, handling the cigarette lighter that stood beside a plain flat silver cigarette-case in front of him, twisting a lock of hair on the side of his head, using the handkerchief on his face and neck. Occasionally he put a finger greedily to his mouth and worried a nail. Even at a distance Bond could see that every finger-nail was bitten down to the quick.

The hands themselves were strong and capable but the thumbs had something ungainly about them which it took Bond a moment or two to define. He finally detected that they were unnaturally long and reached level with the top joint of the index finger.

Bond concluded his inspection with Drax's clothes

which were expensive and in excellent taste – a dark blue pinstripe in lightweight flannel, double-breasted with turnback cuffs, a heavy white silk shirt with a stiff collar, an unobtrusive tie with a small grey and white check, modest cuff-links, which looked like Cartier, and a plain gold Patek Philippe watch with a black leather strap.

Bond lit another cigarette and concentrated on the game, leaving his subconscious to digest the details of Drax's appearance and manner that had seemed to him significant and that might help to explain the riddle of his cheating, the nature of which had still to be discovered.

Half an hour later the cards had completed the circle.

'My deal,' said Drax with authority. 'Game all and we have a satisfactory inflation above the line. Now then, Max, see if you can't pick up a few aces. I'm tired of doing all the work.' He dealt smoothly and slowly round the table, keeping up a running fire of rather heavy-handed banter with the company. 'Long rubber,' he said to M who was sitting smoking his pipe between Drax and Basildon. 'Sorry to have kept you out so long. How about a challenge after dinner? Max and I'll take on you and Commander Thingummy. What did you say his name was? Good player?'

'Bond,' said M. 'James Bond. Yes, I think we'd like that very much. What do you say, James?'

Bond's eyes were glued to the bent head and slowly

moving hands of the dealer. Yes, that was it! Got you, you bastard. A Shiner. A simple, bloody Shiner that wouldn't have lasted five minutes in a pro's game. M saw the glint of assurance in Bond's eyes as they met across the table.

'Fine,' said Bond cheerfully. 'Couldn't be better.' He made an imperceptible movement of the head. 'How about showing me the Betting Book before dinner? You always say it'll amuse me.'

M nodded. 'Yes. Come along. It's in the Secretary's office. Then Basildon can come down and give us a cocktail and tell us the result of this death-struggle.' He got up.

'Order what you want,' said Basildon with a sharp glance at M. 'I'll be down directly we've polished them off.'

'Around nine then,' said Drax, glancing from M to Bond. 'Show him the bet about the girl in the balloon.' He picked up his hand. 'Looks like I shall have the Casino's money to play with,' he said after a rapid glance at his cards. 'Three No Trumps.' He shot a triumphant glance at Basildon. 'Put that in your pipe and smoke it.'

Bond, following M out of the room, missed Basildon's reply.

They walked down the stairs and along to the Secretary's office in silence. The room was in darkness. M switched on the light and went and sat down in the swivel chair in front of the busy-looking desk. He turned the chair to face Bond who had walked over to the empty fireplace and was taking out a cigarette.

'Any luck?' he asked looking up at him.

'Yes,' said Bond. 'He cheats all right.'

'Ah,' said M unemotionally. 'How does he do it?'

'Only on the deal,' said Bond. 'You know that silver cigarette-case he has in front of him, with his lighter? He never takes cigarettes from it. Doesn't want to get fingermarks on the surface. It's plain silver and very highly polished. When he deals, it's almost concealed by the cards and his big hands. And he doesn't move his hands away from it. Deals four piles quite close to him. Every card is reflected in the top of the case. It's just as good as a mirror although it looks perfectly innocent lying there. As he's such a good businessman it would be normal for him to have a first-class memory. You remember I told you about 'Shiners'? Well, that's just a version of one. No wonder he brings off these miraculous finesses every once in a while. That double we watched was easy. He knew his partner had the guarded queen. With his two aces the double was a certainty. The rest of the time he just plays his average game. But knowing all the cards on every fourth deal is a terrific edge. It's not surprising he always shows a profit.'

'But one doesn't notice him doing it,' protested M.

'It's quite natural to look down when one's dealing,' said Bond. 'Everybody does. And he covers up with a lot of banter, much more than he produces when someone else is dealing. I expect he's got very good peripheral vision – the thing they mark us so highly for when we take our medical for the Service. Very wide angle of sight.'

The door opened and Basildon came in. He was bristling. He shut the door behind him. 'That dam' shut-out bid of Drax's,' he exploded. 'Tommy and I could have made four hearts if we could have got around to bidding it. Between them they had the ace of hearts, six club tricks, and the ace, king of diamonds and a bare guard in spades. Made nine tricks straight off. How he had the face to open Three No Trumps I can't imagine.' He calmed down a little. 'Well, Miles,' he said, 'has your friend got the answer?'

M gestured to Bond, who repeated what he had told M. Lord Basildon's face got angrier as Bond talked.

'Damn the man,' he exploded when Bond had finished. 'What the hell does he want to do that for? Bloody millionaire. Rolling in money. Fine scandal we're in for. I'll simply have to tell the Committee. Haven't had a cheating case since the 'fourteen-eighteen war.' He paced up and down the room. The club was quickly forgotten as he remembered the significance of Drax himself. 'And they say this rocket of his is going to be ready before long. Only comes up here once or twice a week for a bit of relaxation. Why, the man's a public hero! this is terrible.'

Basildon's anger was chilled by the thought of his responsibility. He turned to M for help. 'Now, Miles, what am I to do? He's won thousands of pounds in this club and others have lost it. Take this evening. It doesn't matter about my losses, of course. But what about Dangerfield? I happen to know he's been having a bad time on the stock market lately. I don't see how I can avoid telling the Committee. Can't shirk it — whoever Drax is. And you know what that'll mean. There are ten on the Committee. Bound to be a leak. And then look at the scandal. They tell me the Moonraker can't exist without Drax and the papers say the whole future of the country depends on the thing. This is a damned serious business.' He paused and shot a hopeful glance at M and then at Bond. 'Is there any alternative?'

Bond stubbed out his cigarette. 'He could be stopped,' he said quietly. That is,' he added with a thin smile, 'if you don't mind paying him out in his own coin.'

'Do anything you bloody well like,' said Basildon emphatically. 'What are you thinking of?' Hope dawned in his eyes at Bond's assurance.

'Well,' said Bond. 'I could show him I'd spotted him and at the same time flay the hide off him at his own game. Of course Meyer'd get hurt in the process. Might lose a lot of money as Drax's partner. Would that matter?'

'Serve him right,' said Basildon, overcome with relief and ready to grasp at any solution. 'He's been riding along on Drax's back. Making plenty of money playing with him. You don't think . . .'

'No,' said Bond. 'I'm sure he doesn't know what's going on. Although some of Drax's bids must come as a bit of a shock. Well,' he turned to M, 'is it all right with you, sir?'

M reflected. He looked at Basildon. There was no doubt of his view.

He looked at Bond. 'All right,' he said. 'What must be, must be. Don't like the idea, but I can see Basildon's point. So long as you can bring it off and,' he smiled, 'as long as you don't want me to palm any cards or anything of that sort. No talent for it.'

'No,' said Bond. He put his hands in his coat pockets and touched the two silk handkerchiefs. 'And I think it should work. All I need is a couple of packs of used cards, one of each colour, and ten minutes in here alone.'

5 / DINNER AT BLADES

It was eight o'clock as Bond followed M through the tall doors, across the well of the staircase from the card room, that opened into the beautiful white and gold Regency dining-room of Blades.

M chose not to hear a call from Basildon who was presiding over the big centre table where there were still two places vacant. Instead, he walked firmly across the room to the end one of a row of six smaller tables, waved Bond into the comfortable armed chair that faced outwards into the room, and himself took the one on Bond's left so that his back was to the company.

The head steward was already behind Bond's chair. He placed a broad menu card beside his plate and handed another to M. 'Blades' was written in fine gold script across the top. Below there was a forest of print.

'Don't bother to read through all that,' said M, 'unless you've got no ideas. One of the first rules of the club, and one of the best, was that any member may speak for any dish, cheap or dear, but he must pay for it. The same's true today, only the odds are one doesn't have to pay for it. Just order what you feel like.' He looked up at the steward. 'Any of that Beluga caviar left, Porterfield?'

'Yes, sir. There was a new delivery last week.'

'Well,' said M. 'Caviar for me. Devilled kidney and a slice of your excellent bacon. Peas and new potatoes. Strawberries in kirsch. What about you, James?'

'I've got a mania for really good smoked salmon,' said Bond. Then he pointed down the menu. 'Lamb cutlets. The same vegetables as you, as it's May. Asparagus with Béarnaise sauce sounds wonderful. And perhaps a slice of pineapple.' He sat back and pushed the menu away.

'Thank heaven for a man who makes up his mind,' said M. He looked up at the steward. 'Have you got all that, Porterfield?'

'Yes, sir.' The steward smiled. 'You wouldn't care for a marrow bone after the strawberries, sir? We got half a dozen in today from the country, and I'd specially kept one in case you came in.'

'Of course. You know I can't resist them. Bad for me but it can't be helped. God knows what I'm celebrating this evening. But it doesn't often happen. Ask Grimley to come over, would you.'

'He's here now, sir,' said the steward, making way for the wine-waiter.

'Ah, Grimley, some vodka, please.' He turned to Bond. 'Not the stuff you had in your cocktail. This is real pre-war Wolfschmidt from Riga. Like some with your smoked salmon?'

'Very much,' said Bond.

'Then what?' asked M. 'Champagne?' Personally

I'm going to have a half-bottle of claret. The Mouton Rothschild '34, please, Grimley. But don't pay any attention to me, James. I'm an old man. Champagne's no good for me. We've got some good champagnes, haven't we, Grimley?' None of that stuff you're always telling me about, I'm afraid, James. Don't often see it in England. Taittinger, wasn't it?'

Bond smiled at M's memory. 'Yes,' he said, 'but it's only a fad of mine. As a matter of fact, for various reasons I believe I would like to drink champagne this evening. Perhaps I could leave it to Grimley.'

The wine-waiter was pleased. 'If I may suggest it, sir, the Dom Perignon '46. I understand that France only sells it for dollars, sir, so you don't often see it in London. I believe it was a gift from the Regency Club in New York, sir. I have some on ice at the moment. It's the Chairman's favourite and he's told me to have it ready every evening in case he needs it.'

Bond smiled his agreement.

'So be it, Grimley,' said M. 'The Dom Perignon. Bring it straight away, would you?'

A waitress appeared and put racks of fresh toast on the table and a silver dish of Jersey butter. As she bent over the table her black skirt brushed Bond's arm and he looked up into two pert, sparkling eyes under a soft fringe of hair. The eyes held his for a fraction of a second and then she whisked away. Bond's eyes followed the white bow at her waist and the starched collar and cuffs of her uniform as she went down the long room.

His eyes narrowed. He recalled a pre-war establishment in Paris where the girls were dressed with the same exciting severity. Until they turned round and showed their backs.

He smiled to himself. The *Marthe Richards* law had changed all that.

M turned from studying their neighbours behind him. 'Why were you so cryptic about drinking champagne?'

'Well, if you don't mind, sir,' Bond explained, 'I've got to get a bit tight tonight. I'll have to seem very drunk when the time comes. It's not an easy thing to act unless you do it with a good deal of conviction. I hope you won't get worried if I seem to get frayed at the edges later on.'

M shrugged his shoulders. 'You've got a head like a rock, James,' he said. Drink as much as you like if it's going to help. Ah, here's the vodka.'

When M poured him three fingers from the frosted carafe Bond took a pinch of black pepper and dropped it on the surface of the vodka. The pepper slowly settled to the bottom of the glass leaving a few grains on the surface which Bond dabbed up with the tip of a finger. Then he tossed the cold liquor well to the back of his throat and put his glass, with the dregs of the pepper at the bottom, back on the table.

M gave him a glance of rather ironical inquiry.

'It's a trick the Russians taught me that time you attached me to the Embassy in Moscow,' apologized

Bond. 'There's often quite a lot of fusel oil on the surface of this stuff – at least there used to be when it was badly distilled. Poisonous. In Russia, where you get a lot of bath-tub liquor, it's an understood thing to sprinkle a little pepper in your glass. It takes the fusel oil to the bottom. I got to like the taste and now it's a habit. But I shouldn't have insulted the club Wolfschmidt,' he added with a grin.

M grunted. 'So long as you don't put pepper in Basildon's favourite champagne,' he said drily.

A harsh bray of laughter came from a table at the far end of the room. M looked over his shoulder and then turned back to his caviar.

'What do you think of this man Drax?' he said through a mouthful of buttered toast.

Bond helped himself to another slice of smoked salmon from the silver dish beside him. It had the delicate glutinous texture only achieved by Highland curers – very different from the desiccated products of Scandinavia. He rolled a wafer-thin slice of brown bread-and-butter into a cylinder and contemplated it thoughtfully.

'One can't like his manner much. At first I was rather surprised that you tolerate him here.' He glanced at M, who shrugged his shoulders. 'But that's none of my business and anyway clubs would be very dull without a sprinkling of eccentrics. And in any case he's a national hero and a millionaire and obviously an adequate card-player. Even when he isn't helping himself to the odds,' he added. 'But I can see he's the sort of man I always imagined. Full-blooded, ruthless, shrewd. Plenty of guts. I'm not surprised he's managed to get where he is. What I don't understand is why he should be quite happy to throw it all away. This cheating of his. It's really beyond belief. What's he trying to prove with it? That he can beat everyone at everything? He seems to put so much passion into his cards – as if it wasn't a game at all, but some sort of trial of strength. You've only got to look at his finger-nails. Bitten to the quick. And he sweats too much. There's a lot of tension there somewhere. It comes out in those ghastly jokes of his. They're harsh. There's no light touch about them. He seemed to want to squash Basildon like a fly. Hope I shall be able to keep my temper. That manner of his is pretty riling. He even treats his partner as if he was muck. He hasn't quite got under my skin, but I shan't at all mind sticking a very sharp pin in him tonight.' He smiled at M 'If it comes off, that is.'

'I know what you mean,' said M. 'But you may be being a bit hard on the man. After all, it's a big step from the Liverpool docks, or wherever he came from, to where he is now. And he's one of those people who was born with naturally hairy heels. Nothing to do with snobbery. I expect his mates in Liverpool found him just as loud-mouthed as Blades does. As for his cheating, there's probably a crooked streak in him somewhere. I dare say he took plenty of short cuts on his way up. Somebody said that to become very rich you have to be helped by a combination of remarkable circumstances and an unbroken run of luck. It certainly isn't only the qualities of people that make them rich. At least that's my experience. At the beginning, getting together the first ten thousand, or the first hundred thousand, things have got to go damn right. And in that commodity business after the war, with all the regulations and restrictions, I expect it was often a case of being able to drop a thousand pounds in the right pocket. Officials. The ones who understand nothing but addition, division – and silence. The useful ones.'

M paused while the next course came. With it arrived the champagne in a silver ice-bucket, and the small wicker-basket containing M's half-bottle of claret.

The wine-steward waited until they had delivered a favourable judgement on the wines and then moved away. As he did so a page came up to their table. 'Commander Bond?' he asked.

Bond took the envelope that was handed to him and slit it open. He took out a thin paper packet and carefully opened it under the level of the table. It contained a white powder. He took a silver fruit knife off the table and dipped the tip of the blade into the packet so that about half its contents were transferred to the knife. He reached for his glass of champagne and tipped the powder into it.

'Now what?' said M with a trace of impatience.

There was no hint of apology in Bond's face. It wasn't

M who was going to have to do the work that evening. Bond knew what he was doing. Whenever he had a job of work to do he would take infinite pains beforehand and leave as little as possible to chance. Then if something went wrong it was the unforeseeable. For that he accepted no responsibility.

'Benzedrine,' he said. 'I rang up my secretary before dinner and asked her to wangle some out of the surgery at Headquarters. It's what I shall need if I'm going to keep my wits about me tonight. It's apt to make one a bit overconfident, but that'll be a help too.' He stirred the champagne with a scrap of toast so that the white powder whirled among the bubbles. Then he drank the mixture down with one long swallow. 'It doesn't taste,' said Bond, 'and the champagne is quite excellent.'

M smiled at him indulgently. 'It's your funeral,' he said. – 'Now we'd better get on with our dinner. How were the cutlets?'

'Superb,' said Bond. 'I could cut them with a fork. The best English cooking is the best in the world – particularly at this time of the year. By the way, what stakes will we be playing for this evening? I don't mind very much. We ought to end up the winners. But I'd like to know how much it will cost Drax.'

'Drax likes to play for what he calls "One and One",' said M, helping himself from the strawberries that had just been put on the table. 'Modest sounding stake, if you don't know what it stands for. In fact it's one tenner a hundred and one hundred pounds on the rubber.'

'Oh,' said Bond respectfully. 'I see.'

'But he's perfectly happy to play for Two and Two or even Three and Three. Mounts up at those figures. The average rubber of bridge at Blades is about ten points. That's £200 at One and One. And the bridge here makes for big rubbers. There are no conventions so there's plenty of gambling and bluffing. Sometimes it's more like poker. They're a mixed lot of players. Some of them are the best in England, but others are terribly wild. Don't seem to mind how much they lose. General Bealey, just behind us.' M made a gesture with his head, 'Doesn't know the reds from the blacks. Nearly always a few hundred down at the end of the week. Doesn't seem to care. Bad heart. No dependants. Stacks of money from jute. But Duff Sutherland, the scruffy-looking chap next to the chairman, is an absolute killer. Makes a regular ten thousand a year out of the club. Nice chap. Wonderful card manners. Used to play chess for England.'

M was interrupted by the arrival of his marrow bone. It was placed upright in a spotless lace napkin on the silver plate. An ornate silver marrow-scoop was laid beside it.

After the asparagus, Bond had little appetite for the thin slivers of pineapple. He tipped the last of the ice-cold champagne into his glass. He felt wonderful. The effects of the benzedrine and champagne had more than offset the splendour of the food. For the first time he took his mind away from the dinner and his conversation with M and glanced round the room.

It was a sparkling scene. There were perhaps fifty men in the room, the majority in dinner jackets, all at ease with themselves and their surroundings, all stimulated by the peerless food and drink, all animated by a common interest – the prospect of high gambling, the grand slam, the ace pot, the key-throw in a 64 game at backgammon. There might be cheats or possible cheats amongst them, men who beat their wives, men with perverse instincts, greedy men, cowardly men, lying men; but the elegance of the room invested each one with a kind of aristocracy.

At the far end, above the cold table, laden with lobsters, pies, joints and delicacies in aspic, Romney's unfinished full-length portrait of Mrs Fitzherbert gazed provocatively across at Fragonard's *Jeu de Cartes*, the broad conversation-piece which half-filled the opposite wall above the Adam fireplace. Along the lateral walls, in the centre of each gilt-edged panel, was one of the rare engravings of the Hell-Fire Club in which each figure is shown making a minute gesture of scatological or magical significance. Above, marrying the walls into the ceiling, ran a frieze in plaster relief of carved urns and swags interrupted at intervals by the capitals of the fluted pilasters which framed the windows and the tall double doors, the latter delicately carved with a design showing the Tudor Rose interwoven with a ribbon effect.

The central chandelier, a cascade of crystal ropes terminating in a broad basket of strung quartz, sparkled warmly above the white damask tablecloths and George IV silver. Below, in the centre of each table, branched candlesticks distributed the golden light of three candles, each surmounted by a red silk shade, so that the faces of the diners shone with a convivial warmth which glossed over the occasional chill of an eye or cruel twist of a mouth.

Even as Bond drank in the warm elegance of the scene, some of the groups began to break up. There was a drift towards the door accompanied by an exchange of challenges, side-bets, and exhortations to hurry up and get down to business. Sir Hugo Drax, his hairy red face shining with cheerful anticipation, came towards them with Meyer in his wake.

'Well, gentlemen,' he said jovially as he reached their table. 'Are the lambs ready for the slaughter and the geese for the plucking?' He grinned and in wolfish pantomime drew a finger across his throat. 'We'll go ahead and lay out the axe and the basket. Made your wills?'

'Be with you in a moment,' said M edgily. 'You go along and stack the cards.'

Drax laughed. 'We shan't need any artificial aids,' he said. 'Don't be long.' He turned and made for the door. Meyer enveloped them in an uncertain smile and followed him.

M grunted. 'We'll have coffee and brandy in the card

room,' he said to Bond. 'Can't smoke here. Now then. Any final plans?'

'I'll have to fatten him up for the kill, so please don't worry if I seem to be getting high,' said Bond. 'We'll just have to play our normal game till the time comes. When it's his deal, we'll have to be careful. Of course, he can't alter the cards and there's no reason why he shouldn't deal us good hands, but he's bound to bring off some pretty remarkable coups. Do you mind if I sit on his left?'

'No,' said M. 'Anything else?'

Bond reflected for a moment. 'Only one thing, sir,' he said. 'When the time comes, I shall take a white handerchief out of my coat pocket. That will mean that you are about to be dealt a Yarborough. Would you please leave the bidding of that hand to me?'

Drax and Meyer were waiting for them. They were
leaning back in their chairs, smoking Cabinet Havanas.

On the small tables beside them there was coffee and
large balloons of brandy. As M and Bond came up, Drax
was tearing the paper cover off a new pack of cards.
The other pack was fanned out across the green baize
in front of him.

'Ah, there you are,' said Drax. He leant forward and
cut a card. They all followed suit. Drax won the cut
and elected to stay where he was and take the red
cards.

Bond sat down on Drax's left.

M beckoned to a passing waiter. 'Coffee and the club
brandy,' he said. He took out a thin black cheroot and
offered one to Bond who accepted it. Then he picked
up the red cards and started to shuffle them.

'Stakes?' asked Drax, looking at M. 'One and One?
Or more? I'll be glad to accommodate you up to Five
and Five.'

'One and One'll be enough for me,' said M. 'James?'

Drax cut in, 'I suppose your guest knows what he's
in for?' he asked sharply.

Bond answered for M. 'Yes,' he said briefly. He smiled

at Drax. 'And I feel rather generous tonight. What would you like to take off me?'

'Every penny you've got,' said Drax cheerfully. 'How much can you afford?'

'I'll tell you when there's none left,' said Bond. He suddenly decided to be ruthless. 'I'm told that Five and Five is your limit. Let's play for that.'

Almost before the words were out of his mouth he regretted them. £50 a hundred! £500 side-bets! Four bad rubbers would be double his income for a year. If something went wrong he'd look pretty stupid. Have to borrow from M. And M wasn't a particularly rich man. Suddenly he saw that this ridiculous game might end in a very nasty mess. He felt the prickle of sweat on his forehead. That damned benzedrine. And, for him of all people to allow himself to be needled by a blustering loud-mouthed bastard like Drax. And he wasn't even on a job. The whole evening was a bit of a social pantomime that meant less than nothing to him. Even M had only been dragged into it by chance. And all of a sudden he'd let himself be swept up into a duel with this multimillionaire, into a gamble for literally all Bond possessed, for the simple reason that the man had got filthy manners and he'd wanted to teach him a lesson. And supposing the lesson didn't come off? Bond cursed himself for an impulse that earlier in the day would have seemed unthinkable. Champagne and benzedrine! Never again.

Drax was looking at him in sarcastic disbelief. He

turned to M who was still unconcernedly shuffling the cards. 'I suppose your guest is good for his commitments,' he said. Unforgivably.

Bond saw the blood rush up M's neck and into his face. M paused for an instant in his shuffling. When he continued Bond noticed that his hands were quite calm. M looked up and took the cheroot very deliberately out from between his teeth. His voice was perfectly controlled. 'If you mean "Am I good for my guest's commitments",' he said coldly, 'the answer is yes.'

He cut the cards to Drax with his left hand and with his right knocked the ash off his cheroot into the copper ashtray in the corner of the table. Bond heard the faint hiss as the burning ash hit the water.

Drax squinted sideways at M. He picked up the cards. 'Of course, of course,' he said hastily. 'I didn't mean . . .' He left the sentance unfinished and turned to Bond. 'Right, then,' he said, looking rather curiously at Bond. 'Five and Five it is. Meyer,' he turned to his partner, 'how much would you like to take? There's Six and Six to cut up.'

'One and One's enough for me, Hugger,' said Meyer apologetically. 'Unless you'd like me to take some more.'

He looked anxiously at his partner.

'Of course not,' said Drax. 'I like a high game. Never get enough on, generally. Now then,' he started to deal. 'Off we go.'

And suddenly Bond didn't care about the high stakes. Suddenly all he wanted to do was to give this hairy ape the lesson of his life, give him a shock which would make him remember this evening for ever, remember Bond, remember M, remember the last time he would cheat at Blades, remember the time of day, the weather outside, what he had had for dinner.

For all its importance, Bond had forgotten the Moonraker. This was a private affair between two men.

As he watched the casual downward glance at the cigarette-case between the two hands and felt the cool memory ticking up the card values as they passed over its surface, Bond cleared his mind of all regrets, absolved himself of all blame for what was about to happen, and focused his attention on the game. He settled himself more comfortably into his chair and rested his hands on the padded leather arms. Then he took the thin cheroot from between his teeth, laid it on the burnished copper surround of the ashtray beside him and reached for his coffee. It was very black and strong. He emptied the cup and picked up the balloon glass with its fat measure of pale brandy. As he sipped it and then drank again, more deeply, he looked over the rim at M. M met his eye and smiled briefly.

'Hope you like it,' he said. 'Comes from one of the Rothschild estates at Cognac. About a hundred years ago one of the family bequeathed us a barrel of it every year in perpetuity. During the war they hid a barrel for us every year and then sent us over the whole lot in 1945. Ever since then we've been drinking doubles. And,' he gathered up his cards, 'now we shall have to concentrate.'

Bond picked up his hand. It was average. A bare two-and-a-half quick tricks, the suits evenly distributed. He reached for his cheroot and gave it a final draw, then killed it in the ashtray.

'Three clubs,' said Drax.

No bid from Bond.

Four clubs from Meyer.

No bid from M.

Hm, thought Bond. He's not quite got the cards for a game call this time. Shut-out call – knows that his partner has got a bare raise. M may have got a perfectly good bid. We may have all the hearts between us, for instance. But M never gets a bid. Presumably they'll make four clubs.

They did, with the help of one finesse through Bond. M turned out not to have had hearts, but a long string of diamonds, missing only the king, which was in Meyer's hand and would have been caught. Drax didn't have nearly enough length for a three call. Meyer had the rest of the clubs.

Anyway, thought Bond as he dealt the next hand, we were lucky to escape without a game call.

Their good luck continued. Bond opened a No Trump, was put up to three by M, and they made it with an over-trick. On Meyer's deal they went one down in five diamonds, but on the next hand M opened four spades and Bond's three small trumps and an outside king, queen were all M needed for the contract.

First rubber to M and Bond. Drax looked annoyed. He had lost £900 on the rubber and the cards seemed to be running against them.

'Shall we go straight on?' he asked. 'No point in cutting.'

M smiled across at Bond. The same thought was in both their minds. So Drax wanted to keep the deal. Bond shrugged his shoulders.

'No objection,' said M. 'These seats seem to be doing their best for us.'

'Up to now,' said Drax, looking more cheerful.

And with reason. On the next hand he and Meyer bid and made a small slam in spades that required two hair-raising finesses, both of which Drax, after a good deal of pantomime and hemming and hawing, negotiated smoothly, each time commenting loudly on his good fortune.

'Hugger, you're wonderful,' said Meyer fulsomely. 'How the devil do you do it?'

Bond thought it time to sow a tiny seed. 'Memory,' he said.

Drax looked at him, sharply. 'What do you mean, memory?' he said. 'What's that got to do with taking a finesse?'

'I was going to add "and card sense",' said Bond

smoothly. 'They're the two qualities that make great card-players.'

'Oh,' said Drax slowly. 'Yes, I see.' He cut the cards to Bond and as Bond dealt he felt the other man's eyes examining him carefully.

The game proceeded at an even pace. The cards refused to get hot and no one seemed inclined to take chances. M doubled Meyer in an incautious four-spade bid and got him two down vulnerable, but on the next hand Drax went out with a lay down three No Trumps. Bond's win on the first rubber was wiped out and a bit more besides.

'Anyone care for a drink?' asked M as he cut the cards to Drax for the third rubber. 'James. A little more champagne. The second bottle always tastes better.'

'I'd like that very much,' said Bond.

The waiter came. The others ordered whiskies and sodas.

Drax turned to Bond. 'This game needs livening up,' he said. 'A hundred we win this hand.' He had completed the deal and the cards lay in neat piles in the centre of the table.

Bond looked at him. The damaged eye glared at him redly. The other was cold and hard and scornful. There were beads of sweat on either side of the large, beaky nose.

Bond wondered if he was having a fly thrown over him to see if he was suspicious of the deal. He decided to leave the man in doubt. It was a hundred down the drain, but it would give him an excuse for increasing the stakes later.

'On your deal?' he said with a smile. 'Well,' he weighed imaginary chances. 'Yes. All right.' An idea seemed to come to him. 'And the same on the next hand. If you like,' he added.

'All right, all right,' said Drax impatiently. 'If you want to throw good money after bad.'

'You seem very certain about this hand,' said Bond indifferently, picking up his cards. They were a poor lot and he had no answer to Drax's opening No Trump except to double it. The bluff had no effect on Drax's partner. Meyer said 'Two No Trumps' and Bond was relieved when M, with no long suit, said 'No bid'. Drax left it in two No Trumps and made the contract.

'Thanks,' he said with relish, and wrote carefully on his score. 'Now let's see if you can get it back.'

Much to his annoyance, Bond couldn't. The cards still ran for Meyer and Drax and they made three hearts and the game.

Drax was pleased with himself. He took a long swallow at his whisky and soda and wiped down his face with his bandana handkerchief.

'God is with the big battalions,' he said jovially. 'Got to have the cards as well as play them. Coming back for more or had enough?'

Bond's champagne had come and was standing beside him in its silver bucket. There was a glass goblet three-quarters full beside it on the side table. Bond picked it up and drained it, as if to give himself Dutch courage. Then he filled it again.

'All right,' he said thickly, 'a hundred on the next two hands.'

And promptly lost them both, and the rubber.

Bond suddenly realized that he was nearly £1500 down. He drank another glass of champagne. 'Save trouble if we just double the stakes on this rubber,' he said rather wildly. 'All right with you?'

Drax had dealt and was looking at his cards. His lips were wet with anticipation. He looked at Bond who seemed to be having difficulty lighting his cigarette. 'Taken,' he said quickly. 'A hundred pounds a hundred and a thousand on the rubber.' Then he felt he could risk a touch of sportsmanship. Bond could hardly cancel the bet now. 'But I seem to have got some good tickets here,' he added. 'Are you still on?'

'Of course, of course,' said Bond, clumsily picking up his hand. 'I made the bet, didn't I?'

'All right, then,' said Drax with satisfaction. 'Three No Trumps here.'

He made four.

Then, to Bond's relief, the cards turned. Bond bid and made a small slam in hearts and on the next hand M ran out in three No Trumps.

Bond grinned cheerfully into the sweating face. Drax was picking angrily at his nails. 'Big battalions,' said Bond, rubbing it in.

Drax growled something and busied himself with the score. Bond looked across at M, who was putting a match, with evident satisfaction at the way the game had gone, to his second cheroot of the evening, an almost unheard of indulgence.

''Fraid this'll have to be my last rubber,' said Bond. 'Got to get up early. Hope you'll forgive me.'

M looked at his watch. 'It's past midnight,' he said. 'What about you, Meyer?'

Meyer, who had been a silent passenger for most of the evening and who had the look of a man caught in a cage with a couple of tigers, seemed relieved at being offered a chance of making his escape. He leapt at the idea of getting back to his quiet flat in Albany and the soothing companionship of his collection of Battersea snuff-boxes.

'Quite all right with me, Admiral,' he said quickly. 'What about you, Hugger? Nearly ready for bed?'

Drax ignored him. He looked up from his score-sheet at Bond. He noticed the signs of intoxication. The moist forehead, the black comma of hair that hung untidily over the right eyebrow, the sheen of alcohol in the grey-blue eyes.

'Pretty miserable balance so far,' he said. 'I make it you win a couple of hundred or so. Of course if you want to run out of the game you can. But how about some fireworks to finish up with? Treble the stakes on the last rubber? Fifteen and fifteen? Historic match. Am I on?'

Bond looked up at him. He paused before answering. He wanted Drax to remember every detail of this last rubber, every word that had been spoken, every gesture.

'Well,' said Drax impatiently. 'What about it?'

Bond looked into the cold left eye in the flushed face. He spoke to it alone.

'One hundred and fifty pounds a hundred, and £1500 on the rubber,' he said distinctly. 'You're on.'

There was a moment's silence at the table. It was broken by the agitated voice of Meyer.

'Here I say,' he said anxiously. 'Don't include me in on this, Hugger.' He knew it was a private bet with Bond, but he wanted to show Drax that he was thoroughly nervous about the whole affair. He saw himself making some ghastly mistake that would cost his partner a lot of money.

'Don't be ridiculous, Max,' said Drax harshly. 'You play your hand. This is nothing to do with you. Just an enjoyable little bet with our rash friend here. Come along, come along. My deal, Admiral.'

M cut the cards and the game began.

Bond lit a cigarette with hands that had suddenly become quite steady. His mind was clear. He knew exactly what he had to do, and when, and he was glad that the moment of decision had come.

He sat back in his chair and for a moment he had the impression that there was a crowd behind him at each elbow, and that faces were peering over his shoulder, waiting to see his cards. He somehow felt that the ghosts were friendly, that they approved of the rough justice that was about to be done.

He smiled as he caught himself sending this company of dead gamblers a message, that they should see that all went well.

The background noise of the famous gaming room broke in on his thoughts. He looked round. In the middle of the long room, under the central chandelier, there were several onlookers round the poker game. 'Raise you a hundred.' 'And a hundred.' 'And a hundred.' 'Damn you. I'll look', and a shout of triumph followed by a hubbub of comment. In the distance he could hear the rattle of a croupier's rake against the counters at the Shemmy game. Nearer at hand, at his end of the room, there were three other tables of bridge over which the smoke of cigars and cigarettes rose towards the barrelled ceiling.

Nearly every night for more than a hundred and fifty years there had been just such a scene, he reflected, in this famous room. The same cries of victory and defeat, the same dedicated faces, the same smell of tobacco and drama. For Bond, who loved gambling, it was the most exciting spectacle in the world. He gave it a last glance to fix it all in his mind and then he turned back to his table.

He picked up his cards and his eyes glittered. For once, on Drax's deal, he had a cast-iron game hand; seven spades with the four top honours, the ace of hearts, and the ace, king of diamonds. He looked at Drax. Had he and Meyer got the clubs? Even so Bond could overbid. Would Drax try and force him too high and risk a double? Bond waited.

'No bid,' said Drax, unable to keep the bitterness of his private knowledge of Bond's hand out of his voice.

'Four spades,' said Bond.

No bid from Meyer; from M; reluctantly from Drax. M provided some help, and they made five.

One hundred and fifty points below the line. A hundred above for honours.

'Humph,' said a voice at Bond's elbow. He looked up. It was Basildon. His game had finished and he had strolled over to see what was happening on this separate battlefield.

He picked up Bond's score-sheet and looked at it.

'That was a bit of a beetle-crusher,' he said cheerfully. 'Seems you're holding the champions. What are the stakes?'

Bond left the answer to Drax. He was glad of the diversion. It could not have been better timed. Drax had cut the blue cards to him. He married the two halves and put the pack just in front of him, near the edge of the table.

'Fifteen and fifteen. On my left,' said Drax.

Bond heard Basildon draw in his breath.

'Chap seemed to want to gamble, so I accommodated him. Now he goes and gets all the cards . . .'

Drax grumbled on.

Across the table, M saw a white handkerchief materialize in Bond's right hand. M's eyes narrowed. Bond seemed to wipe his face with it. M saw him glance sharply at Drax and Meyer, then the handkerchief was back in his pocket.

A blue pack was in Bond's hands and he had started to deal.

'That's the hell of a stake,' said Basildon. 'We once had a thousand-pound side-bet on a game of bridge. But that was in the rubber boom before the fourteen-eighteen war. Hope nobody's going to get hurt.' He meant it. Very high stakes in a private game generally led to trouble. He walked round and stood between M and Drax.

Bond completed the deal. With a touch of anxiety he picked up his cards.

He had nothing but five clubs to the ace, queen, ten, and eight small diamonds to the queen.

It was all right. The trap was set.

He almost felt Drax stiffen as the big man thumbed through his cards, and then, unbelieving, thumbed them through again. Bond knew that Drax had an incredibly good hand. Ten certain tricks, the ace, king of diamonds, the four top honours in spades, the four top honours in hearts, and the king, knave, nine of clubs.

Bond had dealt them to him – in the Secretary's room before dinner.

Bond waited, wondering how Drax would react to the huge hand. He took an almost cruel interest in watching the greedy fish come to the lure.

Drax exceeded his expectations.

Casually he folded his hand and laid it on the table. Nonchalantly he took the flat carton out of his pocket, selected a cigarette and lit it. He didn't look at Bond. He glanced up at Basildon.

'Yes,' he said, continuing the conversation about their stakes. 'It's a high game, but not the highest I've ever played. Once played for two thousand a rubber in Cairo. At the Mahomet Ali as a matter of fact. They've really got guts there. Often bet on every trick as well as on the game and rubber. 'Now,' he picked up his hand and looked slyly at Bond. 'I've got some good tickets here. I'll admit it. But then you may have too, for all I know.' (Unlikely, you old shark, thought Bond, with three of the ace-kings in your own hand.) 'Care to have something extra just on this hand?'

Bond made a show of studying his cards with the minuteness of someone who is nearly very drunk. 'I've got a promising lot too.' he said thickly. 'If my partner fits and the cards lie right I might make a lot of tricks myself. What are you suggesting?'

'Sounds as if we're pretty evenly matched,' lied Drax. 'What do you say to a hundred a trick on the side? From what you say it shouldn't be too painful.'

Bond looked thoughtful and rather fuddled. He took another careful look at his hand, running through the cards one by one. 'All right,' he said. 'You're on. And frankly you've made me gamble. You've obviously got a big hand, so I must shut you out and chance it.'

Bond looked blearily across at M. 'Pay your losses on this one, partner,' he said. 'Here we go. Er – seven clubs.'

In the dead silence that followed, Basildon, who had seen Drax's hand, was so startled that he dropped his whisky and soda on the floor. He looked dazedly down at the broken glass and let it lie.

Drax said 'What?' in a startled voice and hastily ran through his cards again for reassurance.

'Did you say grand slam in clubs?' he asked, looking curiously at his obviously drunken opponent. 'Well, it's your funeral. What do you say, Max?'

'No bid,' said Meyer, feeling in the air the electricity of just that crisis he had hoped to avoid. Why the hell hadn't he gone home before this last rubber? He groaned inwardly.

'No bid,' said M apparently unperturbed. 'Double.' The word came viciously out of Drax's mouth. He put down his hand and looked cruelly, scornfully at this tipsy oaf who had at last, inexplicably, fallen into his hands.

'That mean you double the side-bets too?' asked Bond.

'Yes,' said Drax greedily. 'Yes. That's what I meant.'

'All right,' said Bond. He paused. He looked at Drax and not at his hand. 'Redouble. The contract and the side-bets. £400 a trick on the side.'

It was at that moment that the first hint of a dreadful,

incredible doubt entered Drax's mind. But again he looked at his hand, and again he was reassured. At the very worst he couldn't fail to make two tricks.

A muttered 'No bid' from Meyer. A rather strangled 'No bid' from M. An impatient shake of the head from Drax.

Basildon stood, his face very pale, looking intently across the table at Bond.

Then he walked slowly round the table, scrutinizing all the hands. What he saw was this:

BOND
◇ Queen, 8, 7, 6, 5, 4, 3, 2
♣ Ace, queen, 10, 8, 4

DRAX	MEYER
♠ Ace, king, queen, knave	♠ 6, 5, 4, 3, 2
♡ Ace, king, queen, knave	♡ 10, 9, 8, 7, 2
◇ Ace, king	◇ Knave, 10, 9
♣ King, knave, 9	

M
♠ 10, 9, 8, 7
♡ 6, 5, 4, 3
♣ 7, 6, 5, 3, 2

And suddenly Basildon understood. It was a laydown Grand Slam for Bond against any defence. Whatever Meyer led, Bond must get in with a trump in his own hand or on the table. Then, in between clearing trumps, finessing of course against Drax, he would play two rounds of diamonds, trumping them in dummy and catching Drax's ace and king in the process. After five plays he would be left with the remaining trumps and six winning diamonds. Drax's aces and kings would be totally valueless.

It was sheer murder.

Basildon, almost in a trance, continued round the table and stood between M and Meyer so that he could watch Drax's face, and Bond's. His own face was impassive, but his hands, which he had stuffed into his trouser pockets so that they would not betray him, were sweating. He waited, almost fearfully, for the terrible punishment that Drax was about to receive – thirteen separate lashes whose scars no card-player would ever lose.

'Come along, come along,' said Drax impatiently. 'Lead something. Max. Can't be here all night.'

You poor fool, thought Basildon. In ten minutes you'll wish that Meyer had died in his chair before he could pull out that first card.

In fact, Meyer looked as if at any moment he might have a stroke. He was deathly pale, and the perspiration was dropping off his chin on to his shirt front. For all he knew, his first card might be a disaster.

At last, reasoning that Bond might be void in his own long suits, spades and hearts, he led the knave of diamonds.

It made no difference what he led, but when M's hand went down showing chicane in diamonds, Drax snarled across at his partner. 'Haven't you got anything else, you dam' fool? Want to hand it to him on a plate? Whose side are you on, anyway?'

Meyer cringed into his clothes. 'Best I could do, Hugger,' he said miserably, wiping his face with his handkerchief.

But by this time Drax had got his own worries.

Bond trumped on the table, catching Drax's king of diamonds, and promptly led a club. Drax put up his nine. Bond took it with his ten and led a diamond, trumping it on the table. Drax's ace fell. Another club from the table, catching Drax's knave.

Then the ace of clubs.

As Drax surrendered his king, for the first time he saw what might be happening. His eyes squinted anxiously at Bond, waiting fearfully for the next card. Had Bond got the diamonds? Hadn't Meyer got them guarded? After all, he had opened with them. Drax waited, his cards slippery with sweat.

Morphy, the great chess player, had a terrible habit. He would never raise his eyes from the game until he knew his opponent could not escape defeat. Then he would slowly lift his great head and gaze curiously at the man across the board. His opponent would feel the gaze and would slowly, humbly raise his eyes to meet Morphy's. At that moment he would know that it was no good continuing the game. The eyes of Morphy said so. There was nothing left but surrender.

Now, like Morphy, Bond lifted his head and looked straight into Drax's eyes. Then he slowly drew out the queen of diamonds and placed it on the table. Without waiting for Meyer to play he followed it, deliberately, with the 8, 7, 6, 5, 4, and the two winning clubs.

Then he spoke. 'That's all, Drax,' he said quietly, and sat slowly back in his chair.

Drax's first reaction was to lurch forward and tear Meyer's cards out of his hand. He faced them on the table, scrabbling feverishly among them for a possible winner.

Then he flung them back across the baize.

His face was dead white, but his eyes blazed redly at Bond. Suddenly he raised one clenched fist and crashed it on the table among the pile of impotent aces and kings and queens in front of him.

Very low, he spat the words at Bond. 'You're a che . . .'

'That's enough, Drax.' Basildon's voice came across the table like a whiplash. 'None of that talk here. I've been watching the whole game. Settle up. If you've got any complaints, put them in writing to the Committee.'

Drax got slowly to his feet. He stood away from his chair and ran a hand through his wet red hair. The colour came slowly back into his face and with it an expression of cunning. He glanced down at Bond and there was in his good eye a contemptuous triumph which Bond found curiously disturbing.

He turned to the table. 'Good night, gentlemen,' he said, looking at each of them with the same oddly scornful expression. 'I owe about £15,000. I will accept Meyer's addition.'

He leant forward and picked up his cigarette-case and lighter.

Then he looked again at Bond and spoke very quietly, the red moustache lifting slowly from the splayed upper teeth.

'I should spend the money quickly, Commander Bond,' he said.

Then he turned away from the table and walked swiftly out of the room.

Part Two / *Tuesday, Wednesday*

Although he had not got to bed until two, Bond walked into his headquarters punctually at ten the next morning. He was feeling dreadful. As well as acidity and liver as a result of drinking nearly two whole bottles of champagne, he had a touch of the melancholy and spiritual deflation that were partly the after-effects of the benzedrine and partly reaction to the drama of the night before.

When he went up in the lift towards another routine day, the bitter taste of the midnight hours was still with him.

After Meyer had scuttled thankfully off to bed, Bond had taken the two packs of cards out of the pockets of his coat and had put them on the table in front of Basildon and M. One was the blue pack that Drax had cut to him and that he had pocketed, substituting instead, under cover of his handkerchief, the stacked blue pack in his right-hand pocket. The other was the stacked red pack in his left-hand pocket which had not been needed.

He fanned the red pack out on the table and showed M and Basildon that it would have produced the same freak grand slam that had defeated Drax.

'It's a famous Culbertson hand,' he explained. 'He used it to spoof his own quick-trick conventions. I had to doctor a red and a blue pack. Couldn't know which colour I would be dealing with.'

'Well, it certainly went with a bang,' said Basildon gratefully. 'I expect he'll put two and two together and either stay away or play straight in future. Expensive evening for him. Don't let's have any arguments about your winnings,' he added. 'You've done everyone – and particularly Drax – a good turn tonight. Things might have gone wrong. Then it would have been your fingers that would have got burned. Cheque will reach you on Saturday.'

They had said good-night and Bond, in a mood of anticlimax, had gone off to bed. He had taken a mild sleeping pill to try and clear his mind of the bizarre events of the evening and prepare himself for the morning and the office. Before he slept he reflected, as he had often reflected in other moments of triumph at the card table, that the gain to the winner is, in some odd way, always less than the loss to the loser.

When he closed the door behind him Loelia Ponsonby looked curiously at the dark shadows under his eyes. He noticed the glance, as she had intended.

He grinned. 'Partly work and partly play,' he explained. 'In strictly masculine company,' he added. 'And thanks very much for the benzedrine. It really was badly needed. Hope I didn't interfere with your evening?'

'Of course not,' she said, thinking of the dinner and the library book she had abandoned when Bond telephoned. She looked down at her shorthand pad. 'The Chief of Staff telephoned half an hour ago. He said that M would be wanting you today. He couldn't say when. I told him that you've got Unarmed Combat at three and he said to cancel it. That's all, except the dockets left over from yesterday.'

'Thank heavens,' said Bond. 'I couldn't have stood being thrown about by that dam' Commando chap today. Any news of 008?'

'Yes,' she said. 'They say he's all right. He's been moved to the military hospital at Wahnerheide. Apparently it's only shock.'

Bond knew what 'shock' might mean in his profession. 'Good,' he said without conviction. He smiled at her and went into his office and closed the door.

He walked decisively round his desk to the chair, sat down, and pulled the top file towards him. Monday was gone. This was Tuesday. A new day. Closing his mind to his headache and to thoughts about the night, he lit a cigarette and opened the brown folder with the Top Secret red star on it. It was a memorandum from the Office of the Chief Preventive Officer of the United States Customs Branch and it was headed *The Inspectoscope.*

He focused his eyes.

'The Inspectoscope,' he read, 'is an instrument using fluoroscopic principles for the detection of contraband.

It is manufactured by the Sicular Inspectoscope Company of San Francisco and is widely used in American prisons for the secret detection of metal objects concealed in the clothing or on the person of criminals and prison visitors. It is also used in the detection of IDB (Illicit Diamond Buying) and diamond smuggling in the diamond fields of Africa and Brazil. The instrument costs seven thousand dollars, is approximately eight feet long by seven feet high and weighs nearly three tons. It requires two trained operators. Experiments have been made with this instrument in the customs hall of the International Airport at Idlewild with the following results . . .'

Bond skipped two pages containing details of a number of petty smuggling cases and studied the 'Summary of Conclusions' from which he deduced, with some irritation, that he would have to think of some place other than his armpit for carrying his .25 Beretta the next time he travelled abroad. He made a mental note to discuss the problem with the Technical Devices Section.

He ticked and initialled the distribution slip and automatically reached for the next folder entitled *Philopon. A Japanese murder-drug.*

'Philopon', his mind was trying to wander and he dragged it sharply back to the typewritten pages.

'Philopon is the chief factor in the increase in crime in Japan. According to the Welfare Ministry there are now 1,500,000 addicts in the country, of whom one million are under the age of 20, and the Tokyo Metropolitan Police attribute 70 per cent of juvenile crime to the influences of the drug.

'Addiction, as in the case of marijuana in the United States, begins with one "shot". The effect is "stimulating" and the drug is habit-forming. It is also cheap – about ten yen (sixpence) a shot – and the addict rapidly increases his shots to the neighbourhood of one hundred a day. In these quantities the addiction becomes expensive and the victim automatically turns to crime to pay for the drug. That the crime often includes physical assault and murder is due to a peculiar property of the drug. It induces an acute persecution complex in the addict who becomes prey to the illusion that people want to kill him and that he is always being followed with harmful intent. He will turn with his feet and fists, or with a razor, on a stranger in the streets who he thinks has scrutinized him offensively. Less advanced addicts tend to avoid an old friend who has reached the one hundred shots a day dosage, and this of course merely increases his feeling of persecution.

'In this way murder becomes an act of self-defence, virtuous and justified, and it will readily be seen what a dangerous weapon it can become in the handling and direction of organized crime by a "master-mind".

'Philopon has been traced as the motive power behind the notorious Bar Mecca murder case and as a result of that unpleasant affair the police rounded up more than 5000 *purveyors* of the drug in a matter of weeks.

'As usual Korean nationals are being blamed . . .'

Suddenly Bond rebelled. What the hell was he doing reading all this stuff? When would he conceivably require to know about a Japanese murder-drug called Philopon?

Inattentively he skimmed through the remaining pages, ticked himself off the distribution slip, and threw the docket into his out-tray.

His headache was still sitting over his right eye as if it had been nailed there. He opened one of the drawers of his desk and took out a bottle of Phensic. He considered asking his secretary for a glass of water, but he disliked being cosseted. With distaste he crunched two tablets between his teeth and swallowed down the harsh powder.

Then he lit a cigarette and got up and stood by the window. He looked across the green panorama far below him and, without seeing it, let his eyes wander aimlessly along the jagged horizon of London while his mind focused on the strange events of the night before.

And the more he thought about it, the stranger it all seemed.

Why should Drax, a millionaire, a public hero, a man with a unique position the country, why should this remarkable man cheat at cards? What could he achieve by it? What could he prove to himself? Did he think that he was so much a law unto himself, so far above the common herd and their puny canons of behaviour that he could spit in the face of public opinion?

Bond's mind paused. Spit in their faces. That just about described his manner at Blades. The combination of superiority and scorn. As if he was dealing with human muck so far beneath contempt that there was no need to put up even a pretence of decent behaviour in its company.

Presumably Drax enjoyed gambling. Perhaps it eased the tensions in him, the tensions that showed in his harsh voice, his nail-biting, the constant sweating. But he mustn't lose. It would be contemptible to lose to these inferior people. So, at whatever risk, he must cheat his way to victory. As for the possibility of detection, presumably he thought that he could bluster his way out of any corner. If he thought about it at all. And people with obsessions, reflected Bond, were blind to danger. They even courted it in a perverse way. Kleptomaniacs would try to steal more and more difficult objects. Sex maniacs would parade their importunities as if they were longing to be arrested. Pyromaniacs often made no attempt to avoid being linked with their fire-raising.

But what obsession was it that was consuming this man? What was the origin of the compulsive urge that was driving him down the steep hill into the sea?

All the signs pointed to paranoia. Delusions of grandeur and, behind that, of persecution. The contempt in his face. The bullying voice. The expression of secret triumph with which he had met defeat after a moment of bitter collapse. The triumph of the maniac who knows that whatever the facts may say he is right. Whoever may try to thwart him he can overcome. For him there is no defeat because of his secret power. He knows how to make gold. He can fly like a bird. He is almighty – the man in the padded cell who is God.

Yes, thought Bond, gazing blindly out over Regent's Park. That is the solution. Sir Hugo Drax is a raving paranoiac. That is the power which has driven him on, by devious routes, to make his millions. That is the mainspring of the gift to England of this giant rocket that will annihilate our enemies. Thanks to the all-powerful Drax.

But who can tell how near to breaking-point this man is? Who has penetrated behind that bluster, behind all that red hair on his face, who has read the signs as more than the effect of his humble origins or of sensitivity about his war wounds?

Apparently no one. Then was he, Bond, right in his analysis? What was it based on? Was this glimpse through a shuttered window into a man's soul sufficient evidence? Perhaps others had caught such a glimpse. Perhaps there had been other moments of supreme tension in Singapore, Hong Kong, Nigeria, Tangier, when some merchant sitting across a table from Drax had noticed the sweat and the bitten nails and the red blaze of the eyes in the face from which all the blood had suddenly been drained.

If one had time, thought Bond, one ought to seek those people out, if they existed, and really find out about this man, perhaps get him in the killing-bottle before it was too late.

Too late? Bond smiled to himself. What was he being so dramatic about? What had this man done to him? Made him a present of £15,000. Bond shrugged. It was none of his business anyway. But that last remark of his, 'Spend it quickly, Commander Bond.' What had he meant by that? It must be those words, Bond reflected, that had stayed in the back of his mind and made him ponder so carefully over the problem of Drax.

Bond turned brusquely away from the window. To hell with it, he thought. I'm getting obsessed myself. Now then. Fifteen thousand pounds. A miraculous windfall. All right then, he *would* spend it quickly. He sat down at his desk and picked up a pencil. He thought for a moment and then wrote carefully on a memorandum pad headed 'Top Secret':

(1) Rolls-Bentley Convertible, say £5000.

(2) Three diamond clips at £250 each, £750.

He paused. That still left nearly £10,000. Some clothes, paint the flat, a set of the new Henry Cotton irons, a few dozen of the Taittinger champagne. But those could wait. He would go that afternoon and buy the clips and talk to Bentley's. Put all the rest into gold shares. Make a fortune. Retire.

In angry protest the red telephone splintered the silence 'Can you come up? M wants you.' It was the Chief of Staff, speaking urgently.

'Coming,' said Bond, suddenly alert. 'Any clue?'

'Search me,' said the Chief of Staff. 'Hasn't touched his signals yet. Been over at the Yard and the Ministry of Supply all the morning.'

He rang off.

A few minutes later Bond was walking through the familiar door and the green light had gone on over the entrance. M looked sharply at him. 'You look pretty dreadful, 007,' he said. 'Sit down.'

It's business, thought Bond, his pulse quickening. No Christian names today. He sat down. M was studying some pencilled notes on a scratch-pad. He looked up. His eyes were no longer interested in Bond.

'Trouble down at Drax's plant last night,' he said. 'Double killing. Police tried to get hold of Drax. Didn't think of Blades apparently. Caught up with him when he got back to the Ritz about half-past one this morning. Two men from the Moonraker got shot in a public house near the plant. Both dead. Drax told the police he couldn't care less and then hung up. Typical of the man. He's down there now. Taking the thing a bit more seriously, I gather.'

'Curious coincidence,' said Bond thoughtfully. 'But where do we come in, sir? Isn't it a police job?'

'Partly,' said M, 'but it happens that we're responsible for a lot of the key personnel down there. Germans,' he added. 'I'd better explain.' He looked down at his pad. 'It's an RAF establishment and the cover-plan is that it's part of the big radar network along the East Coast. The RAF are responsible for guarding the perimeter and the Ministry of Supply only has authority at the centre where the work is going on. It's on the edge of the cliffs between Dover and Deal. The whole area covers about a thousand acres, but the site itself is about two hundred. On the site there are only Drax and fifty-two others left. All the construction team have gone.'

Pack of cards and a joker, reflected Bond.

'Fifty of these are Germans,' continued M. 'More or less all the guided missile experts the Russians didn't get. Drax paid for them to come over here and work on the Moonraker. Nobody was very happy with the arrangement but there was no alternative. The Ministry of Supply couldn't spare any of their experts from Woomera. Drax had to find his men where he could. To strengthen the RAF security people, the Ministry of Supply appointed their own security officer to live on the site. Man called Major Tallon.'

M paused and looked up at the ceiling.

'He was one of the two who got killed last night. Shot by one of the Germans, who then shot himself.'

M lowered his eyes and looked at Bond. Bond said nothing, waiting for the rest of the story.

'It happened in a public house near the site. Plenty of witnesses. Apparently it's an inn on the edge of the site that is in bounds to the men. Must have somewhere to go to, I suppose.' M paused. He kept his eyes on Bond. 'Now you asked where we come in on all this. We come in because we cleared this particular German, and all the others, before they were allowed to come over here. We've got the dossiers of all of them. So when this happened the first thing RAF Security and Scotland Yard wanted was the dossier of the dead man. They got on to the Duty Officer last night and he dug the papers out of Records and sent them over to the Yard. Routine job. He noted it in the log. When I got here this morning and saw the entry in the log I suddenly got interested.' M spoke quietly. 'After spending the evening with Drax, it was, as you remarked, a curious coincidence.'

'Very curious, sir,' said Bond, still waiting.

'And there's one more thing,' concluded M. 'And this is the real reason why I've let myself get involved instead of keeping clear of the whole business. This has got to take priority over everything.' M's voice was very quiet. 'They're going to fire the Moonraker on Friday. Less than four days' time. Practice shoot.'

M paused and reached for his pipe and busied himself lighting it.

Bond said nothing. He still couldn't see what all this had to do with the Secret Service whose jurisdiction runs only outside the United Kingdom. It seemed a job for the Special Branch of Scotland Yard, or conceivably for MI5. He waited. He looked at his watch. It was noon.

M got his pipe going and continued.

'But quite apart from that,' said M, 'I got interested because last night I got interested in Drax.'

'So did I, sir,' said Bond.

'So when I read the log,' said M, ignoring Bond's comment, 'I telephoned Vallance at the Yard and asked him what it was all about. He was rather worried and asked me to come over. I said I didn't want to tread on Five's corns but he said he had already spoken to them. They maintained it was a matter between my department and the police since it was we who had cleared the German who did the killing. So I went along.'

M paused and looked down at his notes.

'The place is on the coast about three miles north of Dover,' he said. 'There's this inn nearby on the main coast road, the 'World Without Want', and the men from the site go there in the evening. Last night, about seven-thirty, the Security man from the Ministry, this man Tallon, went along there and was having a whisky and soda and chatting away with some of the Germans when the murderer, if you like to call him that, came in and walked straight up to Tallon. He pulled out a Luger – no serial numbers by the way – out of his shirt and said,' M looked up, '"I love Gala Brand. You shall not have her". Then he shot Tallon through the heart and put the smoking gun in his own mouth and pulled the trigger.'

'What a ghastly business,' said Bond. He could see

every detail of the shambles in the crowded taproom of a typical English public house. 'Who's the girl?'

'That's another complication,' said M. 'She's an agent of the Special Branch. Bilingual in German. One of Vallance's best girls. She and Tallon were the only two non-Germans Drax had with him on the site. Vallance is a suspicious chap. Has to be. This Moonraker plan is obviously the most important thing happening in England. Without telling anyone and acting more or less on instinct, he planted this Brand girl on Drax and somehow fixed for her to be taken on as his private secretary. Been on the site since the beginning. She's had absolutely nothing to report. Says that Drax is an excellent chief, except for his manners, and drives his men like hell. Apparently he started by making passes at her, even after she'd spun the usual yarn about being engaged, but after she'd shown she could defend herself, which of course she can, he gave up and she says they're perfectly good friends. Naturally she knew Tallon, but he was old enough to be her father, besides being happily married with four children, and she told Vallance's man who got a word with her this morning that he's taken her to the cinema in a paternal sort of way twice in eighteen months. As for the killer, man called Egon Bartsch, he was an electronics expert whom she barely knew by sight.'

'What do his friends say about all this?' asked Bond.

'The man who shared his room with him backs up

Bartsch. Says he was madly in love with the Brand woman and put his whole lack of success down to "The Englishman". He says Bartsch had been getting very moody and reserved lately and that he wasn't a bit surprised to hear of the shooting.'

'Sounds pretty corroborative,' said Bond. 'Somehow one can see the picture. One of those highly strung nervous chaps with the usual German chip on the shoulder. What does Vallance think?'

'He's not sure,' said M. 'He's mainly concerned with protecting his girl from the Press and seeing that her cover doesn't get blown. All the papers are on to it, of course. It'll be in the midday editions. And they're all howling for a picture of the girl. Vallance is having one cooked up and got down to her that'll look more or less like any girl, but just sufficiently like her. She'll send it out this evening. Fortunately the reporters can't get near the place. She's refusing to talk and Vallance is praying that some friend or relation won't blow the gaff. They're holding the inquest today and Vallance is hoping that the case will be officially closed by this evening and that the papers will have to let it die for lack of material.'

'What about this practice shoot?' asked Bond.

'They're sticking to the schedule,' said M. 'Noon on Friday. They're using a dummy warhead and firing her vertically with only three-quarter tanks. They're clearing about a hundred square miles of the North Sea from about Latitude 52 up. That's north of a line joining

The Hague and the Wash. Full details are going to be given out by the PM on Thursday night.'

M stopped talking. He swivelled his chair round so that he could look out of the window. Bond heard a distant clock chime the four quarters. One o'clock. Was he going to miss his lunch again? If M would stop ferreting about in the business of other Departments he could have a quick lunch and get round to Bentley's. Bond shifted slightly in his chair.

M turned back and faced him again across the desk.

'The people who are most worried about all this,' he said, 'are the Ministry of Supply. Tallon was one of their best men. His reports had been completely negative all along. Then he suddenly rang up the Assistant Under-Secretary yesterday afternoon and said he thought something fishy was going on at the site and he asked to see the Minister personally at ten o'clock this morning. Wouldn't say anything more on the telephone. And a few hours later he gets shot. Another funny coincidence, wasn't it?'

'Very funny,' said Bond. 'But why don't they close down the site and have a wholesale inquiry? After all, this thing's too big to take a chance on.'

'The Cabinet met early this morning,' said M, 'and the Prime Minister asked the obvious question. What evidence was there of any attempt, or even of any intention, to sabotage the Moonraker? The answer was none. There were only fears which had been brought to the surface in the last twenty-four hours by Tallon's vague message and the double murder. Everyone agreed that unless there was a grain of evidence, which so far hasn't turned up, both these incidents could be put down to the terrific nervous tension on the site. The way things are in the world at the moment it was decided that the sooner the Moonraker could give us an independent say in world affairs the better for us and,' M shrugged his shoulders, 'quite possibly for the world. And it was agreed that for a thousand reasons why the Moonraker should be fired the reasons against didn't stand up. The Minister of Supply had to agree, but he knows as well as you or I that, whatever the facts, it would be a colossal victory for the Russians to sabotage the Moonraker on the eve of her practice shoot. If they did it well enough they might easily get the whole project shelved. There are fifty Germans working on the thing. Any one of them could have relatives still being held in Russia whose lives could be used as a lever.' M paused. He looked up at the ceiling. Then his eyes came down and rested thoughtfully on Bond.

'The Minister asked me to go and see him after the Cabinet. He said that the least he could do was replace Tallon at once. The new man must be bilingual in German, a sabotage expert, and have had plenty of experience of our Russian friends. MI5 have put up three candidates. They're all on cases at the moment, but they could be extricated in a few hours. But then the Minister asked my opinion. I gave it. He talked to the Prime Minister and a lot of red tape got cut very quickly.'

Bond looked sharply, resentfully, into the grey, uncompromising eyes.

'So,' said M flatly, 'Sir Hugo Drax has been notified of your appointment and he expects you down at his headquarters in time for dinner this evening.'

At six o'clock that Tuesday evening towards the end of May, James Bond was thrashing the big Bentley down the Dover road along the straight stretch that runs into Maidstone.

Although he was driving fast and with concentration, part of his mind was going back over his movements since he had left M's office four and a half hours earlier.

After giving a brief outline of the case to his secretary and eating a quick lunch at a table to himself in the canteen, he had told the garage for God's sake to hurry up with his car and deliver it, filled up, to his flat not later than four o'clock. Then he had taken a taxi down to Scotland Yard where he had an appointment with Assistant Commissioner Vallance at a quarter to three.

The courtyards and cul-de-sacs of the Yard had reminded him as usual of a prison without roofs. The overhead strip lighting in the cold corridor took the colour out of the cheeks of the police sergeant who asked his business and watched him sign the apple-green chit. It did the same for the face of the constable who led him up the short steps and along the bleak passage between the rows of anonymous doors to the waiting-room.

A quiet, middle-aged woman with the resigned eyes of someone who had seen everything came in and said the Assistant Commissioner would be free in five minutes. Bond had gone to the window and had looked out into the grey courtyard below. A constable, looking naked without his helmet, had come out of a building and walked across the yard munching a split roll with something pink between the two halves. It had been very quiet and the noise of the traffic on Whitehall and on the Embankment had sounded far away. Bond had felt dispirited. He was getting tangled up with strange departments. He would be out of touch with his own people and his own Service routines. Already, in this waiting-room, he felt out of his element. Only criminals or informers came and waited here, or influential people vainly trying to get out of a dangerous driving charge or desperately hoping to persuade Vallance that their sons were not really homosexuals. You could not be in the waiting-room of the Special Branch for any innocent purpose. You were either prosecuting or defending.

At last the woman came for him. He stubbed out his cigarette in the top of the Player's cigarette tin that serves as an ashtray in the waiting-rooms of government departments, and followed her across the corridor.

After the gloom of the waiting-room the unseasonable fire in the hearth of the large cheerful room had seemed like a trick, like the cigarette offered you by the Gestapo.

It had taken Bond a full five minutes to shake off his depression and realize that Ronnie Vallance was relieved to see him, that he was not interested in inter-departmental jealousies and that he was only looking to Bond to protect the Moonraker and get one of his best officers out of what might be a bad mess.

Vallance was a man of great tact. For the first few minutes he had spoken only of M. And he had spoken with inside knowledge and with sincerity. Without even mentioning the case he had gained Bond's friend-ship and co-operation.

As Bond swung the Bentley through the crowded streets of Maidstone he reflected that Vallance's gift had come from twenty years of avoiding the corns of MI5, of working in with the uniformed branch of the police, and of handling ignorant politicians and affronted foreign diplomats.

When Bond had left him after a quarter of an hour's hard talking, each man knew that he had acquired an ally. Vallance had sized up Bond and knew that Gala Brand would get all Bond's help and whatever protec-tion she needed. He also respected Bond's professional approach to the assignment and his absence of depart-mental rivalry with the Special Branch. As for Bond, he was full of admiration for what he had learned about Vallance's agent, and he felt that he was no longer naked and that he had Vallance and the whole of Vallance's department behind him.

Bond had left Scotland Yard with the feeling that he had achieved Clausewitz's first principle. He had made his base secure.

His visit to the Ministry of Supply had added nothing to his knowledge of the case. He had studied Tallon's record and his reports. The former was quite straightforward – a lifetime in Army Intelligence and Field Security – and the latter painted a picture of a very lively and well-managed technical establishment – one or two cases of drunkenness, one of petty theft, several personal vendettas leading to fights and mild bloodshed but otherwise a loyal and hardworking team of men.

Then he had had an inadequate half-hour in the Operations Room of the Ministry with Professor Train, a fat, scruffy, undistinguished-looking man who had been runner-up for the Physics Division of the Nobel Prize the year before and who was one of the greatest experts on guided missiles in the world.

Professor Train had walked up to a row of huge wall maps and had pulled down the cord of one of them. Bond was faced with a ten-foot horizontal scale diagram of something that looked like a V2 with big fins.

'Now,' said Professor Train, 'you know nothing about rockets so I'm going to put this in simple terms and not fill you up with a lot of stuff about Nozzle Expansion

Ratios, Exhaust Velocity, and the Keplerian Ellipse. The Moonraker, as Drax chooses to call it, is a single-stage rocket. It uses up all its fuel shooting itself into the air and then it homes on to the objective. The V2's trajectory was more like a shell fired from a gun. At the top of its 200-mile flight it had climbed to about 70 miles. It was fuelled with a very combustible mixture of alcohol and liquid oxygen which was watered down so as not to burn out the mild steel which was all they were allocated for the engine. There are far more powerful fuels available but until now we hadn't been able to achieve very much with them for the same reason, their combustion temperature is so high that they would burn out the toughest engine.'

The professor paused and stuck a finger in Bond's chest 'All you, my dear sir, have to remember about this rocket is that, thanks to Drax's Columbite, which has a melting point of about 3500 degrees Centigrade, compared with 1300 in the V2 engines, we can use one of the super fuels without burning out the engine. In fact,' he looked at Bond as if Bond should be impressed, 'we are using fluorine and hydrogen.'

'Oh, really,' said Bond reverently.

The Professor looked at him sharply. 'So we hope to achieve a speed in the neighbourhood of 1500 miles an hour and a vertical range of about 1000 miles. This should produce an operational range of about 4000 miles, bringing every European capital within reach of England. Very useful,' he added drily, 'in certain circumstances. But, for the scientists, chiefly desirable as a step towards escape from the earth. Any questions?'

'How does it work?' asked Bond dutifully.

The Professor gestured brusquely towards the diagram.

'Let's start from the nose,' he said. 'First comes the warhead. For the practice shoot this will contain upper-atmosphere instruments, radar and suchlike. Then the gyro compasses to make it fly straight – pitch-and-yaw gyro and roll gyro. Then various minor instruments, servo motors, power supply. And then the big fuel tanks – 30,000 pounds of the stuff.

'At the stern you get two small tanks to drive the turbine. Four hundred pounds of hydrogen peroxide mixes with forty pounds of potassium permanganate and makes steam which drives the turbines underneath them. These drive a set of centrifugal pumps which force the main fuel into the rocket motor. Under terrific pressure. Do you follow me?' He cocked a dubious eyebrow at Bond.

'Sounds much the same principle as a jet plane,' said Bond.

The Professor seemed pleased. 'More or less,' he said. 'But the rocket carries all its fuel inside it, instead of sucking in oxygen from outside like the Comet. Well then,' he continued, 'the fuel gets ignited in the motor and squirts out at the end in a continuous blast. Rather like a continuous recoil from a gun. And this blast forces the rocket into the air like any other firework. Of course it's at the stern that the Columbite comes in. It's allowed us to make a motor that won't be melted by the fantastic heat. And then,' he pointed, 'those are the tail fins to keep it steady at the beginning of its flight. Also made of Columbite alloy or they'd break away with the colossal air pressure. Anything else?'

'How can you be certain it'll come down where you mean it to?' asked Bond. 'What's to prevent it falling on The Hague next Friday?'

'The gyros will see to that. But as a matter of fact we're taking no chances on Friday and we're using a radar homing device on a raft in the middle of the sea. There'll be a radar transmitter in the nose of the rocket which will pick up an echo from our gadget in the sea and home on to it automatically. Of course,' the Professor grinned, 'if we ever had to use the thing in wartime it would be a great help to have a homing device transmitting energy from the middle of Moscow or Warsaw or Prague or Monte Carlo or wherever we might be shooting at. It'll probably be up to you chaps to get one there. Good luck to you.'

Bond smiled non-committally. 'One more question,' he said. 'If you wanted to sabotage the rocket what would be the easiest way?'

'Any number,' said the Professor cheerfully. 'Sand in the fuel. Grit in the pumps. A small hole anywhere on the fuselage or the fins. With that power and at those speeds the smallest fault would finish it.'

'Thanks very much,' said Bond. 'It seems you've got fewer worries about the Moonraker than I have.'

'It's a wonderful machine,' said the Professor. 'She'll fly all right if nobody interferes with her. Drax has done a sound job. Wonderful organizer. That's a brilliant team he put together. And they'll do anything for him. We've got a lot to thank him for.'

Bond did a racing change and swung the big car left at the Charing fork, preferring the clear road by Chilham and Canterbury to the bottlenecks of Ashford and Folkestone. The car howled up to eighty in third and he held it in the same gear to negotiate the hairpin at the top of the long gradient leading up to the Molash road.

And, he wondered, going back into top and listening with satisfaction to the relaxed thunder of the exhaust, and what about Drax? What sort of a reception was Drax going to give him this evening? According to M, when his name had been suggested over the telephone, Drax had paused for a moment and then said, 'Oh yes. I know the fellow. Didn't know he was mixed up in that racket. I'd be interested to have another look at him. Send him along. I'll expect him in time for dinner.' Then he had rung off.

The people at the Ministry had their own view of Drax. In their dealings with him they had found him a dedicated man, completely bound up in the Moonraker, living for nothing but its success, driving his men to the limit, fighting for priorities in material with other departments, goading the Ministry of Supply into clearing his requirements at Cabinet level. They disliked his hectoring manners but they respected him for his know-how and his drive and his dedication. And, like the rest of England, they considered him a possible saviour of the country.

Well, thought Bond, accelerating down the straight stretch of road past Chilham Castle, he could see that picture too and if he was going to work with the man he must adjust himself to the heroic version. If Drax was willing, he would put the whole affair at Blades out of his mind and concentrate on protecting Drax and his wonderful project from their country's enemies. There were only about three days to go. The security precautions were already minute and Drax might resent suggestions for increasing them. It was not going to be easy and a great deal of tact would have to be used. Tact. Not Bond's long suit and not, he reflected, connected in any way with that he knew of Drax's character.

Bond took the short cut out of Canterbury by the Old Dover road and looked at his watch. It was six-thirty. Another fifteen minutes to Dover and then another ten minutes along the Deal road. Were there any other plans to be made? The double killing was out of his hands, thank heaven. 'Murder and suicide while of unsound mind' had been the coroner's verdict. The girl had not even been called. He would stop for a drink at the 'World Without Want' and have a quick word with the innkeeper. The next day he would have to try and smell out the 'something fishy' that Tallon had wanted to see the Minister about. No clue about that. Nothing had been found in Tallon's room, which presumably he would now be taking over. Well, at any rate that would give him plenty of leisure to go through Tallon's papers.

Bond concentrated on his driving as he coasted down into Dover. He kept left and was soon climbing out of the town again past the wonderful cardboard castle.

There was a patch of low cloud on top of the hill and a spit of rain on his windshield. There was a cold breeze coming in from the sea. The visibility was bad and he switched on his lights as he motored slowly along the coast-road, the ruby-spangled masts of the Swingate radar station rising like petrified Roman candles on his right.

The girl? He would have to be careful how he contacted her and careful not to upset her. He wondered if she would be any use to him. After a year on the site she would have had all the opportunities of a private secretary to 'The Chief' to get under the skin of the whole project – and of Drax. And she had a mind trained to his own particular craft. But he would have to be prepared for her to be suspicious of the new broom and perhaps resentful. He wondered what she was really like. The photograph on her record-sheet at the Yard had shown an attractive but rather severe girl and any hint of seductiveness had been abstracted by the cheerless jacket of her policewoman's uniform.

Hair: Auburn. Eyes: Blue. Height: 5 ft 7. Weight: 9 stone. Hips: 38. Waist: 26. Bust: 38. Distinguishing marks: Mole on upper curvature of right breast.

Hm! thought Bond.

He put the statistics out of his mind as he came to the turning to the right. There was a signpost that said Kingsdown, and the lights of a small inn.

He pulled up and switched off the engine. Above his head a sign which said 'World Without Want' in faded gold lettering groaned in the salt breeze that came over the cliffs half a mile away. He got out, stretched and walked over to the door of the public bar. It was locked. Closed for cleaning? He tried the next door, which opened and gave access to the small private bar. Behind the bar a stolid-looking man in shirt-sleeves was reading an evening paper.

He looked up as Bond entered, and put his paper down. 'Evening, sir,' he said, evidently relieved to see a customer.

'Evening,' said Bond. 'Large whisky and soda, please.' He sat up at the bar and waited while the man poured two measures of Black and White and put the glass in front of him with a syphon of soda.

Bond filled the glass with soda and drank. 'Bad business you had here last night,' he said, putting the glass down.

'Terrible, sir,' said the man. 'And bad for trade.

Would you be from the Press, sir? Had nothing but reporters and policemen in and out of the house all day long.'

'No,' said Bond. 'I've come to take over the job of the fellow who got shot. Major Tallon. Was he one of your regular customers?'

'Never came here but the once, sir, and that was the end of him. Now I've been put out of bounds for a week and the public has got to be painted from top to bottom. But I will say that Sir Hugo has been very decent about it. Sent me fifty quid this afternoon to pay for the damage. He must be a fine gentleman that. Made himself well liked in these parts. Always very generous and a cheery word for all.'

'Yes. Fine man,' said Bond. 'Did you see it all happen?'

'Didn't see the first shot, sir. Serving a pint at the time. Then of course I looked up. Dropped the ruddy pint on the floor.'

'What happened then?'

'Well, everybody's standing back of course. Nothing but Germans in the place. About a dozen of them. There's the body on the floor and the chap with the gun looking down at him. Then suddenly he stands to attention and sticks his left arm up in the air. "Eil!" he shouts like the silly bastards used to do during the war. Then he puts the end of the gun in his mouth. Next thing,' the man made a grimace, 'he's all over my ruddy ceiling.'

'That was all he said after the shot?' asked Bond. 'Just "*Heil*"?'

'That's all, sir. Don't seem to be able to forget the bloody word, do they?'

'No,' said Bond thoughtfully, 'they certainly don't.'

Five minutes later Bond was showing his Ministry pass to the uniformed guard on duty at the gate in the high wire fence.

The RAF sergeant handed it back to him and saluted. 'Sir Hugo's expecting you, sir. It's the big house up in the woods there.' He pointed to some lights a hundred yards further on towards the cliffs.

Bond heard him telephoning to the next guard point. He motored slowly along the new tarmac road that had been laid across the fields behind Kingsdown. He could hear the distant boom of the sea at the foot of the tall cliffs and from somewhere close at hand there was a high-pitched whine of machinery which grew louder as he approached the trees.

He was stopped again by a plain-clothes guard at a second wire fence through which a five-bar gate gave access to the interior of the wood, and as he was waved through he heard the distant baying of police dogs which suggested some form of night patrol. All these precautions seemed efficient. Bond decided that he wouldn't have to worry himself with problems of external security.

Once through the trees the car was running over a

flat concrete apron the limits of which, in the bad light, were out of range even of the huge twin beams of his Marchal headlamps. A hundred yards to his left, on the edge of the trees, there were the lights of a large house half-hidden behind a wall six feet thick, that rose straight up off the surface of the concrete almost to the height of the house. Bond slowed the car down to walking pace and turned its bonnet away from the house towards the sea and towards a dark shape that suddenly glinted white in the revolving beams of the South Goodwin Lightship far out in the Channel. His lights cut a path down the apron to where, almost on the edge of the cliff and at least half a mile away, a squat dome surged up about fifty feet out of the concrete. It looked like the top of an observatory and Bond could distinguish the flange of a joint running east and west across the surface of the dome.

He turned the car back and slowly ran it up between what he now assumed to be a blast-wall and the front of the house. As he pulled up outside the house the door opened and a manservant in a white jacket came out. He smartly opened the door of the car.

'Good evening, sir. This way please.'

He spoke woodenly and with a trace of accent. Bond followed him into the house and across a comfortable hall to a door on which the butler knocked.

'In.'

Bond smiled to himself at the harsh tone of the well-remembered voice and at the note of command in the single monosyllable.

At the far end of the long, bright, chintzy living-room Drax was standing with his back to an empty grate, a huge figure in a plum-coloured velvet smoking-jacket that clashed with the reddish hair on his face. There were three other people standing near him, two men and a woman.

'Ah, my dear fellow,' said Drax boisterously, striding forward to meet him and shaking him cordially by the hand.

'So we meet again. And so soon. Didn't realize you were a ruddy spy for my Ministry or I'd have been more careful about playing cards against you. Spent that money yet?' he asked, leading him towards the fire.

'Not yet,' smiled Bond. 'Haven't seen the colour of it.'

'Of course. Settlement on Saturday. Probably get the cheque just in time to celebrate our little firework display, what? Now let's see.' He led Bond up to the woman. 'This is my secretary, Miss Brand.'

Bond looked into a pair of very level blue eyes.

'Good evening.' He gave her a friendly smile.

There was no answering smile in the eyes which looked calmly into his. No answering pressure of her hand. 'How do you do,' she said indifferently, almost, Bond sensed, with hostility.

It crossed Bond's mind that she had been well-chosen. Another Loelia Ponsonby. Reserved efficient,

loyal, virginal. Thank heavens, he thought. A professional.

'My right-hand man, Dr Walter.' The thin elderly
man with a pair of angry eyes under the shock of black
hair seemed not to notice Bond's outstretched hand.
He sprang to attention and gave a quick nod of the
head. 'Valter,' said the thin mouth above the black
imperial, correcting Drax's pronunciation.

And my – what shall I say – my dogsbody. What you
might call my ADC, Willy Krebs.' There was the touch
of a slightly damp hand. 'Ferry pleased to meet you,'
said an ingratiating voice and Bond looked into a pale
round unhealthy face now split in a stage smile which
died almost as Bond noticed it. Bond looked into his
eyes. They were like two restless black buttons and
they twisted away from Bond's gaze.

Both men wore spotless white overalls with plastic
zip fasteners at the sleeves and ankles and down the
back. Their hair was close-cropped so that the skin
shone through and they would have looked like people
from another planet but for the untidy black moustache
and imperial of Dr Walter and the pale wispy moustache of Krebs. They were both caricatures – a mad
scientist and a youthful version of Peter Lorre.

The colourful ogreish figure of Drax was a pleasant
contrast in this chilly company and Bond was grateful
to him for the cheerful roughness of his welcome and
for his apparent wish to bury the hatchet and make the
best of his new security officer.

Drax was very much the host. He rubbed his hands together. 'Now, Willy,' he said, 'how about making one of your excellent dry Martinis for us? Except, of course, for the Doctor. Doesn't drink or smoke,' he explained to Bond, returning to his place by the mantelpiece. 'Hardly breathes.' He barked out a short laugh. 'Thinks of nothing but the rocket. Do you, my friend?'

The Doctor looked stonily in front of him. 'You are pleased to joke,' he said.

'Now, now,' said Drax, as if to a child. 'We will go back to those leading edges later. Everybody's quite happy about them except you.' He turned to Bond. 'The good Doctor is always frightening us,' he explained indulgently. 'He's always having nightmares about something. Now it's the leading edges of the fins. They're already as sharp as razor blades – hardly any wind resistance at all. And he suddenly gets it into his head that they're going to melt. Friction of the air. Of course everything's possible, but they've been tested at over 3000 degrees and, as I tell him, if they're going to melt then the whole rocket will melt. And that's just not going to happen,' he added with a grim smile.

Krebs came up with a silver tray with four full glasses and a frosted shaker. The Martini was excellent and Bond said so.

'You are ferry kind,' said Krebs with a smirk of satisfaction. 'Sir Hugo is ferry exacting.'

'Fill up his glass,' said Drax, 'and then perhaps our friend would like to wash. We dine at eight sharp.'

As he spoke there came the muffled wail of a siren and almost immediately the sound of a body of men running in strict unison across the concrete apron outside.

'That's the first night shift,' explained Drax. 'Barracks are just behind the house. Must be eight o'clock. We do everything at the double here,' he added with a gleam of satisfaction in his eye. 'Precision. Lot of scientists about, but we try to run the place like a military establishment. Willy, look after the Commander. We'll go ahead. Come along, my dear.'

As Bond followed Krebs to the door through which he had entered, he saw the other two with Drax in the lead make for the double doors at the end of the room which had opened as Drax finished speaking. The manservant in the white coat stood in the entrance. As Bond went out into the hall it crossed his mind that Drax would certainly go into the dining-room ahead of Miss Brand. Forceful personality. Treated his staff like children. Obviously a born leader. Where had he got it from? The Army? Or did it grow on one with millions of money? Bond followed the slug-like neck of Krebs and wondered.

The dinner was excellent. Drax was a genial host and at his own table his manners were faultless. Most of his conversation consisted in drawing out Dr Walter for the benefit of Bond, and it covered a wide range of technical matters which Drax took pains to explain briefly after each topic had been exhausted. Bond was impressed by the confidence with which Drax handled each abstruse problem as it was raised, and by his immense grasp of detail. A genuine admiration for the man gradually developed in him and overshadowed much of his previous dislike. He felt more than ever inclined to forget the Blades affair now that he was faced with the other Drax, the creator and inspired leader of a remarkable enterprise.

Bond sat between his host and Miss Brand. He made several attempts to engage her in conversation. He failed completely. She answered with polite monosyllables and would hardly meet his eye. Bond became mildly irritated. He found her physically very attractive and it annoyed him to be unable to extract the smallest response. He felt that her frigid indifference was overacted and that security would have been far better met with an easy, friendly approach instead of this exaggerated reticence. He felt a strong urge to give her a sharp kick on the ankle. The idea entertained him and he found himself observing her with a fresh eye — as a girl and not as an official colleague. As a start, and under cover of a long argument between Drax and Walter, in which she was required to join, about the collation of weather reports from the Air Ministry and from Europe, he began to add up his impressions of her.

She was far more attractive than her photograph had suggested and it was difficult to see traces of the severe competence of a policewoman in the seductive girl beside him. There was authority in the definite line of the profile, but the long black eyelashes over the dark blue eyes and the rather wide mouth might have been painted by Marie Laurencin. Yet the lips were too full for a Laurencin and the dark brown hair that curved inwards at the base of the neck was of a different fashion. There was a hint of northern blood in the high cheekbones and in the very slight upward slant of the eyes, but the warmth of her skin was entirely English. There was too much poise and authority in her gestures and in the carriage of her head for her to be a very convincing portrait of a secretary. In fact she seemed almost a member of Drax's team, and Bond noticed that the men listened with attention as she answered Drax's questions.

Her rather severe evening dress was in charcoal black grosgrain with full sleeves that came below the elbow. The wrap-over bodice just showed the swell of her breasts, which were as splendid as Bond had guessed from the measurements on her record sheet. At the point of the vee there was a bright blue cameo brooch, a Tassie intaglio, Bond guessed, cheap but imaginative. She wore no other jewellery except a half-hoop of small diamonds on her engagement finger. Apart from the warm rouge on her lips, she wore no make-up and her nails were square-cut with a natural polish.

Altogether, Bond decided, she was a very lovely girl and beneath her reserve, a very passionate one. And, he reflected, she might be a policewoman and an expert at jujitsu, but she also had a mole on her right breast.

With this comforting thought Bond turned the whole of his attention to the conversation between Drax and Walter and made no further attempts to make friends with the girl.

Dinner ended at nine. 'Now we will go over and introduce you to the Moonraker,' said Drax, rising abruptly from the table. 'Walter will accompany us. He has much to do. Come along, my dear Bond.'

Without a word to Krebs or the girl he strode out of the room. Bond and Walter followed him.

They left the house and walked across the concrete towards the distant shape on the edge of the cliff. The moon had risen and in the distance the squat dome shone palely in its light.

A hundred yards from the site Drax stopped. 'I will explain the geography,' he said. 'Walter, you go ahead. They will be waiting for you to have another look at those fins. Don't worry about them, my dear fellow. Those people at High Duty Alloys know what they're doing. Now,' he turned to Bond and gestured towards the milk-white dome, 'in there is the Moonraker. What you see is the lid of a wide shaft that has been cut about forty foot down into the chalk. The two halves of the dome are opened hydraulically and folded back flush with that twenty-foot wall. If they were open now, you would see the nose of the Moonraker just protruding above the level of the wall. Over there,' he pointed to a square shape that was almost out of sight in the direction of Deal, 'is the firing point. Concrete block-house. Full of radar tracking gadgets – Doppler velocity radar and flightpath radar, for instance. Information is fed to them by twenty telemetering channels in the nose of the rocket. There's a big television screen in there too so that you can watch the behaviour of the rocket inside the shaft after the pumps have been started. Another television set to follow the beginning of its climb. Alongside the blockhouse there's a hoist down the face of the cliff. Quite a lot of gear has been brought to the site by sea and then sent up on the hoist. That whine you hear is from the power house over there,' he gestured vaguely in the direction of Dover. 'The men's barracks and the house are protected by the blast-wall, but when we fire there won't be anyone within a mile of the site, except the Ministry experts and the BBC team who are going to be in the firing point. Hope it'll stand up to the blast. Walter says that the site and a lot of the concrete apron will be melted by the heat. That's all. Nothing else you need to know about until we get inside. Come along.'

Bond noted again the abrupt tone of command. He followed in silence across the moonlit expanse until they came to the supporting wall of the dome. A naked red bulb glowed over a steel-plated door in the wall. It illuminated a bold sign which said in English and German: MORTAL DANGER. ENTRY FORBIDDEN WHEN RED LAMP SHOWS. RING AND WAIT.

Drax pressed the button beneath the notice and there

was the muffled clang of an alarm bell. 'Might be some-body working with oxy-acetylene or doing some other delicate job,' he explained. 'Take his mind off his job for a split second as somebody comes in and you could have an expensive mistake. Everybody downs tools when the bell rings and then starts up again when they see what it is.' Drax stood away from the door and pointed upwards to a row of four-foot wide gratings just below the top of the wall. 'Ventilator shafts,' he explained. 'Air-conditioned inside to 70 degrees.'

The door was opened by a man with a truncheon in his hand and a revolver at his hip. Bond followed Drax through into a small anteroom. It contained nothing but a bench and a neat row of felt slippers.

'Have to put these on,' said Drax sitting down and kicking off his shoes. 'Might slip up and knock into someone. Better leave your coat here, too. Seventy degrees is quite warm.'

'Thanks,' said Bond remembering the Beretta at his armpit. 'As a matter of fact I don't feel the heat.'

Feeling like a visitor to an operating theatre, Bond followed Drax through a communicating door out on to an iron catwalk and into a blaze of spotlights that made him automatically put a hand up to his eyes as he grasped the guard-rail in front of him.

When he took his hand away he was greeted by a scene of such splendour that for several minutes he stood speechless, his eyes dazzled by the terrible beauty of the greatest weapon on earth.

It was like being inside the polished barrel of a huge gun. From the floor, forty feet below, rose circular walls of polished metal near the top of which he and Drax clung like two flies. Up through the centre of the shaft, which was about thirty feet wide, soared a pencil of glistening chromium, whose point, tapering to a needle-sharp antenna, seemed to graze the roof twenty feet above their heads.

The shimmering projectile rested on a blunt cone of latticed steel which rose from the floor between the tips of three severely back-swept delta fins that looked as sharp as surgeons' scalpels. But otherwise nothing marred the silken sheen of the fifty feet of polished chrome steel except the spidery fingers of two light gantries which stood out from the walls and clasped the waist of the rocket between thick pads of foam-rubber.

Where they touched the rocket, small access doors stood open in the steel skin and, as Bond looked down, a man crawled out of one door on to the narrow platform of the gantry and closed the door behind him with a gloved hand. He walked gingerly along the narrow bridge to the wall and turned a handle. There was a sharp whine of machinery and the gantry took its padded hand off the rocket and held it poised in the air like the forelegs of a praying mantis. The whine altered to a deeper tone and the gantry slowly telescoped in on itself. Then it reached out again and seized the rocket ten feet lower down. Its operator crawled out along its arm and opened another small access door and disappeared inside.

'Probably checking the fuel-feed from the after tanks,' said Drax. 'Gravity feed. Tricky bit of design What do you think of her?' He looked with pleasure at Bond's rapt expression.

'One of the most beautiful things I've ever seen,' said Bond. It was easy to talk. There was hardly a sound in the great steel shaft and the voices of the men clustered below under the tail of the rocket were no more than a murmur.

Drax pointed upwards. 'Warhead,' he explained. 'Experimental one now. Full of instruments. Telemeters and so forth. Then the gyros just opposite us here. Then mostly fuel tanks all the way down until you get to the turbines near the tail. Driven by superheated steam, made by decomposing hydrogen peroxide. The fuel, fluorine and hydrogen' (he glanced sharply at Bond. 'That's top-secret by the way') 'falls down the feed tubes and gets ignited as soon as it's forced into the motor. Sort of controlled explosion which shoots the rocket into the air. That steel floor under the rocket slides away. There's a big exhaust pit underneath.

Comes out at the base of the cliff. You'll see it tomorrow. Looks like a huge cave. When we ran a static test the other day the chalk melted and ran out into the sea like water. Hope we don't burn down the famous white cliffs when we come to the real thing. Like to come and have a look at the works?'

Bond followed silently as Drax led the way down the steep iron ladder that curved down the side of the steel wall. He felt a glow of admiration and almost of reverence for this man and his majestic achievement. How could he ever have been put off by Drax's childish behaviour at the card-table? Even the greatest men have their weaknesses. Drax must have an outlet for the tension of the fantastic responsibility he was carrying. It was clear from the conversation at dinner that he couldn't shed much on to the shoulders of his highly strung deputy. From him alone had to spring the vitality and confidence to buoy up his whole team. Even in such a small thing as winning at cards it must be important to him to be constantly reassuring himself, constantly searching out omens of good fortune and success, even to the point of creating these omens for himself. Who, Bond asked himself, wouldn't sweat and bite his nails when so much had been dared, when so much was at stake?

As they filed down the long curve of the stairway, their figures grotesquely reflected back at them by the mirror of the rocket's chromium skin, Bond almost felt the man-in-the-street's affection for the man whom, only a few hours previously, he had been dissecting without pity, almost with loathing.

When they reached the steel-plated floor of the shaft, Drax paused and looked up. Bond followed his eyes. Seen from that angle it seemed as if they were gazing up a thin straight shaft of light into the blazing heaven of the arcs, a shaft of light that was not pure white but a shot mother-of-pearl satin. There were shimmers of red in it picked up from the crimson canisters of a giant foam fire-extinguisher that stood near them, a man in an asbestos suit beside it aiming its nozzle at the base of the rocket. There was a streak of violet whose origin was a violet bulb on the board of an instrument panel in the wall, which controlled the steel cover over the exhaust pit. And there was a whisper of emerald green from the shaded light over a plain deal table at which a man sat and wrote down figures as they were called to him from the group gathered directly beneath the Moonraker's tail.

Gazing up this pastel column, so incredibly slim and graceful, it seemed unthinkable that anything so delicate could withstand the pressures which it had been designed to meet on Friday – the howling stream of the most powerful controlled explosion that had ever been attempted; the impact of the sound barrier; the unknown pressures of the atmosphere at 15,000 miles an hour; the terrible shock as it plunged back from a thousand miles up and hit the atmospheric envelope of the earth.

Drax seemed to read his thoughts. He turned to Bond. 'It will be like committing murder,' he said. Then surprisingly, he burst into a braying laugh. 'Walter,' he called to the group of men. 'Come here.' Walter detached himself and came over. 'Walter, I was saying to our friend the Commander that when we fire the Moonraker it will be like committing murder.'

Bond was not surprised to see a look of puzzled incredulity come over the Doctor's face.

Drax said irritably, 'Child murder. Murder of our child,' he gestured at the rocket. 'Wake up. Wake up. What's the matter with you?'

Walter's face cleared. Frostily he beamed his appreciation of the simile. 'Murder. Yes, that is good. Ha! ha! And now, Sir Hugo. The graphite slats in the exhaust vent. The Ministry is quite happy about their melting-point? They do not feel that . . .' Still talking, Walter led Drax under the tail of the rocket. Bond followed.

The faces of the ten men were turned towards them as they came up. Drax introduced him with a wave of the hand. 'Commander Bond, our new security officer,' he said briefly.

The group eyed Bond in silence. There was no move to greet him and the ten pairs of eyes were incurious.

'Now then, what's all this fuss about the graphite? . . .' The group closed round Drax and Walter. Bond was left standing alone.

He was not surprised by the coolness of his reception. He would have regarded the intrusion of an amateur into the secrets of his own department with much the same indifference mixed with resentment. And he sympathized with these hand-picked technicians who had lived for months among the highest realms of astronautics, and were now on the threshold of the final arbitration. And yet, he reminded himself, the innocent among them must know that Bond had his own duty to perform, his own vital part in this project. Supposing one pair of those uncommunicative eyes concealed a man within a man, an enemy, perhaps at this very moment exulting in his knowledge that the graphite which Walter seemed to mistrust was indeed under-strength. It was true that they had the look of a well-knit team, almost of a brotherhood, as they stood round Drax and Walter, hanging on their words, their eyes intent on the mouths of the two men. But was part of one brain moving within the privacy of some secret orbit, ticking off its hidden calculus like the stealthy mechanism of an infernal machine?

Bond moved casually up and down the triangle made by the three points of the fins as they rested in their rubber-lined cavities in the steel floor, interesting himself in whatever met his eyes, but every now and then focusing the group of men from a new angle.

With the exception of Drax they all wore the same tight nylon overalls fastened with plastic zips. There was nowhere a hint of metal and none wore spectacles. As in the case of Walter and Krebs their heads were close-shaved, presumably, Bond would have thought, to prevent a loose hair falling into the mechanism. And yet, and this struck Bond as a most bizarre characteristic of the team, each man sported a luxuriant moustache to whose culture it was clear that a great deal of attention had been devoted. They were in all shapes and tints: fair or mousy or dark; handlebar, walrus, Kaiser, Hitler – each face bore its own hairy badge amongst which the rank, reddish growth of Drax's facial hair blazed like the official stamp of their paramount chief.

Why, wondered Bond, should every man on the site wear a moustache? He had never liked the things, but combined with these shaven heads, there was something positively obscene about this crop of hairy tufts. It would have been just bearable if they had all been cut to the same pattern, but this range of individual fashions, this riot of personalized growth, had something particularly horrible about it against the background of naked round heads.

There was nothing else to notice; the men were of average height and they were all on the slim side – tailored, Bond supposed, more or less to the requirements of their work. Agility would be needed on the gantries, and compactness for manoeuvring through the access doors and around the tiny compartments in the rocket. Their hands looked relaxed and spotlessly clean, and their feet in the felt slippers were motionless with concentration. He never once caught any of them glancing in his direction and, as for penetrating their minds or weighing up their loyalties, he admitted to himself that the task of unmasking the thoughts of fifty of these robot-like Germans in three days was quite hopeless. Then he remembered. It was fifty no longer. Only forty-nine. One of these robots had blown his top (apt expression, reflected Bond). And what had come out of Bartsch's secret thoughts? Lust for a woman and a Heil Hitler. Would he be far wrong, wondered Bond, if he guessed that, forgetting the Moonraker, those were also the dominant thoughts inside forty-nine other heads?

'Doctor Walter! That is an order.' Drax's voice of controlled anger broke in on Bond's thoughts as he stood fingering the sharp leading edge of the tail of one of the Columbite fins. 'Back to work. We have wasted enough time.'

The men scattered smartly about their duties and Drax came up to where Bond was standing, leaving Walter hanging about indecisively beneath the exhaust vent of the rocket.

Drax's face was thunderous. 'Damn fool. Always seeing trouble,' he muttered. And then abruptly, as if he wanted to clear his deputy out of his mind, 'Come along to my office. Show you the flight plan. Then we'll go off to bed.'

Bond followed him across the floor. Drax turned a small handle flush with the steel wall and a narrow door opened with a soft hiss. Three feet inside there was another steel door and Bond noticed that they were both edged with rubber. Air-lock. Before closing the outer door Drax paused on the threshold and pointed along the circular wall to a number of similar inconspicuous flat knobs in the wall. 'Workshops,' he said. 'Electricians, generators, fuelling control, washrooms, stores.' He pointed to the adjoining door. 'My secretary's room.' He closed the outer door before he opened the second and walked into his office and shut the inner door behind Bond.

It was a severe room painted pale grey, containing a broad desk and several chairs of tubular metal and dark blue canvas. The floor was carpeted in grey. There were two green filing cabinets and a large metal radio set. A half-open door showed part of a tiled bathroom. The desk faced a wide blank wall which seemed to be made of opaque glass. Drax walked up to the walls and snapped down two switches on its extreme right. The whole wall lit up and Bond was faced with two maps each about six feet square traced on the back of the glass.

The left-hand map showed the eastern quarter of England from Portsmouth to Hull and the adjoining waters from Latitude 50 to 55. From the red dot near Dover which was the site of the Moonraker, arcs showing the range in ten-mile intervals had been drawn up the map. At a point eighty miles from the site, between the Friesian Islands and Hull, there was a red diamond in the middle of the ocean.

Drax waved towards the dense mathematical tables

and columns of compass readings which filled the right-hand side of the map. 'Wind velocities, atmospheric pressure, ready-reckoner for the gyro settings,' he said. 'All worked out using the rocket's velocity and range as constants. We get the weather every day from the Air Ministry and readings from the upper atmosphere every time the RAF jet can get up there. When he's at maximum altitude he releases helium balloons that can get up still further. The earth's atmosphere reaches about fifty miles up. After twenty there's hardly any density to affect the Moonraker. It'll coast up almost in a vacuum. Getting through the first twenty miles is the problem. The gravity pull's another worry. Walter can explain all those things if you're interested. There'll be continuous weather reports during the last few hours on Friday. And we'll set the gryos just before the take-off. For the time being, Miss Brand gets together the data every morning and keeps a table of gyro settings in case they're wanted.'

Drax pointed at the second of the two maps. This was a diagram of the rocket's flight ellipse from firing point to target. There were more columns of figures. 'Speed of the earth and its effect on the rocket's trajectory,' explained Drax. 'The earth will be turning to the east while the rocket's in flight. That factor has to be married in with the figures on the other map. Complicated business. Fortunately you don't have to understand it. Leave it to Miss Brand. Now then,' he switched off the lights and the wall went blank, 'any particular questions about your job? Don't think there'll be much for you to do. You can see that the place is already riddled with security. The Ministry's insisted on it from the beginning.'

'Everything looks all right,' said Bond. He examined Drax's face. The good eye was looking at him sharply. Bond paused. 'Do you think there was anything between your secretary and Major Tallon?' he asked. It was an obvious question and he might just as well ask it now.

'Could have been,' said Drax easily. 'Attractive girl. They were thrown together a lot down here. At any rate she seems to have got under Bartsch's skin.'

'I hear Bartsch saluted and shouted "Heil Hitler" before he put the gun in his mouth,' said Bond.

'So they tell me,' said Drax evenly. 'What of it?'

'Why do all the men wear moustaches?' asked Bond, ignoring Drax's question. Again he had the impression that his question had nettled the other man.

Drax gave one of his short barking laughs. 'My idea,' he said. 'They're difficult to recognize in those white overalls and with their heads shaved. So I told them all to grow moustaches. The thing's become quite a fetish. Like in the RAF during the war. See anything wrong with it?'

'Of course not,' said Bond. 'Rather startling at first. I would have thought that large numbers on their suits with a different colour for each shift would have been more effective.'

'Well,' said Drax, turning away towards the door as if to end the conversation, 'I decided on moustaches.'

On Wednesday morning Bond woke early in the dead man's bed.

He had slept little. Drax had said nothing on their way back to the house and had bidden him a curt goodnight at the foot of the stairs. Bond had walked along the carpeted corridor to where light shone from an open door and had found his things neatly laid out in a comfortable bedroom.

The room was furnished in the same expensive taste as the ground floor and there were biscuits and a bottle of Vichy (not a Vichy bottle of tap-water, Bond established) beside the Heal bed.

There were no signs of the previous occupant except a leather case containing binoculars on the dressing-table and a metal filing cabinet which was locked. Bond knew about filing cabinets. He tilted it against the wall, reached underneath, and found the bottom end of the bar-lock which protrudes downwards when the top section has been locked. Upwards pressure released the drawers one by one and he softly lowered the edge of the cabinet back on to the floor with the unkind reflection that Major Tallon would not have survived very long in the Secret Service.

The top drawer contained scale maps of the site and its component buildings and Admiralty Chart No. 1895 of the Straits of Dover. Bond laid each sheet on the bed and examined them minutely. There were traces of cigarette ash in the folds of the Admiralty chart.

Bond fetched his tool-box – a square leather case that stood beside the dressing-table. He examined the numbers on the wheels of the combination lock and, satisfied that they had not been disturbed, turned them to the code number. The box was closely fitted with instruments. Bond selected a fingerprint powder-spray and a large magnifying glass. He puffed the fine greyish powder foot by foot over the whole expanse of the chart. A forest of fingerprints showed.

By going over these with the magnifying glass he established that they belonged to two people. He isolated two of the best sets, took a Leica with a flashbulb attachment out of the leather case and photographed them. Then he carefully examined through his glass the two minute furrows in the paper which the powder had brought to light.

These appeared to be two lines drawn out from the coast to form a cross-bearing in the sea. It was a very narrow bearing, and both lines seemed to originate from the house where Bond was. In fact, thought Bond, they might indicate observations of some object in the sea made from each wing of the house.

The two lines were drawn not with a pencil, but,

presumably to avoid detection, with a stylus which had barely furrowed the paper.

At the point where they met there was the trace of a question mark, and this point was on the twelve-fathom line about fifty yards from the cliff on a direct bearing from the house to the South Goodwin Lightship.

There was nothing else to be gathered from the chart. Bond glanced at his watch. Twenty minutes to one. He heard distant footsteps in the hall and the click of a light being extinguished. On an impulse he rose and softly switched off the lights in his room, leaving only the shaded reading-light beside the bed.

He heard the heavy footsteps of Drax approaching up the stairs. There was the click of another switch and then silence. Bond could imagine the great hairy face turned down the corridor, looking, listening. Then there was a creak and the sound of a door being softly opened and as softly closed. Bond waited, visualizing the motions of the man as he prepared for bed. There was the muffled sound of a window being thrown open and the distant trumpet of a nose being blown. Then silence.

Bond gave Drax another five minutes then he went over to the filing cabinet and softly pulled out the other drawers. There was nothing in the second and third, but the bottom one was solid with files arranged under index letters. They were the dossiers of all the men working on the site. Bond pulled out the 'A' section and went back to the bed and started to read.

In each case the formula was the same: full name, address, date of birth, description, distinguishing marks, profession or trade since the war, war record, political record and present sympathies, criminal record, health, next of kin. Some of the men had wives and children whose particulars were noted, and with each dossier there were photographs, full face and profile, and the fingerprints of both hands.

Two hours and ten cigarettes later he had worked through all of them and had discovered two points of general interest. First, that every one of the fifty men appeared to have led a blameless life without a breath of political or criminal odium. This seemed so unlikely that he decided to refer every single dossier back to Station D for a thorough recheck at the first opportunity.

The second point was that none of the faces in the photographs bore a moustache. Despite Drax's explanations, this fact raised a second tiny question mark in Bond's mind.

Bond got up from the bed and locked everything away, putting the Admiralty Chart and one of the files in his leather case. He turned the wheels of the combination lock and thrust the case far under his bed so that it rested directly beneath his pillow at the inside angle of the wall. Then he quietly washed and cleaned his teeth in the adjoining bathroom and eased the window wide open.

The moon was still shining: as it must have shone,

Bond thought, when, aroused perhaps by some unusual noise, Tallon had climbed up to the roof, maybe only a couple of nights before, and had seen, out at sea, what he had seen. He would have had his glasses with him and Bond, remembering, turned back from the window and picked them up. They were a very powerful German pair, booty perhaps from the war, and the 7×50 on the top plates told Bond that they were night glasses. And then the careful Tallon must have walked softly (but not softly enough?) to the other end of the roof and had raised his glasses again, estimating the distance from the edge of the cliff to the object in the sea, and from the object to the Goodwin Lightship. Then he would have come back the way he had gone and softly re-entered his room.

Bond saw Tallon, perhaps for the first time since he had been in the house, carefully lock the door and walk over to the filing cabinet and take out the chart which he had hardly glanced at till then and on it softly mark the lines of his rough bearing. Perhaps he looked at it for a long while before putting the minute question mark beside it.

And what had the unknown object been? Impossible to say. A boat? A light? A noise?

Whatever it was Tallon had not been supposed to see it. And somebody had heard him. Somebody had guessed he had seen it and had waited until Tallon had left his room next morning. Then that man had come into his room and had searched it. Probably the chart had revealed nothing, but there were the night glasses by the window.

That had been enough. And that night Tallon had died.

Bond pulled himself up. He was going too fast, building up a case on the flimsiest evidence. Bartsch had killed Tallon and Bartsch was not the man who had heard the noise, the man who had left fingerprints on the chart, the man whose dossier Bond had put away in his leather case.

That man had been the oily ADC, Krebs, the man with the neck like a white slug. They were his prints on the chart. For a quarter of an hour Bond had compared the impressions on the chart with the prints on Krebs's dossier. But who said Krebs had heard a noise or done anything about it if he had? Well, to begin with, he looked like a natural snooper. He had the eyes of a petty thief. And those prints of his had definitely been made on the chart after Tallon had studied it. Krebs's fingers overlaid Tallon's at several points.

But how could Krebs possibly be involved, with Drax's eye constantly on him? The confidential assistant. But what about Cicero, the trusted valet of the British Ambassador in Ankara during the war? The hand in the pocket of the striped trousers hanging over the back of the chair. The Ambassador's keys. The safe. The secrets. This picture looked very much the same.

Bond shivered. He suddenly realized that he had

been standing for a long time in front of the open windows and that it was time to get some sleep.

Before he got into bed he took his shoulder-holster from the chair where it hung beside his discarded clothes and removed the Beretta with the skeleton grip and slipped it under his pillow. As a defence against whom? Bond didn't know, but his intuition told him quite definitely that there was danger about. The smell of it was insistent although it was still imprecise and lingered only on the threshold of his subconscious. In fact he knew his feelings were based on a number of tiny question-marks which had materialized during the past twenty-four hours – the riddle of Drax; Bartsch's 'Heil Hitler'; the bizarre moustaches; the fifty worthy Germans; the chart; the night glasses; Krebs.

First he must pass on his suspicions to Vallance. Then explore the possibilities of Krebs. Then look to the defences of the Moonraker – the seaward side for instance. And then get together with this Brand girl and agree on a plan for the next two days. There wasn't much time to lose.

While he forced sleep to come into his teeming mind, Bond visualized the figure seven on the dial of a clock and left it to the hidden cells of his memory to wake him. He wanted to be out of the house and on the telephone to Vallance as early as possible. If his actions aroused suspicion he would not be dismayed. One of his objects was to attract into his orbit the same forces that had concerned themselves with Tallon, for of one thing he felt reasonably certain, Major Tallon had not died because he loved Gala Brand.

The extra-sensory alarm clock did not fail him. Punctually at seven, his mouth dry with too many cigarettes the night before, he forced himself out of bed and into a cold bath. He had shaved, gargled with a sharp mouthwash, and now, in a battered black and white dogtooth suit, dark blue Sea Island cotton shirt and black silk knitted tie, he was walking softly, but not surreptitiously, along the corridor to the head of the stairs, the square leather case in his left hand.

He found the garage at the back of the house and the big engine of the Bentley answered with the first pressure on the starter. He motored slowly across the concrete apron beneath the indifferent gaze of the curtained windows of the house and pulled up, the engine idling in neutral, at the edge of the trees. His eyes travelled back to the house and confirmed his calculation that a man standing on its roof would be able to see over the top of the blast-wall and get a view of the edge of the cliff and of the sea beyond.

There was no sign of life round the domed emplacement of the Moonraker, and the concrete, already beginning to shimmer in the early morning sun, stretched emptily away towards Deal. It looked like a newly laid aerodrome or rather, he thought, with its three disparate concrete 'things', the beehive dome, the flat-iron blast-wall, and the distant cube of the firing point, each casting black pools of shadow towards him in the early sun, like a Dali desert landscape in which three *objets trouvés* reposed at carefully calculated random.

Out at sea, in the early mist that promised a hot day, the South Goodwin Lightship could just be seen, a dim red barque married for ever to the same compass point and condemned, like a property ship on the stage of Drury Lane, to watch the diorama of the waves and clouds sail busily into the wings while, without papers or passengers or cargo, it lay anchored for ever to the departure point which was also its destination.

At thirty seconds' interval it blared its sad complaint into the mist, a long double trumpet note on a falling cadence. A siren song, Bond reflected, to repel instead of to seduce. He wondered how the seven men of its crew were now supporting the noise as they munched their pork and beans. Did they flinch as it punctuated the Housewife's Choice coming at full strength from the radio in the narrow mess? But a secure life,[1] Bond decided, although anchored to the gates of a graveyard.

He made a mental note to find out if those seven men had seen or heard the thing that Tallon had marked on the chart, then he drove quickly on through the guard posts.

In Dover, Bond pulled up at the Café Royal, a modest little restaurant with a modest kitchen but capable, as he knew of old, of turning out excellent fish and egg dishes. The Italian-Swiss mother and son who ran it

[1] Bond was wrong: Friday, November 26th 1954. R.I.P.

welcomed him as an old friend and he asked for a plate of scrambled eggs and bacon and plenty of coffee to be ready in half an hour. Then he drove on to the police station and put a call in to Vallance through the Scotland Yard switchboard. Vallance was at home having breakfast. He listened without comment to Bond's guarded talk, but he expressed surprise that Bond had not had an opportunity to have a talk with Gala Brand. 'She's a bright girl, that,' he said. 'If Mr K. is up to something she's sure to have an idea what it is. And if T. heard a noise on Sunday night, she may have heard it too. Though I'll admit she's said nothing about it.'

Bond said nothing about the reception he had had from Vallance's agent. 'Going to talk to her this morning,' he said, 'and I'll send up the chart and the Leica film for you to have a look at. I'll give them to the Inspector. Perhaps one of the road patrols could bring them up. By the way, where did T. telephone from when he rang up his employer on Monday?'

'I'll have the call traced and let you know,' said Vallance. 'And I'll have Trinity House ask the South Goodwins and the Coastguards if they can help. Anything else?'

'No,' said Bond. The line went through too many switchboards. Perhaps if it had been M he would have hinted more. It seemed ridiculous to talk to Vallance about moustaches and the creep of danger he had felt the night before and which the daylight had dissipated. These policemen wanted hard facts. They were better, he decided, at solving crimes than at anticipating them. 'No. That's all.' He hung up.

He felt more cheerful after an excellent breakfast. He read the *Express* and *The Times* and found a bare report of the inquest on Tallon. The *Express* had made a big play with the girl's photograph and he was amused to see what a neutral likeness Vallance had managed to produce. He decided that he must try and work with her. He would take her completely into his confidence whether she was receptive or not. Perhaps she also had her suspicions and intuitions which were so vague that she was keeping them to herself.

Bond drove back fast to the house. It was just nine o'clock and as he came through the trees on to the concrete there was the wail of a siren and from the woods behind the house a double file of twelve men appeared running, in purposeful unison, towards the launching dome. They marked time while one of their number rang the bell, then the door opened and they filed through and out of sight.

Scratch a German and you find precision, thought Bond.

Half an hour before, Gala Brand had stubbed out her breakfast cigarette, swallowed the remains of her coffee, left her bedroom and walked across to the site, looking very much the private secretary in a spotless white shirt and dark blue pleated skirt.

Punctually at eight-thirty she was in her office. There was a sheaf of Air Ministry teleprints on her desk and her first action was to transfer a digest of their contents on to a weather map and walk through the communicating door into Drax's office and pin the map to the board that hung in the angle of the wall beside the blank glass wall. Then she pressed the switch that illuminated the wall map, made some calculations based on the columns of figures revealed by the light, and entered the results on the diagram she had pinned to the board.

She had done this, with Air Ministry figures that became more and more precise as the practice shoot drew nearer, every day since the site was completed and the building of the rocket that had begun inside it, and she had become so expert that she now carried in her head the gyro settings for almost every variation in the weather at the different altitudes.

So it irritated her all the more that Drax did not seem to accept her figures. Every day when, punctually at nine, the warning bells clanged and he came down the steep iron stairway and into his office, his first action was to call for the insufferable Dr Walter and together they would work out all her figures afresh and transfer the results to the thin black notebook that Drax always carried in the hip pocket of his trousers. She knew that this was an invariable routine and she had become tired of watching it through an inconspicuous hole she had drilled, so as to be able to send Vallance a weekly record of Drax's visitors, in the thin wall between the two offices. The method was amateurish but effective and she had slowly built up a complete picture of the daily routine she came to find so irritating. It was irritating for two reasons. It meant that Drax didn't trust her figures, and it undermined her chance of having some part, however modest, in the final launching of the rocket.

It was natural that over the months she should have become as immersed in her disguise as she was in her real profession. It was fundamental to the thoroughness of her cover that her personality should be as truly split as possible. And now, while she spied and probed and sniffed the wind around Drax for her Chief in London, she was passionately concerned with the success of the Moonraker and had become as dedicated to its service as anyone else on the site.

And the rest of her duties as Drax's private secretary

were insufferably dull. Every day there was a big post addressed to Drax in London and forwarded down by the Ministry, and that morning she had found the usual batch of about fifty letters waiting on her desk. They would be of three kinds. Begging letters, letters from rocket cranks, and business letters from Drax's stockbroker and from other commercial agents. To these Drax would dictate brief replies and the rest of her day would be occupied with typing and filing.

So it was natural that her one duty connected with the operation of the rocket should bulk very large in the dull round, and that morning, as she checked and rechecked her flight-plan, she was more than ever determined that her figures should be accepted on The Day. And yet, as she often reminded herself, perhaps there was no question but that they would be. Perhaps the daily calculations of Drax and Walter for entry in the little black book were nothing but a recheck of her own figures. Certainly Drax had never queried either her weather plan or the gyro settings she calculated from them. And when one day she had asked straight out whether her figures were correct he had replied with evident sincerity, 'Excellent, my dear. Most valuable. Couldn't manage without them.'

Gala Brand walked back into her own office and started slitting open the letters. Only two more flight plans, for Thursday and Friday and then, on her figures or on a different set, the set in Drax's pocket, the gyros would be finally adjusted and the switch would be pulled in the firing point.

She absentmindedly looked at her finger-nails and then stretched her two hands out with their backs towards her. How often in the course of her training at the Police College had she been sent out among the other pupils and told not to come back without a pocketbook, a vanity case, a fountain pen, even a wristwatch? How often during the courses had the instructor whipped round and caught her wrist with a 'Now, now, Miss. That won't do at all. Might have been an elephant looking for sugar in the keeper's pocket. Try again.'

Coolly she flexed her fingers and then, her mind made up, turned back to the pile of letters.

At a few minutes to nine the alarm bells rang and she heard Drax arrive in the office. A moment later she heard him open the double doors again and call for Walter. Then came the usual mumble of voices whose words were drowned by the soft whirr of the ventilators.

She arranged the letters in their three piles and sat forward relaxed, her elbows resting on the desk and her chin in her left hand.

Commander Bond. James Bond. Clearly a conceited young man like so many of them in the Secret Service. And why had he been sent down instead of somebody she could work with, one of her friends from the Special Branch, or even somebody from MI5? The message from the Assistant Commissioner had said that there was no one else available at short notice, that this was one of the stars of the Secret Service who had the complete confidence of the Special Branch and the blessings of MI5. Even the Prime Minister had had to give permission for him to operate, for just this one assignment, inside England. But what use could he be in the short time that was left? He could probably shoot all right and talk foreign languages and do a lot of tricks that might be useful abroad. But what good could he do down here without any beautiful spies to make love to. Because he was certainly good-looking. (Gala Brand automatically reached into her bag for her vanity case. She examined herself in the little mirror and dabbed at her nose with a powder puff.) Rather like Hoagy Carmichael in a way. That black hair falling down over the right eyebrow. Much the same bones. But there was something a bit cruel in the mouth, and the eyes were cold. Were they grey or blue? It had been difficult to say last night. Well, at any rate she had put him in his place and shown him that she wasn't impressed by dashing young men from the Secret Service, however romantic they might look. There were just as good-looking men in the Special Branch, and they were real detectives, not just people that Phillips Oppenheim had dreamed up with fast cars and special cigarettes with gold bands on them and shoulder-holsters. Oh, she had spotted that all right and had even brushed against him to make sure. Ah well, she supposed she would have to make some sort of show of working along with him, though in what direction heaven only knew. If she had been down there ever since the place had been built without spotting anything, what could this Bond man hope to discover in a couple of days? And what was there to find out? Of course there were one or two things she couldn't understand. Should she tell him about Krebs, for instance? The first thing was to see that he didn't blow her cover by doing something stupid. She would have to be cool and firm and extremely careful. But that didn't mean, she decided, as the buzzer went and she collected her letters and her shorthand book, that she couldn't be friendly. Entirely on her own terms, of course.

Her second decision made, she opened the communicating door and walked into the office of Sir Hugo Drax.

When she came back into her room half an hour later she found Bond sitting back in her chair with *Whitaker's Almanack* open on the desk in front of him. She pursed her lips as Bond got up and wished her a cheerful good morning. She nodded briefly and walked round her desk and sat down. She moved the *Whitaker's* carefully aside and put her letters and notebook in its place.

'You might have a spare chair for visitors,' said Bond with a grin which she defined as impertinent, 'and something better to read than reference books.'

She ignored him. 'Sir Hugo wants you,' she said. 'I was just going to see if you had got up yet.'

'Liar,' said Bond. 'You heard me go by at half-past seven. I saw you peering out between the curtains.'

'I did nothing of the sort,' she said indignantly. 'Why should I be interested in a car going by?'

'I told you you heard the car,' said Bond. He pressed home his advantage. 'And by the way,' he said, 'you shouldn't scratch your head with the blunt end of the pencil when you're taking dictation. None of the best private secretaries do.'

Bond glanced significantly at a point against the jamb of the communicating door. He shrugged his shoulders.

Gala's defences dropped. Damn the man, she thought. She gave him a reluctant smile. 'Oh, well,' she said. 'Come on. I can't spend all the morning playing guessing games. He wants both of us and he doesn't like being kept waiting.' She rose and walked over to the communicating door and opened it. Bond followed her through and shut the door behind him.

Drax was standing looking at the illuminated wall map. He turned as they came in. 'Ah, there you are,' he said with a sharp glance at Bond. 'Thought you might have left us. Guards reported you out at seven thirty this morning.'

'I had to make a telephone call,' said Bond. 'I hope I didn't disturb anyone.'

'There's a telephone in my study,' Drax said curtly. 'Tallon found it good enough.'

'Ah, poor Tallon,' said Bond non-committally. There was a hectoring note in Drax's voice that he particularly disliked and that made him instinctively want to deflate the man. On this occasion he was successful.

Drax shot him a hard glance which he covered up with a short barking laugh and a shrug of the shoulders. 'Do as you please,' he said. 'You've got your job to do. So long as you don't upset the routines down here. You must remember,' he added more reasonably, 'all my men are nervous as kittens just now and I can't have them upset by mysterious goings-on. I hope you're not wanting to ask them a lot of questions today. I'd rather they didn't have anything more to worry about. They haven't recovered from Monday yet. Miss Brand here can tell you all about them, and I believe all their files are in Tallon's room. Have you had a look at them yet?'

'No key to the filing cabinet,' said Bond truthfully.

'Sorry, my fault,' said Drax. He went to the desk and opened a drawer from which he took a small bunch of keys and handed them to Bond. 'Should have given you these last night. The Inspector chap on the case asked me to hand them over to you. Sorry.'

'Thanks very much,' said Bond. He paused. 'By the way, how long have you had Krebs?' He asked the question on an impulse. There was a moment's quiet in the room.

'Krebs?' repeated Drax thoughtfully. He walked over to his desk and sat down. He reached into his trouser pocket and pulled out a packet of his cork-tipped cigarettes. His blunt fingers scrabbled with its cellophane wrapping. He extracted a cigarette and stuffed it into his mouth under the fringe of his reddish moustache and lit it.

Bond was surprised. 'I didn't realize one could smoke down here,' he said, taking out his own case.

Drax's cigarette, a tiny white faggot in the middle of the big red face, waggled up and down as he answered without taking it out of his mouth. 'Quite all right in here,' he said. 'These rooms are air-tight. Doors lined with rubber. Separate ventilation. Have to keep the workshops and generators separate from the shaft and anyway,' his lips grinned round the cigarette, 'I have to be able to smoke.'

Drax took the cigarette out of his mouth and looked at it. He seemed to make up his mind. 'You were asking about Krebs,' he said. 'Well,' he looked meaningly up at Bond, 'just between ourselves I don't entirely trust the fellow.' He held up an admonitory hand. 'Nothing definite, of course, or I'd have had him put away, but I've found him snooping about the house and once I caught him in my study going through my private papers. He had a perfectly good explanation and I let him off with a warning. But quite honestly I have my suspicions of the man. Of course, he can't do any harm. He's part of the household staff and none of them are allowed in here but,' he looked candidly into Bond's eyes, 'I would have said you ought to concentrate on him. Bright of you to have bowled him out so quickly,' he added with respect.

'What put you on to him?'

'Oh, nothing much,' said Bond. 'He's got a shifty look. But what you say's interesting and I'll certainly keep an eye on him.'

He turned to Gala Brand who had remained silent ever since they had entered the room.

'And what do you think of Krebs, Miss Brand?' he asked politely.

The girl spoke to Drax. 'I don't know much about these things, Sir Hugo,' she said with a modesty and a touch of impulsiveness which Bond admired. 'But I don't trust the man at all. I hadn't meant to tell you, but he's been poking around my room, opening letters and so forth. I know he has.'

Drax was shocked. 'Has he indeed?' he said. He bashed his cigarette out in the ashtray and killed the glowing fragments one by one. 'So much for Krebs,' he said, without looking up.

There was a moment's silence in the room during which Bond reflected how odd it was that suspicions should have fallen so suddenly and so unanimously on one man. And did that automatically clear all the others? Might not Krebs be the inside man of a gang? Or was he working on his own and, if so, with what object? And what did his snooping have to do with the death of Talon and Bartsch?

Drax broke the silence. 'Well, that seems to settle it,' he said, looking to Bond for confirmation. Bond gave a non-committal nod. 'Just have to leave him to you. At all events, we must see he is kept well away from the site. As a matter of fact I shall be taking him to London tomorrow. Last-minute details to be settled with the Ministry and Walter can't be spared. Krebs is the only man I've got who can do the work of an ADC. That'll keep him out of trouble. We'll all have to keep an eye on him until then. Unless of course you want to put him under lock and key straight away. I'd prefer not,' he said candidly. 'Don't want to upset the team any more.'

'It shouldn't be necessary,' said Bond. 'Has he got any particular friends among the other men?'

'Never seen him speak to any of them except Walter and the household,' said Drax. 'Daresay he considers himself a cut above the others. Personally, I don't believe there's much harm in the chap or I wouldn't have kept him. He's left alone in that house all day long and I expect he's one of those people who like playing the detective and prying into other people's affairs. What do you say? Perhaps we could leave it like that?'

Bond nodded, keeping his thoughts to himself.

'Well, then,' said Drax, obviously glad to leave a distasteful subject and get back to business, 'we've got other things to talk about. Two more days to go and I'd better tell you the programme.' He got up from his chair and paced heavily up and down the room behind his desk. 'Today is Wednesday,' he said. 'At one o'clock the site will be closed for fuelling. This will be supervised by Dr Walter and myself and two men from the Ministry. Just in case anything goes wrong a television camera will record everything we do. Then, if there is an explosion, our successors will know better next time,' he barked a short laugh. 'Weather permitting, the roof will be opened tonight to allow the fumes to clear. My men will stand guard in watches at ten-yard intervals a hundred yards from the site. There will be three armed men on the beach opposite the exhaust hole in the cliff. Tomorrow morning the site will be opened again until midday for a final check and from that moment, except for the gyro settings, the Moonraker will be ready to go. The guards will be permanently on duty round the site. On Friday morning I shall personally supervise the gyro settings. The men from the Ministry will take over the firing point and the RAF will man the radar. The BBC will set up their vans behind the firing point and will begin their running commentary at eleven-forty-five. At midday exactly I shall press the plunger, a radio beam will break an electric circuit and,' he smiled broadly, 'we shall see what we shall see.' He paused, fingering his chin. 'Now what else? Well now. Shipping will be cleared from the target area from midnight on Thursday. The Navy will provide a patrol of the boundaries of the area all through the morning. There will be a BBC commentator in one of the ships. The Ministry of Supply experts will be in a salvage ship with deep-sea television and after the rocket has landed they will try to bring up the remains. You may be interested to know,' continued Drax, rubbing his hands with almost childish pleasure, 'that a messenger from the Prime Minister has brought me the very welcome news that not only will there be a special Cabinet Meeting to listen to the broadcast, but the Palace will also be listening in to the launching.'

'Splendid,' said Bond, pleased for the man's sake.

'Thank you,' said Drax. 'Now I want to be quite certain that you are satisfied with my security arrangements on the site itself. I don't think we need worry about what goes on outside. The RAF and the police seem to be doing a very thorough job.'

'Everything seems to have been taken care of,' said Bond. 'There doesn't seem to be very much for me to do in the time that's left.'

'Nothing that I can think of,' agreed Drax, 'except our friend Krebs. This afternoon he will be in the television van taking notes, so he will be out of trouble. Why don't you have a look at the beach and the bottom of the cliff while he's out of action? That's the only weak spot I can think of. I've often thought that if someone wanted to get into the site he would try the exhaust pit. Take Miss Brand with you. Two pairs of eyes, and so forth, and she won't be able to use her office until tomorrow morning.'

'Good,' said Bond. 'I'd certainly like to have a look at the seaward side after lunch, and if Miss Brand's got nothing better to do . . .' He turned towards her with his eyebrows raised.

Gala Brand looked down her nose. 'Certainly, if Sir Hugo wishes,' she said without enthusiasm.

Drax rubbed his hands together. 'Then that's settled,' he said. 'And now I must get down to work. Miss Brand, would you ask Dr Walter to come along if he's free. See you at lunch,' he said to Bond, on a note of dismissal.

Bond nodded. 'I think I'll walk over and have a look at the firing point,' he said, not quite knowing why he lied. He turned and followed Gala Brand out through the double doors into the base of the shaft.

A huge black snake of rubber piping meandered over the shining steel floor and Bond watched the girl pick her way among its coils to where Walter was standing alone. He was gazing up at the mouth of the fuel pipe being hoist to where a gantry, outstretched to the threshold of an access door halfway up the rocket, indicated the main fuel tanks.

She said something to Walter and then stood beside him looking upwards as the pipe was delicately man-handled through into the interior of the rocket.

Bond thought she looked very innocent standing there with her brown hair falling back from her head and the curve of her ivory throat sweeping down into the plain white shirt. With her hands clasped behind her back, gazing raptly upwards at the glittering fifty feet of the Moonraker, she might have been a schoolgirl looking up at a Christmas tree – except for the impudent pride of the jutting breasts, swept up by the thrown-back head and shoulders.

Bond smiled to himself as he walked to the foot of the iron stairway and started to climb. That innocent, desirable girl, he reminded himself, is an extremely efficient policewoman. She knows how to kick, and where; she can break my arm probably more easily and quickly than I can break hers, and at least half of her belongs to the Special Branch of Scotland Yard. Of course, he reflected, looking down just in time to see her follow Dr Walters into Drax's office, there is always the other half.

Outside, the brilliant May sunshine seemed particu-larly golden after the blue-white of the arcs and Bond could feel it hot on his back as he walked purposefully across the concrete towards the house. The foghorn from the Goodwins was silent and the morning was so quiet that he could hear the rhythmic thump of a ship's engines as a coaster negotiated the Inner Leads, between the Goodwins and the shore, on its way northwards.

He approached the house under cover of the wide blast-wall and then quickly crossed the few yards to the front door, the crêpe rubber soles of his shoes making no noise. He eased open the door and left it ajar and walked softly into the hall and stood listening. There was the early summer noise of a bumble-bee fussing against the pane of one of the windows and a distant clatter from the barracks behind the house. Otherwise the silence was deep and warm and reassuring.

Bond walked carefully across the hall and up the stairs, placing his feet flat on the ground and using the extreme edges of the steps where the boards would be less likely to creak. There was no noise in the corridor but Bond saw that his door at the far end was open. He took his gun from under his armpit and walked swiftly down the carpeted passage.

Krebs had his back to him. He was kneeling forward in the middle of the floor with his elbows on the ground. His hands were at the wheels of the combination lock of Bond's leather case. His whole attention was focused on the click of the tumblers in the lock.

The target was tempting and Bond didn't hesitate. His teeth showed in a hard smile, he took two quick paces into the room and his foot lashed out.

All his force was behind the point of his shoe and his balance and timing were perfect.

The scream of a jay was driven out of Krebs as, like the caricature of a leaping frog, he hurtled over Bond's case, across a yard or so of carpet, and into the front of the mahogany dressing-table. His head hit the middle of it so hard that the heavy piece of furniture rocked on its base. The scream was abruptly cut off and he crashed in an inert spreadeagle on the floor and lay still.

Bond stood looking at him and listening for the sound of hurrying footsteps, but there was still silence in the house. He walked over to the sprawling figure and bent down and heaved it over on its back. The face around the smudge of yellow moustache was pale and some blood had oozed down over the forehead from a cut in the top of the skull. The eyes were closed and the breathing was laboured.

Bond knelt down on one knee and went carefully through every pocket of Krebs's neat grey pinstripe suit, laying the disappointingly meagre contents on the carpet beside the body. There was no pocketbook and no papers. The only objects of interest were a bunch of skeleton keys, a spring knife with a well-sharpened stiletto blade, and an obscene little truss-shaped black leather cosh. Bond pocketed these and then went to his bedside table and fetched the untouched bottle of Vichy water.

It took five minutes to revive Krebs and get him into a sitting position with his back to the dressing-table and another five for him to be capable of speaking. Gradually the colour came back to his face and the craftiness to his eyes.

'I answer no questions except to Sir Hugo,' he said as Bond started the interrogation. 'You have no right to question me. I was doing my duty.' His voice was surly and assured.

Bond took the empty Vichy bottle by the neck. 'Think again,' he said. 'Or I'll beat the daylight out of you until this breaks and then use the neck for some plastic surgery. Who told you to go over my room?'

'*Leck mich am Arsch.*' Krebs spat the obscene insult at him.

Bond bent down and cracked him sharply across the shins. Krebs's body cringed, but, as Bond raised his arm again, he suddenly shot up from the floor and dived under the descending bottle. The blow caught him hard on the shoulder, but it didn't check his momentum and he was out of the door and halfway down the corridor before Bond started in pursuit.

Bond stopped outside the door and watched the flying figure swerve down the stairs and out of sight. Then, as he heard the scurrying squeak of the rubber-soled shoes as they fled down the stairs and across the hall, he laughed abruptly to himself and went back into his room and locked the door. Short of beating the man's brains out it hadn't looked as if he would get much out of Krebs. He had given him something to think about. Crafty little brute. His injuries couldn't have been so bad after all. Well, it would be up to Drax to punish him. Unless, of course, Krebs had been carrying out Drax's orders.

Bond cleaned up the mess in his room and sat down on his bed and gazed at the opposite wall with unseeing eyes. It had not been only instinct that had made him tell Drax he was going to the firing point instead of to the house. It had seriously crossed his mind that the snooping of Krebs was on Drax's orders, and that Drax ran his own security system. And yet how did that tally with the deaths of Tallon and Bartsch? Or had the double killing been a coincidence unrelated to the marks on the chart and the fingerprints of Krebs?

As if summoned by his thoughts, there came a knock on the door and the butler came in. He was followed by a police sergeant in road patrol uniform who saluted and handed Bond a telegram. Bond took it over to the window. It was signed Baxter, which meant Vallance, and it read:

FIRSTLY CALL WAS FROM HOUSE SECONDLY FOG REQUIRED OPERATION OF FOGHORN SO SHIP HEARD COMMA OBSERVED NOTHING THIRDLY YOUR COMPASS RECKONING TOO NEAR SHORE THUS OUT OF SIGHT OF SAINT MARGARETS OR DEAL COASTGUARD ENDS.

'Thank you,' said Bond. 'No answer.'

When the door was closed Bond put his lighter to the telegram and dropped it in the fireplace, scuffing the charred remains into powder with the sole of his shoe.

Nothing much there except that Tallon's call to the Ministry might indeed have been heard by someone in the house, which might have resulted in the search of his room, which might have resulted in his death. But what about Bartsch? If all this was part of something much bigger how could it be linked up with an attempt to sabotage the rocket? Wasn't it much simpler to conclude that Krebs was a natural snooper, or more likely that he was operating for Drax, who seemed to be meticulously security-conscious and who might want to be sure of the loyalty of his secretary, of Tallon, and certainly, after their encounter at Blades, of Bond? Wasn't it just acting like the chief (and Bond had known many of them who would fit the picture) of some super-secret project during the war who had reinforced official security with his own private spy system?

If that theory was correct there only remained the double killing. Now that Bond had caught the magic and the tension of the Moonraker the facts of the hysterical shooting seemed more reasonable. As for the mark on the chart, that might have been made any day in the past year; the night-glasses were just night-glasses and the moustaches on the men were just a lot of moustaches.

Bond sat on in the silent room, shifting the pieces in the jigsaw so that two entirely different pictures alternated in his mind. In one the sun shone and all was clear and innocent as the day. The other was a dark confusion of guilty motives, obscure suspicions, and nightmare queries.

When the gong sounded for lunch he still did not know which picture to choose. To shelve a decision he cleared his mind of everything but the prospect of his afternoon alone with Gala Brand.

16 / A GOLDEN DAY

It was wonderful afternoon of blue and green and gold. When they left the concrete apron through the guard-gate near the empty firing point, now connected by a thick cable with the launching site, they stopped for a moment on the edge of the great chalk cliff and stood gazing over the whole corner of England where Caesar had first landed two thousand years before.

To their left the carpet of green turf, bright with small wildflowers, sloped gradually down to the long pebble beaches of Walmer and Deal, which curved off towards Sandwich and the Bay. Beyond, the cliffs of Margate, showing white through the distant haze that hid the North Foreland, guarded the grey scar of Manston aerodrome above which American Thunderjets wrote their white scribbles in the sky. Then came the Isle of Thanet and, out of sight, the mouth of the Thames.

It was low tide and the Goodwins were golden and tender in the sparkling blue of the Straits with only the smattering of masts and spars that stretched along their length to tell the true story. The white lettering on the South Goodwins Lightship was easy to read and even the name of her sister ship to the north showed white against the red of her hull.

Between the sands of the coast, along the twelve-fathom channel of the Inner Leads, there were half a dozen ships beating up through the Downs, the thud of their engines coming clearly off the quiet sea, and between the evil sands and the sharp outline of the French coast there were ships of all registries going about their business – liners, merchantmen, ungainly Dutch schuyts, and even a slim corvette hastening down south, perhaps to Portsmouth. As far as the eye could reach the Eastern Approaches of England were dotted with traffic plying towards near or distant horizons, towards a home port, or towards the other side of the world. It was a panorama full of colour and excitement and romance and the two people on the edge of the cliff were silent as they stood for a time and watched it all.

The peace was broken by two blasts on the siren from the house and they turned to gaze back at the ugly concrete world that had been cleaned out of their minds. As they watched, a red flag was broken out above the dome of the launching site and two RAF crash-wagons with red crosses on their sides rolled out of the trees to the edge of the blast-wall and pulled up.

'Fuelling's going to begin,' said Bond. 'Let's get on with our walk. There'll be nothing to see and if there happened to be something we probably wouldn't survive it at this range.'

She smiled at him. 'Yes,' she said. 'And I'm sick of the sight of all this concrete.'

They walked on down the gentle slope and were soon out of sight of the firing point and the high wire fence.

The ice of Gala's reserve melted quickly in the sunshine.

The exotic gaiety of her clothes, a black and white striped cotton shirt tucked into a wide hand-stitched black leather belt above a medium-length skirt in shocking pink, seemed to have infected her, and it was impossible for Bond to recognize the chill woman of the night before in the girl who now walked beside him and laughed happily at his ignorance of the names of the wildflowers, the samphire, Viper's bugloss, and fumitory round their feet.

Triumphantly she found a bee orchis and picked it.

'You wouldn't do that if you knew that flowers scream when they are picked,' said Bond.

Gala looked at him. 'What do you mean?' she asked, suspecting a joke.

'Didn't you know?' He smiled at her reaction. 'There's an Indian called Professor Bhose, who's written a treatise on the nervous system of flowers. He measured their reaction to pain. He even recorded the scream of a rose being picked. It must be one of the most heart-rending sounds in the world. I heard something like it as you picked that flower.'

'I don't believe it,' she said, looking suspiciously at the torn root. 'Anyway,' she said maliciously, 'I wouldn't have thought you were a person to get sentimental. Don't people in your section of the Service make a business of killing? And not just flowers either. People.'

'Flowers can't shoot back,' said Bond.

She looked at the orchis. 'Now you've made me feel like a murderer. It's very unkind of you. But,' she admitted reluctantly, 'I shall have to find out about this Indian and if you're right I shall never pick a flower again as long as I live. What am I to going to do with this one? You make me feel it's bleeding all over my hands.'

'Give it to me,' said Bond. 'According to you, my hands are dripping with blood already. A little more won't hurt.'

She handed it to him and their hands touched. 'You can stick it in the muzzle of your revolver,' she said to cover the flash of contact.

Bond laughed. 'So the eyes aren't only for decoration,' he said. 'Anyway it's an automatic and I left it in my room.' He drew the stalk of the flower through one of the button holes in his blue cotton shirt. 'I thought a shoulder-holster would look a bit conspicuous without a coat to cover it. And I don't think anyone will be going over my room this afternoon.'

By tacit agreement they edged away from the moment of warmth. Bond told her of his discovery of Krebs and of the scene in his bedroom.

'Serves him right,' she said. 'I've never trusted him. But what did Sir Hugo say?'

'I had a word with him before lunch,' said Bond. 'Gave him Krebs's knife and keys as proof. He was furious and went straight off to see the man, muttering with rage. When he came back he said that Krebs seemed to be in a pretty bad way and was I satisfied that he'd been punished enough? All that business about not wanting to upset the team at the last moment and so forth. So I agreed that he'd be sent back to Germany next week and that meanwhile he would consider himself under open arrest – only allowed out of his room under surveillance.'

They scrambled down a steep cliff-path to the beach and turned to the right beside the deserted small-arms range of the Royal Marine Garrison at Deal. They walked along in silence until they came to the two-mile stretch of shingle that runs at low tide beneath the towering white cliffs to St Margaret's Bay.

As they trudged slowly through the deep smooth pebbles Bond told her of all that had gone through his mind since the previous day. He held nothing back and he showed each false hare as it had been started and finally run to earth, leaving nothing but a thin scent of ill-founded suspicions and a muddle of clues that all ended in the same question mark . . . where was a pattern? Where was a plan into which the clues would fit? And always the same answer, that nothing Bond knew or suspected seemed to have any conceivable bearing on the security from sabotage of the Moonraker. And that, when all was said and done, was the only matter with which he and the girl were concerned. Not with the death of Tallon and Bartsch, not with the egregious Krebs, but only with the protection of the whole Moonraker project from its possible enemies.

'Isn't that so?' Bond concluded.

Gala stopped and stood for a moment looking out across the tumbled rocks and seaweed towards the quiet glimmering swell of the sea. She was hot and out of breath from the hard going through the shingle and she thought how wonderful it would be to bathe – to step back for a moment into those childish days beside the sea before her life had been caught up in this strange cold profession with its tensions and hollow thrills. She glanced at the ruthless brown face of the man beside her. Did he have moments of longing for the peaceful simple things of life? Of course not. He liked Paris and Berlin and New York and trains and aeroplanes and expensive food, and, yes certainly, expensive women.

'Well?' said Bond, wondering if she was going to come out with some piece of evidence that he had overlooked.

'What do you think?'

'I'm sorry,' said Gala. 'I was dreaming. No,' she answered his question. 'I think you're right. I've been down here since the beginning and although there've been odd little things from time to time, and of course the shooting, I've seen absolutely nothing wrong. Every one of the team, from Sir Hugo down, is heart and soul behind the rocket. It's all they live for and it's been wonderful to see the whole thing grow. The Germans are terrific workers – and I can quite believe that Bartsch broke under the strain – and they love being driven by Sir Hugo and he loves driving them. They worship him. And as for security, the place is solid with it and I'm sure that anyone who tried to get near the Moonraker would be torn to pieces. I agree with you about Krebs and that he was probably working under Drax's orders. It was because I believed that, that I didn't bother to report him when he went through my things. There was nothing for him to find, of course. Just private letters and so on. It would be typical of Sir Hugo to make absolutely sure. And I must say,' she said candidly, 'that I admire him for it. He's a ruthless man with deplorable manners and not a very nice face under all that red hair, but I love working for him and I'm longing for the Moonraker to be a success. Living with it for so long has made me feel just like his men do about it.'

She looked up to see his reactions.

He nodded. 'After only a day I can understand that,' he said. 'And I suppose I agree with you. There's nothing to go on except my intuition and that will have to look after itself. The main thing is that the Moonraker looks as safe as the Crown Jewels, and probably safer.' He shrugged his shoulders impatiently, dissatisfied with himself for disowning the intuitions that were so much of his trade. 'Come on,' he said, almost roughly. 'We're wasting time.'

Understanding, she smiled to herself and followed.

Round the next bend of the cliff they came up with the base of the hoist, encrusted with seaweed and barnacles. Fifty yards further on they reached the jetty, a strong tubular iron frame paved with latticed iron strips that ran out over the rocks and beyond.

Between the two, and perhaps twenty feet up the cliff face, yawned the wide black mouth of the exhaust tunnel which slanted up inside the cliff to the steel floor beneath the stern of the rocket. From the under-lip of the cave melted chalk drooled like lava and there were splashes of the stuff all over the pebbles and rocks below. In his mind's eye Bond could see the blazing white shaft of flame come howling out of the face of the cliff and he could hear the sea hiss and bubble as the liquid chalk poured into the water.

He looked up at the narrow section of the launching dome that showed above the edge of the cliff two hundred feet up in the sky, and imagined the four men in their gas-masks and asbestos suits watching the gauges as the terrible liquid explosive pulsed down the black rubber tube into the stomach of the rocket. He suddenly realized that they were in range if anything went wrong with the fuelling.

'Let's get away from here,' he said to the girl.

When they had put a hundred yards between themselves and the cave Bond stopped and looked back. He imagined himself with six tough men and all the right gear, and he wondered how he would set about attacking the site from the sea – kayaks to the jetty at low tide; a ladder to the lip of the cave? and then what? Impossible to climb the polished steel walls of the exhaust tunnel. It would be a question of firing an anti-tank weapon through the steel floor beneath the rocket, following up with some phosphorus shells and hoping that something would catch fire. Untidy business, but it might be effective. Getting away afterwards would be nasty. Sitting targets from the top of the cliff. But that wouldn't worry a Russian suicide squad. It was all quite feasible.

Gala had been standing beside him watching the eyes that measured and speculated. 'It's not as easy as you might think,' she said, seeing the frown on his face. 'Even when it's high tide and very rough they have guards along the top of the cliff at night. And they've got searchlights and Brens and grenades. Their orders are to shoot and ask questions afterwards. Of course it would be better to floodlight the cliff at night. But that would only pinpoint the site. I really believe they've thought of everything.'

Bond was still frowning. 'If they had covering fire from a submarine or an X-craft, a good team could still do it,' he said. 'It'll be hell, but I'm going for a swim. The Admiralty chart says there's a twelve-fathom channel out there, but I'd like to have a look. There must be plenty of water at the end of the jetty but I'll be happier when I've seen for myself.' He smiled at her. 'Why don't you have a bathe too? It's going to be dam' cold, but it would do you good after stewing inside that concrete dome all the morning.'

Gala's eyes lit up. 'Do you think I could?' she asked doubtfully. 'I'm frightfully hot. But what are we going to wear?' She blushed at the thought of her brief and almost transparent nylon pants and brassière.

'To hell with that,' said Bond airily. 'You must have got some bits and pieces on underneath and I've got pants on. We shall be perfectly respectable and there's no one to see, and I promise not to look,' he lied cheerfully, leading the way round the next bend in the cliff. 'You undress behind that rock and I'll use this one,' he said. 'Come on. Don't be a goose. It's all in the line of duty.'

Without waiting for her to answer he moved behind the tall rock, taking off his shirt as he did so.

'Oh, well,' said Gala, relieved to have the decision taken out of her hands. She went behind her rock and slowly unbuttoned her skirt.

When she peered nervously out, Bond was already halfway down the strip of coarse brown sand that led out among the pools to where the incoming tide eddied through the green and black moraine of the rocks. He looked lithe and brown. The blue pants were reassuring.

Gingerly she followed him, and then suddenly she was in the water. At once nothing else mattered but the velvet ice of the sea and the beauty of the patches of sand between the waving hair of the seaweed that she could see in the clear green depths below her as she buried her head and swam along parallel with the shore in a fast crawl.

When she was level with the jetty she stopped for a moment to get her breath. There was no sign of Bond whom she had last seen streaking along a hundred yards ahead of her. She trod water hard to keep up her circulation and then started back again, unwillingly thinking of him, thinking of the hard brown body that must be somewhere near her, among the rocks, perhaps, or diving to the sand to gauge the depth of water that would be available to an enemy.

She turned back to look for him again and it was then that he suddenly surged up from the sea beneath her. She felt the quick tight clasp of his arms round her and the swift hard impact of his lips on hers.

'Damn you,' she said furiously, but already he had dived again and by the time she had spat out a mouthful of seawater and got her bearings he was swimming blithely twenty yards away.

She turned and swam aloofly out to sea, feeling rather ridiculous but determined to snub him. It was just as she had thought. These Secret Service people always seemed to have time for sex however important their jobs might be.

But her body obstinately tingled with the shock of the kiss and the golden day seemed to have taken on a new beauty. As she swam further out to sea and then turned back and looked along the snarling milk-white teeth of England to the distant arm of Dover and at the black and white confetti of the ravens and gulls tossed against the vivid backcloth of green fields, she decided that anything was permissible on such a day and that, just this once, she would forgive him.

Half an hour later they were lying, waiting for the sun to dry them, separated by a respectable yard of sand at the foot of the cliff.

The kiss had not been mentioned, but Gala's efforts to preserve an atmosphere of aloofness had collapsed under the excitement of examining a lobster that Bond had dived for and caught with his hands. Reluctantly they put it back into one of the rockpools and watched it scuttle backwards into the shelter of the seaweed. And now they lay, tired and exhilarated by their icy swim, and prayed that the sun would not slip behind the clifftop high above their heads before they were warm and dry enough to get back into their clothes.

But those were not Bond's only thoughts. The beautiful strapping body of the girl beside him, incredibly erotic in the tight emphasis of the clinging brassière and pants, came between him and his concern about the Moonraker. And anyway there was nothing he could do about the Moonraker for another hour. It was not yet five o'clock and the fuelling would not be finished until after six. It would only be then that he could get hold of Drax and make certain that for the next two nights the guards were strengthened on the cliff and that they had the right weapons. For he had seen for himself that there was plenty of water, even at low tide, for a submarine.

So there was at least a quarter of an hour to spare before they would have to start back.

Meanwhile this girl. The half-stripped body splayed above him on the surface as he swam up from below; the soft-hard quick kiss with his arms about her; the pointed hillocks of her breasts, so close to him, and the soft flat stomach descending to the mystery of her tightly closed thighs.

To hell with it.

He wrenched his mind out of its fever and gazed straight up into the endless blue of the sky, forcing himself to watch the soaring beauty of the herring gulls as they ranged effortlessly among the air currents that fountained up over the high clifftop above them. But the soft down of the birds' white underbellies seduced his thoughts back to her and gave him no rest.

'Why are you called Gala?' he said to break his hot crouching thoughts.

She laughed. 'I was teased about it all through school,' she said, and Bond was impatient at the easy, clear voice, 'and then through the Wrens and then by half the police force of London. But my real name's even worse. It's Galatea. She was a cruiser my father was serving in when I was born. I suppose Gala's not too bad. I've almost forgotten what I'm called. I'm always having to change my name now that I'm in the Special Branch.'

'In the Special Branch.' 'In the Special Branch.' 'In the . . .'

When the bomb falls. When the pilot miscalculates and the plane hits short of the runway. When the blood leaves the heart and consciousness goes, there are thoughts in the mind, or words, or perhaps a phrase of music, which ring on for the few seconds before death like the dying clang of a bell.

Bond wasn't killed, but the words were still in his mind, several seconds later, after it had all happened.

Ever since they had lain down on the sand up against the cliff, while his thoughts had been of Gala, his eyes had been carelessly watching two gulls playing around a wisp of straw that was the edge of their nest on a small ledge about ten feet below the distant top of the cliff. They would crane and bow in their love-play, with only their heads visible to Bond against the dazzling white of the chalk, and then the male would soar out and away and at once back to the ledge to take up his love-making again.

Bond was dreamily watching them as he listened to the girl, when suddenly both gulls dashed away from the ledge with a single shrill scream of fear. At the same moment there was a puff of black smoke and a soft boom from the top of the cliff and a great section of the white chalk directly above Bond and Gala seemed to sway outwards, zigzag cracks snaking down its face.

The next thing Bond knew was that he was lying on top of Gala, his face pressed into her cheek, that the air was full of thunder, that his breath was stifled and that the sun had gone out. His back was numb and aching under a great weight and in his left ear, besides the echo of the thunder, there was the end of a choking scream.

He was barely conscious and he had to wait until his senses came halfway back to life.

The Special Branch. What was it she had said about the Special Branch?

He made frantic efforts to move. Only in his right arm, the arm nearest to the cliff, was there any play at all, but as he jerked his shoulder the arm became freer until at last, with a great backward heave, light and air reached down to them. Retching in the fog of chalk-dust, he widened the hole until his head could take its crushing weight off Gala. He felt the feeble movement as she turned her head sideways towards the light and air. A growing trickle of dust and stones into the hole he had cleared made him dig fiercely again. Gradually he enlarged the space until he could get a purchase on his right elbow and then, coughing so that he thought his lungs would burst, he heaved his right shoulder up until suddenly it and his head were free.

His first thought was that there had been an explosion in the Moonraker. He looked up at the cliff and then along the shore. No. They were a hundred yards from the site. It was only in the skyline directly above them that a great mouthful had been bitten out of the cliff.

Then he thought of their immediate danger. Gala moaned and he could feel the frantic thud of her heart against his chest, but the ghastly white mask of her face was now free to the air and he wrenched his body from side to side on top of her to try and ease the pressure on her lungs and stomach. Slowly, inch by inch, his muscles cracking under the strain, he worked his way under the pile of dust and rubble towards the cliff face where he knew the weight would be less.

And then at last his chest was free and he could snake his body into a kneeling position beside her. Blood dripped from his cut back and arms and mingled with the chalk dust that continually poured down the sides of the hole he had made, but he could feel that no bones were broken and, in the rage of the rescue work, he felt no pain.

Grunting and coughing and without a pause to take breath he heaved her up into a sitting position and with a bleeding hand wiped some of the chalk dust from her face. Then, freeing his legs from the tomb of chalk, he somehow manhandled her up on to the top of the mound with her back against the cliff.

He knelt and looked at her, at the terrible white scarecrow that minutes before had been one of the most beautiful girls he had ever seen, and as he looked at her and at the streaks of his blood down her face he prayed that her eyes would open.

When, seconds later, they did, the relief was so great that Bond turned away and was rackingly sick.

When the paroxysm was over he felt Gala's hand in his hair. He looked round and saw her wince at the sight of him. She tugged at his hair and pointed up the cliffs. As she did so a shower of small pieces of chalk rattled down beside them.

Weakly he got to his knees and then to his feet and together they scrambled and slid down off the mountain of chalk and away from the crater against the cliff from which they had escaped.

The harsh sand under their feet was like velvet. They both collapsed full length and lay clutching at it with their horrible white hands as if its rough gold would wash the filthy whiteness away. Then Gala too was mercifully sick and Bond crawled a few paces away to leave her alone. He hauled himself to his feet against a single lump of chalk as big as a small motor-car, and at last his bloodshot eyes took in the hell that had almost engulfed them.

Down to the beginning of the rocks, now lapped by the incoming tide, sprawled the debris of the cliff face, an avalanche of chalk blocks and shapes. The white dust of its collapse covered nearly an acre. Above it a jagged rent had appeared in the cliff and a wedge of blue sky had been bitten out of the distant top where before the line of the horizon had been almost straight. There were no longer any seabirds near them and Bond guessed that the smell of disaster would keep them away from the place for days.

The nearness of their bodies to the cliff was what had saved them, that and the slight protection of the overhang below which the sea had bitten into the base of the cliff. They had been buried by the deluge of smaller stuff. The heavier chunks, any one of which would have crushed them, had fallen outwards, the nearest missing them by a few feet. And their nearness to the cliff was the reason for Bond's right arm having been comparatively free so that they had been able to burrow out of the mound before they were stifled. Bond realized that if some reflex had not hurled him on top of Gala at the moment of the avalanche they would now both be dead.

He felt her hand on his shoulder. Without looking at her he put his arm round her waist and together they got down to the blessed sea and let their bodies fall weakly, thankfully into the shallows.

Ten minutes later it was two comparatively human beings who walked back up the sand to the rocks where their clothes lay, a few yards away from the cliff-fall. They were both completely naked. The rags of their underclothing lay somewhere under the pile of chalk dust, torn off in their struggle to escape. But, like survivors from a shipwreck, their nakedness meant nothing. Washed clean of the cloying gritty chalk dust and with their hair and mouths scoured with the salt water, they felt weak and bedraggled, but by the time they had got their clothes on and had shared Gala's comb there was little to show what they had been through.

They sat with their backs to a rock and Bond lit a first delicious cigarette, drinking the smoke deeply into his lungs and expelling it slowly through his nostrils. When Gala had done the best she could with her powder and lipstick he lit a cigarette for her and, as he handed it to her, for the first time they looked into each other's eyes and smiled. Then they sat and looked silently out to sea, at the golden panorama that was the same and yet entirely new.

Bond broke the silence.

'Well, by God,' he said. 'That was close.'

'I still don't know what happened,' said Gala. 'Except that you saved my life.' She put her hand on his and then took it away.

'If you hadn't been there I should be dead,' said Bond. 'If I'd stayed where I was – ' He shrugged his shoulders.

Then he turned and looked at her. 'I suppose you realize,' he said flatly, 'that someone pushed the cliff down on us?' She looked back at him with wide eyes. 'If we searched around in all that,' he gestured towards the avalanche of chalk, 'we would find the marks of two or three drill-holes and traces of dynamite. I saw the smoke and I heard the bang of the explosion a split second before the cliff came down. And so did the gulls,' he added.

'And what's more,' continued Bond after a pause, 'it can't have been only Krebs. It was done in full view of the site. And it was done by several people, well organized, with spies on us from the moment we went down the cliff path to the beach.'

There was comprehension in Gala's eyes and a flash of fear. 'What are we to do?' she asked anxiously. 'What's it all about?'

'They want us dead,' said Bond calmly. 'So we have to stay alive. As to what it's all about, we'll just have to find that out.

'You see,' he went on, 'I'm afraid even Vallance isn't going to be much help. When they made up their minds we were properly buried, they'll have got away from the top of the cliff as fast as they could. They'd know that even if someone saw the cliff-fall, or heard it, they wouldn't get very excited. There are twenty miles of these cliffs and not many people come here until the summer. If the coastguards heard it they may have made a note in the log. But in the spring I expect they get plenty of falls. The winter frosts thaw out in cracks that may be hundreds of years old. So our friends would wait until we didn't turn up tonight and then get the police and coastguards to search for us. They'd keep quiet until the high tide had made porridge out of a good deal of this.' He gestured towards the shambles of fallen chalk. 'The whole scheme is admirable. And even if Vallance believes us, there's not enough evidence to make the Prime Minister interfere with the Moonraker. The damn thing's so infernally important. All the world's waiting to see if it'll work or not. And anyway, what's our story? What the hell's it all about? Some of those bloody Germans up there seem to want us dead before Friday. But what for?' He paused. 'It's up to us, Gala. It's a lousy business but we've simply got to solve it ourselves.'

He looked into her eyes. 'What about it?'

Gala laughed abruptly. 'Don't be ridiculous,' she said. 'It's what we're paid for. Of course we'll take them on. And I agree we'd get nowhere with London. We'd look absolutely ridiculous telephoning reports about cliffs falling on our heads. What are we doing down here anyway, fooling around without any clothes on instead of getting on with our jobs?'

Bond grinned. 'We only lay down for ten minutes to get dry,' he protested mildly. 'How do you think we ought to have spent the afternoon? Taking everybody's fingerprints all over again? That's about all you police think about.' He felt ashamed when he saw her stiffen. He held his hand up. 'I didn't really mean that,' he said. 'But can't you see what we've done this afternoon? Just what had to be done. We've made the enemy show his hand. Now we've got to take the next step and find out who the enemy is and why he wanted us out of the way. And then if we've got enough evidence that someone's trying to sabotage the Moonraker we'll have the whole place turned inside out, the practice shoot postponed, and to hell with politics.'

She jumped to her feet. 'Oh, of course you're right,' she said impatiently. 'It's just that I want to do something about it in a hurry.' She looked for a moment out to sea, away from Bond. 'You've only just come into the picture. I've been living with this rocket for more than a year and I can't bear the idea that something may happen to it. So much seems to depend on it. For all of us. I want to get back there quickly and to find out who wanted to kill us. It may be nothing to do with the Moonraker, but I want to make sure.'

Bond stood up, showing nothing of the pain from the cuts and bruises on his back and legs. 'Come on,' he said, 'it's nearly six o'clock. The tide's coming in fast but we can get to St Margaret's before it catches us. We'll clean up at the Granville there and have a drink and some food and then we'll go back to the house in the middle of dinner. I shall be interested to see what sort of a reception we get. After that we'll have to concentrate on staying alive and seeing what we can see. Can you make it to St Margaret's?'

'Don't be silly,' said Gala. 'Policewomen aren't made of gossamer.' She gave a reluctant smile at Bond's ironically respectful 'Of course not', and they turned towards the distant tower of the South Foreland lighthouse and set off through the shingle.

At half-past eight the taxi from St Margaret's dropped them at the second guard gate and they showed their passes and walked quietly up through the trees on to the expanse of concrete. They both felt keyed up and in high spirits. A hot bath and an hour's rest at the accommodating Granville had been followed by two stiff brandies-and-sodas for Gala and three for Bond followed by delicious fried soles and Welsh rarebits and coffee. And now, as they confidently approached the house, it would have needed second sight to tell that they were both dead tired and that they were naked and bruised under their walking clothes.

They let themselves quietly in through the front door and stood for a moment in the lighted hall. A cheerful mumble of voices came from the dining-room. There was a pause followed by a burst of laughter which was dominated by the harsh bark of Sir Hugo Drax.

Bond's mouth twisted wryly as he led the way across the hall to the door of the dining-room. Then he fixed a cheerful smile on his face and opened the door for Gala to pass through.

Drax sat at the head of the table, festive in his plum-coloured smoking-jacket. A forkful of food, halfway to his open mouth, had stopped in mid-air as they appeared in the doorway. Unnoticed, the food slid off the fork and fell with a soft, distinct 'plep' on to the edge of the table.

Krebs had been in the act of drinking a glass of red wine and the glass, frozen against his mouth, poured a thin trickle down his chin and thence on to his brown satin tie and yellow shirt.

Dr Walter had had his back to the door and it was not until he observed the unusual behaviour of the others, the bulging eyes, the gape of the mouths, and the blood-drained faces, that he whipped his head round towards the door. His reactions, thought Bond, were slower than the others, or else his nerves were steadier. *'Ach so,'* he said softly. *'Die Engländer.'*

Drax was on his feet. 'My dear chap,' he said thickly. 'My dear chap. We were really very worried. Just wondering whether to send out a search party. Few minutes ago one of the guards came in and reported there seemed to have been a cliff-fall.' He came round towards them, his napkin in one hand and the fork still erect in the other.

With the movement the blood surged back into his face, which became first mottled and then its usual red. 'You really might have let me know,' he spoke to the girl, anger rising in his voice. 'Most extraordinary behaviour.'

'It was my fault,' said Bond, moving forward into the room so that he could keep them all in view. 'The walk was longer than I expected. I thought we might get caught by the tide so we went on to St Margaret's and had something to eat there and took a taxi. Miss Brand wanted to telephone but I thought we would be back before eight. You must put the blame on me. But please go ahead with your dinner. Perhaps I might join you for coffee and dessert. I expect Miss Brand would prefer to go to her room. She must be tired after her long day.'

Bond walked deliberately round the table and took the chair next to Krebs. Those pale eyes, he noticed, after the first shock, had been fixed firmly on his plate. As Bond came up behind him he was delighted to see a large mound of Elastoplast on the crown of Krebs's head.

'Yes, go to bed, Miss Brand, I will talk to you in the morning,' said Drax testily. Gala obediently left the room and Drax went to his chair and sat heavily down.

'Most remarkable those cliffs,' said Bond blithely. 'Quite awe-inspiring walking along wondering if they're going to choose just that moment to collapse on one. Reminded me of Russian roulette. And yet one never reads of people being killed by cliffs falling on them. The odds against getting hurt must be terrific.' He paused. 'By the way, what was that you were saying about a cliff-fall just now?'

There was a faint groan on Bond's right, followed by a crash of glass and china as Krebs's head fell forward on to the table.

Bond looked at him with polite curiosity.

'Walter,' said Drax sharply. 'Can't you see that Krebs is ill? Take the man out and put him to bed. And don't be too soft with him. The man drinks too much. Hurry up.'

Walter, his face crumpled and angry, strode round the table and jerked Krebs's head out of the debris. He took him by his coat collar and hauled him to his feet and away from his chair.

'*Du Scheisskerl,*' hissed Walter at the mottled, vacant face. '*Marsch!*' He turned him round and hustled him to the swing door into the pantry and rammed him through. There were muffled sounds of stumbling and cursing and then a door banged and there was silence.

'He must have had a heavy day,' said Bond looking at Drax.

The big man was sweating freely. He wiped his face with a circular sweep of his napkin. 'Nonsense,' he said shortly. 'He drinks.'

The butler, erect and unperturbed by the apparition of Krebs and Walter in his pantry, brought in the coffee. Bond took some and sipped it. He waited for the pantry door to close again. Another German, he thought. He'll already have passed the news back to the barracks. Or perhaps all the team weren't involved. Perhaps there was a team within a team. And if so, did Drax know about it? His behaviour when Bond and Gala had come through the door had been inconclusive. Had part of his astonishment been affronted dignity, the shock of a vain man whose programme had been upset by a chit of a secretary? He had certainly covered up well. And all the afternoon he had been down the shaft supervising the fuelling. Bond decided to probe a little.

'How did the fuelling go?' he asked, his eyes fixed on the other man.

Drax was lighting a long cigar. He glanced up at Bond through the smoke and the flame of his match.

'Excellently.' He puffed at the cigar to get it going. 'Everything is ready now. The guards are out. An hour or two clearing up down there in the morning and then the site will be closed. By the way,' he added. 'I shall be taking Miss Brand up to London in the car tomorrow afternoon. I shall need a secretary as well as Krebs. Have you got any plans?'

'I have to go to London too,' said Bond on an impulse. 'I have my final report to make to the Ministry.'

'Oh, really?' said Drax casually. 'What about? I thought you were satisfied with the arrangements.'

'Yes,' said Bond non-committally.

'That's all right then,' said Drax breezily. 'And now if you don't mind,' he got up from the table, 'I've got some papers waiting for me in my study. So I'll say good-night.'

'Good-night,' said Bond to the already retreating back.

Bond finished his coffee and went out into the hall and up to his bedroom. It was obvious that it had been searched again. He shrugged his shoulders. There was only the leather case. Its contents would show nothing except that he had come equipped with the tools of his trade.

His Beretta in its shoulder-holster was still where he

had hidden it, in the empty leather case that belonged to Tallon's night-glasses. He took the gun out and slipped it under his pillow.

He took a hot bath and used half a bottle of iodine on the cuts and bruises he could reach. Then he got into bed and turned out the light. His body hurt and he was exhausted.

For a moment he thought of Gala. He had told her to take a sleeping pill and lock her door, but otherwise not to worry about anything until the morning.

Before he emptied his mind for sleep he wondered uneasily about her trip with Drax the next day to London.

Uneasily, but not desperately. In due course many questions would have to be answered and many mysteries probed, but the basic facts seemed solid and unanswerable. This extraordinary millionaire had built this great weapon. The Ministry of Supply were pleased with it and considered it sound. The Prime Minister and Parliament thought so too. The rocket was to be fired in less than thirty-six hours under full supervision and the security arrangements were as strict as they could possibly be. Somebody, and probably several people, wanted him and the girl out of the way. Nerves were stretched down here. There was a lot of tension about. Perhaps there was jealousy. Perhaps some people actually suspected them of being saboteurs. But what would that matter so long as he and Gala kept their eyes open? Not much more than a day to go. They were right out in the open here, in May, in England, in peacetime. It was crazy to worry about a few lunatics so long as the Moonraker was out of danger.

And as for tomorrow, reflected Bond as sleep reached out for him, he would arrange to meet Gala in London and bring her back with him. Or she could even stay up in London for the night. Either way he would look after her until the Moonraker was safely fired and then, before work began on the Mark II weapon, there would have to be a very thorough clean-up indeed.

But these were treacherously comforting thoughts. There was danger about and Bond knew it.

He finally drifted into sleep with one small scene firmly fixed in his mind.

There had been something very disquieting about the dinner-table downstairs. It had been laid for only three people.

Part Three / *Thursday, Friday*

The Mercedes was a beautiful thing. Bond pulled his battered grey Bentley up alongside it and inspected it.

It was a Type 300 S, the sports model with a disappearing hood – one of only half a dozen in England, he reflected. Left-hand drive. Probably bought in Germany. He had seen a few of them over there. One had hissed by him on the Munich Autobahn the year before when he was doing a solid ninety in the Bentley. The body, too short and heavy to be graceful, was painted white, with red leather upholstery. Garish for England, but Bond guessed that Drax had chosen white in honour of the famous Mercedes-Benz racing colours that had already swept the board again since the war at Le Mans and the Nurburgring.

Typical of Drax to buy a Mercedes. There was something ruthless and majestic about the cars, he decided, remembering the years from 1934 to 1939 when they had completely dominated the Grand Prix scene, children of the famous Blitzen Benz that had captured the world's speed record at 142 m.p.h. back in 1911. Bond recalled some of their famous drivers, Caracciola, Lang, Seaman, Brauchitsch, and the days when he had seen them drifting the fast sweeping bends of Tripoli at 190, or screaming along the tree-lined straight at Berne with the Auto Unions on their tails.

And yet, Bond looked across at his supercharged Bentley, nearly twenty-five years older than Drax's car and still capable of beating 100, and yet when Bentleys were racing, before Rolls had tamed them into sedate town carriages, they had whipped the blown SS-K's almost as they wished.

Bond had once dabbled on the fringe of the racing world and he was lost in his memories, hearing again the harsh scream of Caracciola's great white beast of a car as it howled past the grandstands at Le Mans, when Drax came out of the house followed by Gala Brand and Krebs.

'Fast car,' said Drax, pleased with Bond's look of admiration. He gestured towards the Bentley. 'They used to be good in the old days,' he added with a touch of patronage.

'Now they're only built for going to the theatre. Too well-mannered. Even the Continental. Now then you, get in the back.'

Krebs obediently climbed into the narrow back seat behind the driver. He sat sideways, his mackintosh up round his ears, his eyes fixed enigmatically on Bond.

Gala Brand, smart in a dark grey tailor-made and black beret and carrying a lightweight black raincoat and gloves, climbed into the right half of the divided front seat. The wide door closed with the rich double click of a Fabergé box.

No sign passed between Bond and Gala. They had made their plans at a whispered meeting in his room before lunch – dinner in London at half-past seven and then back to the house in Bond's car. She sat demurely, her hands in her lap and her eyes to the front, as Drax climbed in, pressed the starter, and pulled the gleaming lever on the steering wheel back into third. The car surged away with hardly a purr from the exhaust and Bond watched it disappear into the trees before he climbed into the Bentley and moved off in leisurely pursuit.

In the hastening Mercedes, Gala busied herself with her thoughts. The night had been uneventful and the morning had been devoted to clearing the launching site of everything that might possibly burn when the Moonraker was fired. Drax had not referred to the events of the previous day and there had been no change in his usual manner. She had prepared her last firing plan (Drax himself was to do it on the morrow) and as usual Walter had been sent for and through her spy-hole she had seen the figures being entered in Drax's black book.

It was a hot, sunny day and Drax was driving in his shirtsleeves. She glanced down and to the left at the top of the little book protruding from his hip-pocket. This drive might be her last chance. Since the evening before she had felt a different person. Perhaps Bond had aroused her competitive spirit, perhaps it was revulsion from playing the secretary too long, perhaps it was the shock of the cliff-fall and the zest of realizing after so many quiet months that she was playing a dangerous game. But now she felt the time had come to take risks. Discovery of the Moonraker's flight-plan was a routine affair and it would give her personal satisfaction to find out the secret of the black notebook. It would be easy.

Casually she laid her folded coat over the space between herself and Drax. At the same time she made a show of arranging herself comfortably, during the course of which she drew an inch or two nearer Drax and her hand came to rest in the folds of the coat between them. Then she settled herself to wait.

Her chance came, as she had thought it might, in the congested traffic of Maidstone. Drax, intent, was trying to beat the traffic lights at the corner of King Street and Gabriel's Hill, but the line of traffic was too slow and he was checked behind a battered family saloon. Gala could see that when the lights changed he was determined to cut in front of the car in front and teach it a lesson. He was a brilliant driver, but a vindictive and impatient one who was always anxious for any car that held him up to be given something to remember.

As the lights went green he gave a blast on his triple horns, pulled out to the right at the intersection, accelerated brutally and got by, shaking his head angrily at the driver of the saloon as he passed it.

In the middle of this harsh manoeuvre it was natural for Gala to allow herself to be thrown towards him. At the same time her left hand dived under the coat and her fingers touched, felt, and extracted the book in one flow of motion. Then the hand was back in the folds of the coat again and Drax, all his feeling in his feet and hands, was seeing nothing but the traffic ahead and the chances of getting across the zebra outside the Royal Star without hitting two women and a boy who were nearly halfway across it.

Now it was a question of facing Drax's growl of rage as with a maidenly but urgent voice she asked if she could possibly stop for a moment to powder her nose.

A garage would be dangerous. He might decide to fill up with petrol. And perhaps he also carried his money in his hip-pocket. But was there an hotel? Yes, she remembered, the Thomas Wyatt just outside Maidstone. And it had no petrol pumps. She started to fidget slightly. She pulled the coat back on to her lap. She cleared her throat.

'Oh, excuse me, Sir Hugo,' she said in a strangled voice.

'Yes. What is it?'

'I'm terribly sorry, Sir Hugo. But could you possibly stop for just a moment. I want, I mean, I'm terribly sorry but I'd like to powder my nose. It's terribly stupid of me. I'm so sorry.'

'Christ,' said Drax. 'Why the hell didn't you . . . Oh, yes. Well, all right. Find a place.' He grumbled on into his moustache, but brought the big car down into the fifties.

'There's a hotel just around this bend,' said Gala nervously. 'Thank you so much, Sir Hugo. It was stupid of me. I won't be a moment. Yes, here it is.'

The car swerved up to the front of the inn and stopped with a jerk. 'Hurry up. Hurry up,' said Drax as Gala, leaving the door of the car open, sped obediently across the gravel, her coat with its precious secret held tightly in front of her body.

She locked the door of the lavatory and snatched open the notebook.

There they were, just as she had thought. On each page, under the date, the neat columns of figures, the atmospheric pressure, the wind velocity, the temperature, just as she had recorded them from the Air Ministry figures. And at the foot of each page the estimated settings for the gyro compasses.

Gala frowned. At a glance she could see that they were entirely different from hers. Drax's figures simply bore no relation to hers whatsoever.

She turned to the last completed page containing the figures for that day. Why, she was wrong by nearly ninety degrees on the estimated course. If the rocket were fired on her flight plan it would land somewhere in France. She looked wildly at her face in the mirror over the washbasin. How could she have gone so monstrously wrong? And why hadn't Drax ever told her? Why, she ran quickly through the book again, every day she had been ninety degrees out, firing the Moonraker at right angles to its true course. And yet she simply couldn't have made such a mistake. Did the Ministry know these secret figures? And why should they be secret?

Suddenly her bewilderment turned to fright. She must somehow get safely, quietly to London and tell somebody. Even though she might be called a fool and a meddler.

Coldly she turned back several pages in the book, took her nail file out of the bag and, as neatly as she could, cut out a specimen page, rolled it up into a tight ball and stuffed it into the tip of a finger of one of her gloves.

She glanced at her face in the mirror. It was pale and she quickly rubbed her cheeks to bring back the colour. Then she put back the look of an apologetic secretary and hurried out and ran across the gravel to the car, clutching the notebook among the folds of her coat.

The engine of the Mercedes was turning over. Drax glowered at her impatiently as she scrambled back into her seat.

'Come on. Come on,' he said, putting the car into third and taking his foot off the clutch so that she nearly caught her ankle in the heavy door. The tyres churned up the gravel as he accelerated out of the parking place and dry-skidded into the London road.

Gala was jerked back, but she remembered to let the coat with her guilty hand in its folds fall on the seat between her and the driver.

And now the book back into the hip-pocket.

She watched the speedometer hovering in the seventies as Drax flung the heavy car along the crown of the road.

She tried to remember her lessons. Distracting pressure on some other part of the body. Distracting the attention. Distraction. The victim must not be at ease. His senses must be focused away. He must be unaware of the touch on his body. Anaesthetized by a stronger stimulus.

Like now, for instance. Drax, bent forward over the wheel, was fighting for a chance to get past a sixty-foot RAF trailer, but the oncoming traffic was leaving no room on the crown of the road. There was a gap and Drax rammed the lever into second and took it, his horns braying imperiously.

Gala's hand reached to the left under the coat.

But another hand struck like a snake.

'Got you.'

Krebs was leaning half over the back of the driving seat. His hand was crushing hers into the slippery cover of the notebook under the folds of the coat.

Gala sat frozen into black ice. With all her strength she wrenched at her hand. It was no good. Krebs had all his weight on it now.

Drax had got past the trailer and the road was empty. Krebs said urgently in German, 'Please stop the car, *mein Kapitän*. Miss Brand is a spy.'

Drax gave a startled glance to his right. What he saw was enough. He put his hand quickly down to his hip-pocket, and then, slowly, deliberately, put it back on the wheel. The sharp turning to Mereworth was just coming up on his left. 'Hold her,' said Drax. He braked so that the tyres screamed, changed down and wrenched the car into the side-road. A few hundred yards down it he pulled the car into the side and stopped.

Drax looked up and down the road. It was empty. He reached over one gloved hand and wrenched Gala's face towards him.

'What is this?'

'I can explain it, Sir Hugo.' Gala tried to bluff against the horror and desperation she knew was in her face. 'It's a mistake. I didn't mean . . .'

Under cover of an angry shrug of the shoulders, her right hand moved softly behind her and the guilty pair of gloves were thrust behind the leather cushion.

'*Sehen sie her, mein Kapitän.* I saw her edging up close to you. It seemed to me strange.'

With his other hand Krebs had whipped the coat away and there were the bent white fingers of her left hand crushed into the cover of the notebook still a foot away from Drax's hip-pocket.

'So.'

The word was deadly cold and with a shivering finality.

Drax let go her chin, but her horrified eyes remained locked into his.

A kind of frozen cruelty was showing through the

jolly façade of red skin and whiskers. It was a different man. The man behind the mask. The creature beneath the flat stone that Gala Brand had lifted.

Drax glanced again up and down the empty road.

Then, looking carefully into the suddenly aware blue eyes, he drew the leather driving gauntlet off his left hand and with his right whipped her as hard as he could across the face with it.

Only a short cry was forced out of Gala's constricted throat, but tears of pain ran down her cheeks. Suddenly she began to fight like a madwoman.

With all her strength she heaved and fought against the two iron arms that held her. With her free right hand she tried to reach the face that leant over her hand and get at the eyes. But Krebs easily moved his head out of her reach and quietly increased the pressure across her throat, hissing murderously to himself as her nails tore strips of skin off the backs of his hands, but noting with a scientist's eye as her struggles became weaker.

Drax watched carefully, with one eye on the road, as Krebs brought her under control and then he started the car and drove cautiously on along the wooded road. He grunted with satisfaction as he came upon a cart-track into the woods and he turned up it and only stopped when he was well out of sight of the road.

Gala had just realized that there were no noise from the engine when she heard Drax say 'there'. A finger touched her skull behind the left ear. Krebs arm came away from her throat and she slumped gratefully forward, gasping for air. Then something crashed into the back of her head where the finger had touched it, and there was a flash of wonderfully releasing pain and blackness.

An hour later passers-by saw a white Mercedes draw up outside a small house at the Buckingham Palace end of Ebury Street and two kind gentlemen help a sick girl out and through the front door. Those who were near could see that the poor girl's face was very pale and that her eyes were shut and that the kind gentlemen almost had to carry her up the steps. The big gentleman with the red face and whiskers was heard to say quite distinctly to the other man that poor Mildred had promised she wouldn't go out until she was quite well again. Very sad.

Gala came to herself in a large top-floor room that seemed to be full of machinery. She was tied very securely to a chair and apart from the searing pain in her head she could feel that her lips and cheek were bruised and swollen.

Heavy curtains were drawn across the window and there was a musty smell in the room as if it was rarely used. There was dust on the few pieces of conventional furniture and only the chromium and ebonite dials on the machines looked clean and new. She thought that she was probably in hospital. She closed her eyes and wondered. It was not long before she remembered. She spent several minutes controlling herself and then she opened her eyes again.

Drax, his back to her, was watching the dials on a machine that looked like a very large radio set. There were three more similar machines in her line of sight and from one of them a thin steel aerial reached up to a rough hole that had been cut for it in the plaster of the ceiling. The room was brightly lit by several tall standard lamps, each of which held a naked high wattage bulb.

To her left there was a noise of tinkering and by swivelling her half-closed eyes in their sockets, which made the pain in her head much worse, she saw the figure of Krebs bent over an electric generator on the floor. Beside it there was a small petrol engine and it was this that was giving trouble. Every now and then Krebs would grasp the starting-handle and crank it hard and a feeble stutter would come from the engine before he went back to his tinkering.

'You dam' fool,' said Drax in German, 'hurry up. I've got to go and see those bloody oafs at the Ministry.'

'At once, *mein Kapitän*,' said Krebs dutifully. He seized the handle again. This time after two or three coughs the engine started up and began to purr.

'It won't make too much noise?' asked Drax.

'No, *mein Kapitän*. The room has been sound-proofed,' answered Krebs. 'Dr Walter assures me that nothing will be heard outside.'

Gala closed her eyes and decided that her only hope

was to feign unconsciousness for as long as possible. Did they intend to kill her? Here in this room? And what was all this machinery? It looked like wireless, or perhaps radar. That curved glass screen above Drax's head that had given an occasional flicker as Drax fiddled with the knobs below the dials.

Slowly her mind started to work again. Why, for instance, was Drax suddenly talking perfect German? And why did Krebs address him as *Herr Kapitän*? And the figures in the black book. Why did they nearly kill her because she had seen them? What did they mean?

Ninety degrees, ninety degrees.

Lazily her mind turned the problem over.

Ninety degrees difference. Supposing her figures had been right all the time for the target eighty miles away in the North Sea. Just supposing she had been right. Then she wouldn't have been aiming the rocket into the middle of France after all. But Drax's figures. Ninety degrees to the left of her North Sea target? Somewhere in England presumably. Eighty miles from Dover. Yes, of course. That was it. Drax's figures. The firing plan in the little black book. They would drop the Moonraker just about in the middle of London.

But on London! On London!!

So one's heart really does go into one's throat. How extraordinary. Such a commonplace and yet there it is and it really does almost stop one breathing.

And now, let me see, so this is a radar homing device. How ingenious. The same as there would be on the raft in the North Sea. This would bring the rocket down within a hundred yards of Buckingham Palace. But would that matter with a warhead full of instruments?

It was probably the cruelty of Drax's blow across her face that settled it, but suddenly she *knew* that somehow it would be a real warhead, an atomic warhead, and that Drax was an enemy of England and that tomorrow at noon he was going to destroy London.

Gala made a last effort to understand.

Through this ceiling, through this chair, into the ground.

The thin needle of the rocket. Dropping fast as light out of a clear sky. The crowds in the streets. The Palace. The nursemaids in the park. The birds in the trees. The great bloom of flame a mile wide. And then the mushroom cloud. And nothing left. Nothing. Nothing. Nothing.

'No. Oh, *no*!'

But the scream was only in her mind and Gala, her body a twisted black potato crisp amongst a million others, had already fainted.

Bond sat at his favourite restaurant table in London, the right-hand corner table for two on the first floor, and watched the people and the traffic in Piccadilly and down the Haymarket.

It was 7.45 and his second Vodka dry Martini with a large slice of lemon peel had just been brought to him by Baker, the head waiter. He sipped it, wondering idly why Gala was late. It was not like her. She was the sort of girl who would telephone if she had been kept at the Yard. Vallance, whom he had visited at five, had said that Gala was due with him at six.

Vallance had been very anxious to see her. He was a worried man and when Bond reported briefly on the security of the Moonraker, Vallance seemed to be listening with only half his mind.

It appeared that all that day there had been heavy selling of sterling. It had started in Tangier and quickly spread to Zurich and New York. The pound had been fluctuating wildly in the money markets of the world and the arbitrage dealers had made a killing. The net result was that the pound was a whole three cents down on the day and the forward rates were still weaker. It was front-page news in the evening papers and at the close of business the Treasury had got on to Vallance and told him the extraordinary news that the selling wave had been started by Drax Metals Ltd. in Tangier. The operation had begun that morning and by close of business the firm had managed to sell British currency short to the tune of twenty million pounds. This had been too much for the markets, and the Bank of England had had to step in and buy in order to stop a still sharper run. It was then that Drax Metals had come to light as the seller.

Now the Treasury wanted to know what it was all about – whether it was Drax himself selling or one of the big commodify interests who were clients of his firm. The first thing they did was to tackle Vallance. Vallance could only think that in some way the Moonraker was to be a failure and that Drax knew it and wanted to profit by his knowledge. He at once spoke to the Ministry of Supply, but they pooh-poohed the idea. There was no reason to think the Moonraker would be a failure and even if its practice flight was not successful the fact would be covered up with talk of technical hitches and so forth. In any case, whether the rocket was a success or not, there could be no possible reaction on British financial credit. No, they certainly wouldn't think of mentioning the matter to the Prime Minister. Drax Metals was a big trading organization. They were probably acting for some foreign government. The Argentine. Perhaps even Russia. Someone with big sterling balances. Anyway it was nothing to do with the Ministry, or with the Moonraker, which would be launched punctually at noon the next day.

This had made sense to Vallance, but he was still worried. He didn't like mysteries and he was glad to share his concern with Bond. Above all he wanted to ask Gala if she had seen any Tangier cables and if so whether Drax had made any comment on them.

Bond was sure Gala would have mentioned anything of the sort to him, and he said so to Vallance. They had talked some more and then Bond had left for his headquarters where M was expecting him.

M had been interested in everything, even the shaven heads and moustaches of the men. He questioned Bond minutely and when Bond finished his story with the gist of his last conversation with Vallance M sat for a long time lost in thought.

'007,' he said at last, 'I don't like any part of this. There's something going on down there but I can't for the life of me make any sense out of it. And I don't see where I can possibly interfere. All the facts are known to the Special Branch and to the Ministry and, God knows, I've got nothing to add to them. Even if I had a word with the PM, which would be damned unfair on Vallance, what am I to tell him? What facts? What's it all about? There's nothing but the smell of it all. And it's a bad smell. And,' he added, 'a very big one, if I'm not mistaken.

'No,' he looked across at Bond and his eyes held an unusual note of urgency. 'It looks as if it's all up to you.

And that girl. You're lucky she's a good one. Anything you want? Anything I can do to help?'

'No, thank you, sir,' Bond had said and he had walked out through the familiar corridors and down in the lift to his own office where he had terrified Loelia Ponsonby by giving her a kiss as he said good-night. The only times he ever did that were at Christmas, on her birthday, and just before there was something dangerous to be done.

Bond drank down the rest of his Martini and looked at his watch. Now it was eight o'clock and suddenly he shivered.

He got straight up from his table and walked out to the telephone.

The switchboard at the Yard said that the Assistant Commissioner had been trying to reach him. He had had to go to a dinner at the Mansion House. Could Commander Bond please stay by the telephone? Bond waited impatiently. All his fears surged up at him from the chunk of black bakelite. He could see the rows of polite faces. The uniformed waiter slowly edging his way round to Vallance. The quickly pulled-back chair. The unobtrusive exit. Those echoing stone lobbies. The discreet booth.

The telephone screamed at him. 'That you, Bond? Vallance here. Seen anything of Miss Brand?'

Bond's heart went cold. 'No,' he said sharply. 'She's half an hour late for dinner. Didn't she turn up at six?'

'No, and I've had a "trace" sent out and there's no

sign of her at the usual address she stays at when she comes to London. None of her friends have seen her. If she left in Drax's car at two-thirty she should have been in London by half-past four. There's been no crash on the Dover road during the afternoon and the AA and the RAC are negative.' There was a pause. 'Now listen.' There was urgent appeal in Vallance's voice. 'She's a good girl that, and I don't want anything to happen to her. Can you handle it for me? I can't put out a general call for her. The killing down there has made her news and we'd have the whole Press round our ears. It will be even worse after ten tonight. Downing Street are issuing a communiqué about the practice shoot and tomorrow's papers are going to be nothing but Moonraker. The PM's going to broadcast. Her disappearance would turn the whole thing into a crime story. Tomorrow's too important for that and anyway the girl may have had a fainting fit or something. But I want her found. Well? What do you say? Can you handle it? You can have all the help you want. I'll tell the Duty Officer that he's to accept your orders.'

'Don't worry,' said Bond. 'Of course I'll look after it.' He paused, his mind racing. 'Just tell me something. What do you know about Drax's movements?'

'He wasn't expected at the Ministry until seven,' said Vallance. 'I left word . . .' There was a confused noise on the line and Bond heard Vallance say 'Thanks.' He came back on the line. 'Just got a report passed on by the City police,' he said. 'The Yard couldn't get me on the 'phone. Talking to you. Let's see,' he read, '"Sir Hugo Drax arrived Ministry 1900 left at 2000. Left message dining at Blades if wanted. Back at site 2300."' Vallance commented: 'That means he'll be leaving London about nine. Just a moment.' He read on: '"Sir Hugo stated Miss Brand felt unwell on arrival in London but at her request he left her at Victoria Station bus terminal at 16.45. Miss Brand stated she would rest with some friends, address unknown, and contact Sir Hugo at Ministry at 1900. She had not done so."' And that's all,' said Vallance. 'Oh, by the way, we made the inquiry about Miss Brand on your behalf. Said you had arranged to meet her at six and she hadn't turned up.'

'Yes,' said Bond, his thoughts elsewhere. 'That doesn't seem to get us anywhere. I'll have to get busy. Just one more thing. Has Drax got a place in London, flat or anything like that?'

'He always stays at the Ritz nowadays,' said Vallance. 'Sold his house in Grosvenor Square when he moved down to Dover. But we happen to know he's got some sort of an establishment in Ebury Street. We checked there. But there was no answer to the bell and my man said the house looked unoccupied. Just behind Buckingham Palace. Some sort of hideout of his. Keeps it very quiet. Probably takes his women there. Anything else? I ought to be getting back or all this big brass will think the Crown Jewels have been stolen.'

'You go ahead,' said Bond. 'I'll do my best and if I

get stuck I'll call on your men to help. Don't worry if you don't hear from me. So long.'

'So long,' said Vallance with a note of relief in his voice. 'And thanks. Best of luck.'

Bond rang off.

He picked up the receiver again and called Blades.

'This is the Ministry of Supply,' he said. 'Is Sir Hugo Drax in the club?'

'Yes, sir,' it was the friendly voice of Brevett. 'He's in the dining-room. Do you wish to speak to him?'

'No, it's all right,' said Bond. 'I just wanted to make certain he hadn't left yet.'

Without noticing what he was eating Bond wolfed down some food and left the restaurant at 8.45. His car was outside waiting for him and he said good-night to the driver from Headquarters and drove to St James's Street. He parked under cover of the central row of taxis outside Boodle's and settled himself behind an evening paper over which he could keep his eyes on a section of Drax's Mercedes which he was relieved to see standing in Park Street, unattended.

He had not long to wait. Suddenly a broad shaft of yellow light shone out from the doorway of Blades and the big figure of Drax appeared. He wore a heavy ulster up round his ears and a cap pulled down over his eyes. He walked quickly to the white Mercedes, slammed the door, and was away across to the left-hand side of St James's Street and braking to turn opposite St James's Palace while Bond was still in third.

God, the man moves quickly, thought Bond, doing a racing change round the island in The Mall with Drax already passing the statue in front of the Palace. He kept the Bentley in third and thundered in pursuit. Buckingham Palace Gate. So it looked like Ebury Street. Keeping the white car just in view, Bond made hurried plans. The lights at the corner of Lower Grosvenor Place were green for Drax and red for Bond. Bond jumped them and was just in time to see Drax swing left into the beginning of Ebury Street. Gambling on Drax making a stop at his house, Bond accelerated to the corner and pulled up just short of it. As he jumped out of the Bentley, leaving the engine ticking over, and took the few steps towards Ebury Street, he heard two short blasts on the Mercedes' horn and as he carefully edged round the corner he was in time to see Krebs helping the muffled figure of a girl across the pavement. Then the door of the Mercedes slammed and Drax was off again.

Bond raced back to his car, whipped into third, and went after him.

Thank God the Mercedes was white. There it went, its stop-lights blazing briefly at the intersections, the headlamps full on and the horn blaring at any hint of a check in the sparse traffic.

Bond set his teeth and rode his car as if she was a Lipizaner at the Spanish Riding School in Vienna. He could not use headlights or horn for fear of betraying his presence to the car in front. He just had to play on his brakes and gears and hope for the best.

The deep note of his two-inch exhaust thundered back at him from the houses on either side and his tyres screamed on the tarmac. He thanked heavens for the new set of racing Michelins that were only a week old. If only the lights would be kind. He seemed to be getting nothing but amber and red while Drax was always being swept on by the green. Chelsea Bridge. So it did look like the Dover road by the South Circular! Could he hope to keep up with the Mercedes on A20? Drax had two passengers. His car might not be tuned. But with that independent springing he could corner better than Bond. The old Bentley was a bit high off the ground for this sort of work. Bond stamped on his brakes and risked a howl on his triple klaxons as a homeward-bound taxi started to weave over to the right. It jerked back to the left and Bond heard a four-letter yell as he shot past.

Clapham Common and the flicker of the white car through the trees. Bond ran the Bentley up to eighty along the safe bit of road and saw the lights go red just in time to stop Drax at the end of it. He put the Bentley into neutral and coasted up silently. Fifty yards away. Forty, thirty, twenty. The lights changed and Drax was over the crossing and away again, but not before Bond had seen that Krebs was beside the driver and there was no sign of Gala except the hump of a rug over the narrow back seat.

So there was no question. You don't take a sick girl

for a drive like a sack of potatoes. Not at that speed for the matter of that. So she was a prisoner. Why? What had she done? What had she discovered? What the hell, in fact, was all this about?

Each dark conjecture came and for a moment settled like a vulture on Bond's shoulder and croaked into his ear that he had been a blind fool. Blind, blind, blind. From the moment he had sat in his office after the night at Blades and made his mind up about Drax being a dangerous man he should have been on his toes. At the first smell of trouble, the marks on the chart for instance, he should have taken action. But what action? He had passed on each clue, each fear. What could he have done except kill Drax? And get hanged for his pains? Well, then. What about the present? Should he stop and telephone the Yard? And let the car get away? For all he knew Gala was being taken for a ride and Drax planned to get rid of her on the way to Dover. And that Bond might conceivably prevent if only his car could take it.

As if to echo his thoughts the tortured rubber screamed as he left the South Circular road into the A20 and took the roundabout at forty. No. He had told M that he would stay with it. He had told Vallance the same. The case had been dumped firmly into his lap and he must do what he could. At least if he kept up with the Mercedes he might shoot up its tyres and apologize afterwards. To let it get away would be criminal.

So be it, said Bond to himself.

He had to slow for some lights and he used the pause to pull a pair of goggles out of the dashboard compartment and cover his eyes with them. Then he leant over to the left and twisted the big screw on the windscreen and then eased the one beside his right hand. He pressed the narrow screen flat down on the bonnet and tightened the screws again.

Then he accelerated away from Swanley Junction and was soon doing ninety astride the Cats eyes down the Farningham by-pass, the wind howling past his ears and the shrill scream of his supercharger riding with him for company.

A mile ahead the great eyes of the Mercedes hooded themselves as they went over the crest of Wrotham Hill and disappeared down into the moonlit panorama of the Weald of Kent.

There were three separate sources of pain in Gala's body. The throbbing ache behind her left ear, the bite of the flex at her wrists, and the chafing of the strap round her ankles.

Every bump in the road, every swerve, every sudden pressure of Drax's foot on the brakes or the accelerator awoke one or another of these pains and rasped at her nerves. If only she had been wedged into the back seat more tightly. But there was just room enough for her body to roll a few inches on the occasional seat so that she was constantly having to twist her bruised face away from contact with the walls of shiny pigskin.

The air she breathed was stuffy with a smell of new leather upholstery, exhaust fumes, and the occasional sharp stench of burning rubber as Drax flayed the tyres on a sharp corner.

And yet the discomfort and pain were nothing.

Krebs! Curiously enough her fear and loathing of Krebs tormented her most. The other things were too big. The mystery of Drax and his hatred of England. The riddle of his perfect command of German. The Moonraker. The secret of the atomic warhead. How to save London. These were matters which she had long ago put away in the back of her mind as insoluble.

But the afternoon alone with Krebs was present and dreadful and her mind went back and back to the details of it like a tongue to an aching tooth.

Long after Drax had gone she had kept up her pretence of unconsciousness. At first Krebs had occupied himself with the machines, talking to them in German in a cooing baby-talk. 'There, my *Liebchen*. That's better now, isn't it? A drop of oil for you, my *Pupperl*? But certainly. Coming up at once. No, no, lazybones. I said a thousand revolutions. Not nine hundred. Come along now. We can do better than that, can't we. Yes, my *Schatz*. That's it. Round and round we go. Up and down. Round and round. Let me wipe your pretty face for you so that we can see what the little dial is saying. *Jesu Maria, bist du ein braves Kind!*'

And so it had gone on with intervals of standing in front of Gala, picking his nose and sucking his teeth in a horribly ruminative way. Until he stayed longer and longer in front of her, forgetting the machines, wondering, making up his mind.

And then she had felt his hand undo the top button of her dress and the automatic recoil of her body had had to be covered by a realistic groan and a pantomime of consciousness returning.

She had asked for water and he had gone into a bathroom and fetched some for her in a toothglass. Then he had pulled a kitchen chair up in front of her and had sat down astride it, his chin resting on the top rail of its back, and had gazed at her speculatively from under his pale drooping lids.

She had been the first to break the silence. 'Why have I been brought here?' she asked. 'What are all those machines?'

He licked his lips and the little pouting red mouth opened under the smudge of yellow moustache and formed itself slowly into a rhomboid-shaped smile. 'That is a lure for little birds,' he said. 'Soon it will lure a little bird into this warm nest. Then the little bird will lay an egg. Oh, such a big round egg! Such a beautiful fat egg.' The lower half of his face giggled with delight while his eyes mooned. 'And the pretty girl is here because otherwise she might frighten the little bird away. And that would be so sad, wouldn't it,' he spat out the next three words, 'filthy English bitch?'

His eyes became intent and purposeful. He hitched his chair nearer so that his face was only a foot away from hers and she was enveloped in the miasma of his breath. 'Now, English bitch. Who are you working for?' He waited. 'You must answer me, you know,' he said softly. 'We are all alone here. There is no one to hear you scream.'

'Don't be stupid,' said Gala desperately. 'How could I be working for anyone except Sir Hugo?' (Krebs smiled at the name.) 'I was just curious about the flight plan . . .' she went into a rambling explanation about her figures and Drax's figures and how she had wanted to share in the success of the Moonraker.

'Try again,' whispered Krebs when she had finished. 'You must do better than that,' and suddenly his eyes had turned hot with cruelty and his hands had reached towards her from behind the back of his chair . . .

In the rear of the hurtling Mercedes Gala ground her teeth together and whimpered at the memory of the soft crawling fingers on her body, probing, pinching, pulling, while all the time the hot vacant eyes gazed curiously into hers until finally she gathered the saliva in her mouth and spat full in his face.

He hadn't even paused to wipe his face, but suddenly he had really hurt her and she had screamed once and then mercifully fainted.

And then she had found herself being pushed into the back of the car, a rug was thrown over her, and they were hurtling through the streets of London and she could hear other cars near them, the frantic ringing of a bicycle bell, an occasional shout, the animal growl of an old klaxon, the whirring putter of a motor-scooter, a scream of brakes, and she had realized that she was back in the real world, that English people, friends, were all around her. She had struggled to get to her knees and scream, but Krebs must have felt her movement because his hands were suddenly at her ankles, strapping them to the foot-rail along the floor, and she knew that she was lost and suddenly the tears were pouring down her cheeks and she was praying that somehow, somebody would be in time.

That had been less than an hour ago and now she could tell from the slow pace of the car and the noise of other traffic that they had reached a large town — Maidstone if she was being taken back to the site.

In the comparative silence of their progress through the town she suddenly heard Krebs's voice. There was a note of urgency in it.

'*Mein Kapitän*,' he said. 'I have been watching a car for some time. It is certainly following us. It has seldom been using its lights. It is only a hundred metres behind us now. I think it is the car of Commander Bond.'

Drax grunted with surprise and she could hear his big body shift round to get a quick look.

He swore sharply and then there was silence and she could feel the big car weaving and straining in the thin traffic. '*Ja, sowas!*' said Drax finally. His voice was thoughtful. 'So that old museum-piece of his can still move. So much the better, my dear Krebs. He seems to be alone.' He laughed harshly. 'So we will give him a run for his money and if he survives it we will get him in the bag with the woman. Turn on the radio. Home Service. We will soon find out if there is a hitch.'

There was a short crackle of static and then Gala could hear the voice of the Prime Minister, the voice of all the great occasions in her life, coming through in broken fragments as Drax put the car into third and accelerated out of the town, '. . . weapon devised by the ingenuity of man . . . a thousand miles into the firmament . . . area patrolled by Her Majesty's ships . . . designed exclusively for the defence of our beloved island . . . a long era of peace . . . development for Man's great journey away from the confines of this planet . . . Sir Hugo Drax, that great patriot and benefactor of our country . . .'

Gala heard Drax's roar of laughter above the howling of the wind, a great scornful bray of triumph, and then the set was switched off.

'James,' whispered Gala to herself. 'There's only you left. Be careful. But make haste.'

Bond's face was a mask of dust and filthy with the blood of flies and moths that had smashed against it. Often he had had to take a cramped hand off the wheel to clear his goggles but the Bentley was going beautifully and he felt sure of holding the Mercedes.

He was touching ninety-five on the straight just before the entrance to Leeds Castle when great lights were suddenly switched on behind him and a four-tone windhorn sounded its impudent 'pom-pim-pom-pam' almost in his ear.

The apparition of a third car in the race was almost unbelievable. Bond had hardly troubled to look in his driving-mirror since he left London. No one but a racing-driver or a desperate man could have kept up with them, and his mind was in a turmoil as he automatically pulled over to the left and saw out of the corner of his eye a low, fire-engine-red car come up level with him and draw away with a good ten miles an hour extra on its clock.

He caught a glimpse of the famous Alfa radiator and along the edge of the bonnet in bold white script the words *Attaboy II*. Then there was the grinning face of a youth in shirtsleeves who stuck two rude fingers in the air before he pulled away in the welter of sound which an Alfa at speed compounds from the whine of its supercharger, the Gatling crackle of its exhaust, and the thunderous howl of its transmission.

Bond grinned in admiration as he raised a hand to the driver. Alfa-Romeo supercharged straight-eight, he thought to himself. Must be nearly as old as mine. 'Thirty-two or '33 probably. And only half my c.c. Targa Florio in 1931 and did well everywhere after that. Probably a hot-rod type from one of the RAF stations round here. Trying to get back from a party in time to sign in before he's put on the report. He watched affectionately as the Alfa wagged its tail in the S-bend abreast of Leeds Castle and then howled off on the long wide road towards the distant Charing-fork.

Bond could imagine the grin of delight as the boy came up with Drax. 'Oh, boy. It's a Merc!' And the rage of Drax at the impudent music of the windhorn. Must be doing 105, reflected Bond. Hope the damn fool doesn't run out of road. He watched the two sets of tail lights closing up, the boy in the Alfa preparing for his trick of coming up behind and suddenly switching everything on when he could see a chance to get by.

There. Four hundred yards away the Mercedes showed white in the sudden twin shafts from the Alfa. There was a mile of clear road ahead, straight as a die. Bond could almost feel the boy's feet stamping the pedal still further into the floorboards. Attaboy!

Up front in the Mercedes Krebs had his mouth close to Drax's ear. 'Another of them,' he shouted urgently. 'Can't see his face. Coming up to pass now.'

Drax let out a harsh obscenity. His bared teeth showed white in the pale glimmer from the dashboard. 'Teach the swine a lesson,' he said, setting his shoulders and gripping the wheel tightly in the great leather gauntlets. Out of the corner of his eye he watched the nose of the Alfa creep up to starboard. 'Pom-pim-pom-pam' chirped the windhorn, softly, delicately, Drax inched the wheel of the Mercedes to the right and, at the horrible crash of metal, whipped it back again to correct the slew of his tail.

'Bravo! Bravo!' screamed Krebs, beside himself with excitement as he knelt on the seat and looked back. 'Double somersault. Jumped the hedge upside down. I think he's burning already. Yes. There are flames.'

'That'll give our fine Mister Bond something to think about,' snarled Drax, breathing heavily.

But Bond, his face a tight mask, had hardly checked his speed and there was nothing but revenge in his mind as he hurtled on after the flying Mercedes.

He had seen it all. The grotesque flight of the red car as it turned over and over, the flying figure of the driver, his arms and legs spreadeagled as he soared out of the driving seat, and the final thunder as the car hurdled the hedge upside down and crashed into the field.

As he flashed by, noting the horrible graffiti of the black skid-marks across the tarmac, his mind recorded one final macabre touch. Somehow undamaged in the holocaust, the windhorn was still making contact and its ululations were going on up to the sky, stridently clearing imaginary roads for the passage of *Attaboy II* – 'Pom-pim-pom-pam.' 'Pom-pim-pom-pam . . .'

So a murder had taken place in front of his eyes. Or at any rate an attempted murder. So, whatever his motives, Sir Hugo Drax had declared war and didn't mind Bond knowing it. This made a lot of things easier. It meant that Drax was a criminal and probably a maniac. Above all it meant certain danger for the Moonraker. That was enough for Bond. He reached under the dashboard and from its concealed holster drew out the long-barrelled .45 Colt Army Special and laid it on the seat beside him. The battle was now in the open and somehow the Mercedes must be stopped.

Using the road as if it was Donington, Bond rammed his foot down and kept it there. Gradually, with the needle twitching either side of the hundred mark he began to narrow the gap.

Drax took the left-hand fork at Charing and hissed up the long hill. Ahead, in the giant beam of his headlights, one of Bowaters' huge eight-wheeled AEC Diesel carriers was just grinding into the first bend of the hair-pin, labouring under the fourteen tons of newsprint it was taking on a night run to one of the East Kent newspapers.

Drax cursed under his breath as he saw the long carrier with the twenty gigantic rolls, each containing five miles of newsprint, roped to its platform. Right in the middle of the tricky S-bend at the top of the hill.

He looked in the driving mirror and saw the Bentley coming into the fork.

And then Drax had his idea.

'Krebs,' the word was a pistol shot. 'Get out your knife.'

There was a sharp click and the stiletto was in Krebs's hand. One didn't dawdle when there was that note in the master's voice.

'I am going to slow down behind this lorry. Take your shoes and socks off and climb out on to the bonnet and when I come up behind the lorry jump on to it. I shall be going at walking-pace. It will be safe. Cut the ropes that hold the rolls of paper. The left ones first. Then the right. I shall have pulled up level with the lorry and when you have cut the second lot jump into the car. Be careful you are not swept off with the paper. *Verstanden? Also. Hals und Beinbruch!'*

Drax dowsed his headlights and swept round the bend at eighty. The lorry was twenty yards ahead and Drax had to brake hard to avoid crashing into its tail.

The Mercedes executed a dry skid until its radiator was almost underneath the platform of the carrier.

Drax changed down to second. 'Now!' He held the car steady as a rock as Krebs, with bare feet, went over the windscreen and scrambled along the shining bonnet, his knife in his hand.

With a leap he was up and hacking at the left-hand ropes. Drax pulled away to the right and crawled up level with the rear wheels of the Diesel, the oily smoke from its exhaust in his eyes and nostrils.

Bond's lights were just showing round the bend.

There was a series of huge thuds as the left-hand rolls poured off the back of the lorry into the road and went hurtling off into the darkness. And more thuds as the right-hand ropes parted. One roll burst as it landed and Drax heard a tearing rattle as the unwinding paper crashed back down the one-in-ten gradient.

Released of its load the lorry almost bounded forward and Drax had to accelerate a little to catch the flying figure of Krebs who landed half across Gala's back and half in the front seat. Drax stamped his foot into the floor and sped off up the hill, ignoring a shout from the lorry-driver above the clatter of the Diesel pistons as he shot ahead.

As he hurtled round the next bend he saw the shaft of two headlights curve up into the sky above the tops of the trees until they were almost vertical. They wavered there for an instant and then the beams whirled away across the sky and went out.

A great barking laugh broke out of Drax as for a split second he took his eyes off the road and raised his face triumphantly towards the stars.

Krebs echoed the maniac laugh with a high giggle. 'A master-stroke, *mein Kapitän*. You should have seen them charge off down the hill. The one that burst. *Wunderschön!* Like the lavatory paper of a giant. That one will have made a pretty parcel of him. He was just coming round the bend. And the second salvo was as good as the first. Did you see the driver's face? *Zum Kotzen!* And the *Firma* Bowater! A fine paperchase they have got on their hands.'

'You did well,' said Drax briefly, his mind elsewhere. Suddenly he pulled into the side of the road with a scream of protest from the tyres.

'*Donnerwetter*,' he said angrily, as he started to turn the car. 'But we can't leave the man there. We must get him.' The car was already hissing back down the road. 'Gun,' ordered Drax briefly.

They passed the lorry at the top of the hill. It was stopped and there was no sign of the driver. Probably telephoning to the company, thought Drax, slowing up as they went round the first bend. There were lights on in the two or three houses and a group of people were standing round one of the rolls of newsprint that lay amongst the ruins of their front gate. There were more rolls in the hedge on the right side of the road. On the left a telegraph pole leant drunkenly, snapped in the middle. Then at the next bend was the beginning of a great confusion of paper stretching away down the long hill, festooning the hedges and the road like the sweepings of some elephantine fancy-dress ball.

The Bentley had nearly broken through the railings that fenced off the right of the bend from a steep bank. Amidst a puzzle of twisted iron stanchions it hung, nose down, with one wheel, still attached to the broken back axle, poised crookedly over its rump like a surrealist umbrella.

Drax pulled up and he and Krebs got out and stood quietly, listening.

There was no sound except the distant rumination of a car travelling fast on the Ashford road and the chirrup of a sleepless cricket.

With their guns out they walked cautiously over to the remains of the Bentley, their feet crunching the broken glass on the road. Deep furrows had been cut across the grass verge and there was a strong smell of petrol and burnt rubber in the air. The hot metal of the car ticked and crackled softly and steam was still fountaining from the shattered radiator.

Bond was lying face downwards at the bottom of the bank twenty feet away from the car. Krebs turned him over. His face was covered with blood but he was breathing. They searched him thoroughly and Drax pocketed the slim Beretta. Then together they hauled him across the road and wedged him into the back seat of the Mercedes, half on top of Gala.

When she realized who it was she gave a cry of horror.

'*Halt's Maul*,' snarled Drax. He got into the front seat and while he turned the car Krebs leant over from the front seat and busied himself with a long piece of flex. 'Make a good job of it,' said Drax. 'I don't want any mistakes.' He had an afterthought. 'And then go back to the wreck and get the number plates. Hurry. I will watch the road.'

Krebs pulled the rug over the two inert bodies and jumped out of the car. Using his knife as a screwdriver he was soon back with the plates, and the big car started to move just as a group of the local residents appeared walking nervously down the hill shining their torches over the scene of devastation.

Krebs grinned happily to himself at the thought of the stupid English having to clean up all this mess. He settled himself back to enjoy the part of the drive he had always liked best, the spring woods full of bluebells and celandines on the way to Chilham.

They had made him particularly happy at night. Lit up amongst the green torches of the young trees by the great headlamps of the Mercedes, they made him think of the beautiful forests of the Ardennes and of the devoted little band with which he had served, and of driving along in a captured American jeep with, just like tonight, his adored leader at the wheel. *Der Tag* had been a long time coming, but now it was here. With young Krebs in the van. At last the cheering crowds, the medals, the women, the flowers. He gazed out at the fleeting hosts of bluebells and felt warm and happy.

Gala could taste Bond's blood. His face was beside hers on the leather seat and she shifted to give him more room. His breathing was heavy and irregular and she wondered how badly he was hurt. Tentatively she whispered into his ear. And then louder. He groaned and his breath came faster.

'James,' she whispered urgently. 'James.'

He mumbled something and she pushed hard against him.

He uttered a string of obscenities and his body heaved.

He lay still again and she could almost feel him exploring his sensations.

'It's me, Gala.' She felt him stiffen.

'Christ,' he said. 'Hell of a mess.'

'Are you all right? Is anything broken?'

She felt him tense his arms and legs. 'Seems all right,' he said. 'Crack on the head. Am I talking sense?'

'Of course,' said Gala. 'Now listen.'

Hurriedly she told him all she knew, beginning with the notebook.

His body was as rigid as a board against her, and he hardly breathed as he listened to the incredible story.

Then they were running into Canterbury and Bond

put his mouth to her ear. 'Going to try and chuck myself over the back,' he whispered. 'Get to a telephone. Only hope.'

He started to heave himself up on his knees, his weight almost grinding the breath out of the girl.

There was a sharp crack and he fell back on top of her.

'Another move out of you and you're dead,' said the voice of Krebs coming softly between the front seats.

Only another twenty minutes to the site! Gala gritted her teeth and set about bringing Bond back to consciousness again.

She had only just succeeded when the car drew up at the door of the launching-dome and Krebs, a gun in his hand, was undoing the bonds round their ankles.

They had a glimpse of the familiar moonlit cement and of the semicircle of guards some distance away before they were hustled through the door and, when their shoes had been torn off by Krebs, out on to the iron catwalk inside the launching-dome.

There the gleaming rocket stood, beautiful, innocent, like a new toy for Cyclops.

But there was a horrible smell of chemicals in the air and to Bond the Moonraker was a giant hypodermic needle ready to be plunged into the heart of England. Despite a growl from Krebs he paused on the stairway and looked up at its glittering nose. A million deaths. A million. A million. A million.

On his hands? For God's sake! On *his* hands?

With Krebs's gun prodding him, he went slowly down the steps on the heels of Gala.

As he turned through the doors of Drax's office, he pulled himself together. Suddenly his mind was clear and all the lethargy and pain had left his body. Something, anything, must be done. Somehow he would find a way. His whole body and mind became focused and sharp as a blade. His eyes were alive again and defeat sloughed off him like the skin of a snake.

Drax had gone ahead and was sitting at his desk. He had a Luger in his hand. It was pointing at a spot halfway between Bond and Gala and it was steady as a rock.

Behind him, Bond heard the double doors thud shut.

'I was one of the best shots in the Brandenburg Division,' said Drax conversationally. 'Tie her to that chair, Krebs. Then the man.'

Gala looked desperately at Bond.

'You won't shoot,' said Bond. 'You'd be afraid of touching off the fuel.' He walked slowly towards the desk.

Drax smiled cheerfully and looked along the barrel at Bond's stomach. 'Your memory is bad, Englishman,' he said flatly. 'I told you this room is cut off from the shaft by the double doors. Another step and you will have no stomach.'

Bond looked at the confident, narrowed eyes and stopped.

'Go ahead, Krebs.'

When they were both tied securely and painfully to the arms and legs of two tubular steel chairs a few feet apart beneath the glass wall-map, Krebs left the room. He came back in a moment with a mechanic's blowtorch.

He set the ugly machine on the desk, pumped air into it with a few brisk strokes of the plunger, and set a match to it. A blue flame hissed out a couple of inches into the room. He picked up the instrument and walked towards Gala. He stopped a few feet to one side of her.

'Now then,' said Drax grimly. 'Let's get this over without any fuss. The good Krebs is an artist with one of those things. We used to call him *Der Zwangsmann* — The Persuader. I shall never forget the way he went over the last spy we caught together. Just south of the Rhine, wasn't it, Krebs?'

Bond pricked up his ears.

'Yes, *mein Kapitän*.' Krebs chuckled reminiscently. 'It was a pig of a Belgian.'

'All right then,' said Drax. 'Just remember, you two. There's no fair play down here. No jolly good sports and all that. This is business.' The voice cracked like a whip on the word. 'You,' he looked at Gala Brand, 'who are you working for?'

Gala was silent.

'Anywhere you like, Krebs.'

Krebs's mouth was half open. His tongue ran up and down his lower lip. He seemed to be having difficulty with his breathing as he took a step towards the girl.

The little flame roared greedily.

'Stop,' said Bond coldly. 'She works for Scotland Yard. So do I.' These things were pointless now. They were of no conceivable use to Drax. In any case, by tomorrow afternoon there might be no Scotland Yard.

'That's better,' said Drax. 'Now, does anybody know you are prisoners? Did you stop and telephone anyone?'

If I say yes, thought Bond, he will shoot us both and get rid of the bodies and the last chance of stopping the Moonraker will be gone. And if the Yard knows, why aren't they here already? No. Our chance may come. The Bentley will be found. Vallance may get worried when he doesn't hear from me.

'No,' he said. 'If I had, they'd be here by now.'

'True,' said Drax reflectively. 'In that case I am no longer interested in you and I congratulate you on making the interview so harmonious. It might have been more difficult if you had been alone. A girl is always useful on these occasions. Krebs, put that down. You may go. Tell the others what is necessary. They will be wondering. I shall entertain our guests for a while and then I shall come up to the house. See the car gets properly washed down. The back seat. And get rid of the marks on the right-hand side. Tell them to take the whole panel off if necessary. Or they can set fire to the dam' thing. We shan't be needing it any more,' he laughed abruptly. '*Verstanden?*'

'Yes, *mein Kapitän*.' Krebs reluctantly placed the softly roaring blowtorch on the desk beside Drax. 'In case you need it,' he said, looking hopefully at Gala and Bond. He went out through the double doors.

Drax put the Luger down on the desk in front of him. He opened a drawer and took out a cigar and lit it from a Ronson desk lighter. Then he settled himself comfortably. There was silence in the room for several minutes while Drax puffed contentedly at his cigar. Then he seemed to make up his mind. He looked benevolently at Bond.

'You don't know how I have longed for an English audience,' he said as if he was addressing a Press conference.

'You don't know how I have longed to tell my story. As a matter of fact, a full account of my operations is now in the hands of a very respectable firm of Edinburgh solicitors. I beg their pardon – Writers to the Signet. Well out of danger.' He beamed from one to the other. 'And these good folk have instructions to open the envelope on the completion of the first successful flight of the Moonraker. But you lucky people shall have a preview of what I have written and then, when tomorrow at noon you see through those open doors,' he gestured to his right, 'the first wisp of steam from the turbines and know that you are to be burnt alive in about half a second, you will have the momentary satisfaction of knowing what it is all in aid of, as,' he grinned wolfishly, 'we English men say.'

'You can spare us the jokes,' said Bond roughly. 'Get on with your story, Kraut.'

Drax's eyes blazed momentarily. 'A Kraut. Yes, I am indeed a *Reichsdeutscher*' – the mouth beneath the red moustache savoured the fine word – 'and even England will soon agree that they have been licked by just one single German. And then perhaps they'll stop calling us Krauts – BY ORDER!' The words were yelled out and the whole of Prussian militarism was in the parade-ground bellow.

Drax glowered across the desk at Bond, the great splayed teeth under the red moustache tearing nervously at one fingernail after another. Then, with an effort, he crammed his right hand into his trouser pocket, as if to put it out of temptation, and picked up his cigar with his left. He puffed at it for a moment and then, his voice still taut, he began.

'My real name,' said Drax, addressing himself to Bond, 'is Graf Hugo von der Drache. My mother was English and because of her I was educated in England until I was twelve. Then I could stand this filthy country no longer and I completed my education in Berlin and Leipzig.'

Bond could imagine that the hulking body with the ogre's teeth had not been very welcome at an English private school. And being a foreign count with a mouthful of names would not have helped much.

'When I was twenty,' Drax's eyes glowed reminiscently, 'I went to work in the family business. It was a subsidiary of the great steel combine *Rheinmetall Borsig*. Never heard of it, I suppose. Well, if you'd been hit by an 88 mm. shell during the war it would probably have been one of theirs. Our subsidiary were experts in special steels and I learned all about them and a lot about the aircraft industry. Our most exacting customers. That's when I first heard about Columbite. Worth diamonds in those days. Then I joined the party and almost immediately we were at war. A wonderful time. I was twenty-eight and a lieutenant in the 140th Panzer Regiment. And we ran through the British

Army in France like a knife through butter. Intoxicating.'

For a moment Drax puffed luxuriously at his cigar and Bond guessed that he was seeing the burning villages of Belgium in the smoke.

'Those were great days, my dear Bond.' Drax reached out a long arm and tapped the ash of his cigar off on to the floor. 'But then I was picked out for the Brandenburg Division and I had to leave the girls and the champagne and go back to Germany and start training for the big water-jump to England. My English was needed in the Division. We were all going to be in English uniforms. It would have been fun, but the damned generals said it couldn't be done and I was transferred to the Foreign Intelligence Service of the SS. The RSHA it was called, and SS *Obergruppenführer* Kaltenbrunner had just taken over the command after Heydrich was assassinated in '42. He was a good man and I was under the direct orders of a still better one, *Obersturmbannführer*,' he rolled out the delicious title with relish, 'Otto Skorzeny. His job in the RSHA was terrorism and sabotage. A pleasant interlude, my dear Bond, during which I was able to bring many an Englishman to book which,' Drax beamed coldly at Bond, 'gave me much pleasure. But then,' Drax's fist crashed down on the desk, 'Hitler was betrayed again by those swinish generals and the English and Americans were allowed to land in France.'

'Too bad,' said Bond drily.

'Yes, my dear Bond, it was indeed too bad.' Drax chose to ignore the irony. 'But for me it was the highspot of the whole war. Skorzeny turned all his saboteurs and terrorists into *SS Jagdverbände* for use behind the enemy lines. Each *Jagdverband* was divided into *Streifkorps* and then into *Kommandos*, each carrying the names of its commanding officer. With the rank of *Oberleutnant*,' Drax swelled visibly, 'at the head of *Kommando* "Drache" I went right through the American lines with the famous 150 Panzer Brigade in the Ardennes breakthrough in December '44. No doubt you will remember the effect of this Brigade in its American uniforms and with its captured American tanks and vehicles. *Kolossal!* When the Brigade had to withdraw I stayed where I was and went to ground in the Forests of Ardennes, fifty miles behind the Allied lines. There were twenty of us, ten good men and ten Hitlerjugend Werewolves. In their teens, but good lads all of them. And, by a coincidence, in charge of them was a young man called Krebs who turned out to have certain gifts which qualified him for the post of executioner and "persuader" to our merry little band.' Drax chuckled pleasantly.

Bond licked his lips as he remembered the crack Krebs's head had made against the dressing-table. Had he kicked him as hard as he possibly could? Yes, his memory reassured him, with every ounce of strength he could put into his shoe.

'We stayed in those woods for six months,' continued

Drax proudly, 'and all the time we reported back to the Fatherland by radio. The location vans never spotted us. Then one day disaster came.' Drax shook his head at the memory. 'There was a big farmhouse a mile away from our hideout in the forest. A lot of Nissen huts had been built round it and it was used as a rear headquarters for some sort of liaison group. English and Americans. A hopeless place. No discipline, no security, and full of hangers-on and shirkers from all over the place. We had kept an eye on it for some time and one day I decided to blow it up. It was a simple plan. In the evening, two of my men, one in American uniform and one in British, were to drive up in a captured scout car containing two tons of explosive. There was a car park – no sentries of course – near the mess hall and they were to run the car in as close to the mess hall as possible, time the fuse for the seven o'clock dinner hour, and then get away. All quite easy and I went off that morning on my own business and left the job to my second in command. I was dressed in the uniform of your Signal Corps and I set off on a captured British motor-cycle to shoot a dispatch rider from the same unit who made a daily run along a near-by road. Sure enough he came along dead on time and I went after him out of a side road. I caught up with him,' said Drax conversationally, 'and shot him in the back, took his papers and put him on top of his machine in the woods and set fire to him.'

Drax saw the fury in Bond's eyes and held up his

hand. 'Not very sporting? My dear chap, the man was already dead. However, to continue. I went on my way and then what should happen? One of our own planes coming back from a reconnaissance came after me down the road with his cannon. One of our own planes! Blasted me right off the road. God knows how long I lay in the ditch. Some time in the afternoon I came to for a bit and had the sense to hide my cap and jacket and the dispatches. In the hedge. They're probably still there. I must go and collect them one day. Interesting souvenirs. Then I set fire to the remains of the motor-cycle and I must have fainted again because the next thing I knew I had been picked up by a British vehicle and we were driving into that damned liaison head-quarters! Believe it or not! And there was the scout car, right up alongside the mess hall! It was too much for me. I was full of shell splinters and my leg was broken. Well, I fainted and when I came round there was half the hospital on top of me and I only had half a face.' He put up his hand and stroked the shiny skin on his left temple and cheek. 'After that it was just a question of acting a part. They had no idea who I was. The car that had picked me up had gone or been blown to pieces. I was just an Englishman in an English shirt and trousers who was nearly dead.'

Drax paused and took out another cigar and lit it. There was silence in the room save for the soft dimin-ished roar of the blowtorch. Its threatening voice was quieter. Pressure running out, reflected Bond.

He turned his head and looked at Gala. For the first time he saw the ugly bruise behind her left ear. He gave her a smile of encouragement and she smiled wryly back.

Drax spoke through the cigar smoke: 'There is not much more to tell,' he said. 'During the year that I was being pushed from one hospital to the next I made my plans down to the smallest detail. They consisted quite simply of revenge on England for what she had done to me and to my country. It gradually became an obsession, I admit it. Every day during the year of the rape and destruction of my country, my hatred and scorn for the English grew more bitter.' The veins on Drax's face started to swell and suddenly he pounded on the desk and shouted across at them, looking with bulging eyes from one to the other. 'I loathe and despise you all. You swine! Useless, idle, decadent fools, hiding behind your bloody white cliffs while other people fight your battles. Too weak to defend your colonies, toadying to America with your hats in your hands. Stinking snobs who'll do anything for money. Hah!' he was triumphant. 'I knew that all I needed was money and the façade of a gentleman. Gentleman! *Pfui Teufel!* To me a gentleman is just someone I can take advantage of. Those bloody fools in Blades for instance. Moneyed oafs. For months I took thousands of pounds off them, swindled them right under their noses until you came along and upset the apple-cart.'

Drax's eyes narrowed. 'What put you on to the cigarette case?' he asked sharply.

Bond shrugged his shoulders. 'My eyes,' he said indifferently.

'Ah well,' said Drax, 'perhaps I was a bit careless that night. But where was I? Ah yes, in hospital. And the good doctors were so anxious to help me find out who I really was.' He let out a roar of laughter. 'It was easy. So easy.' His eyes became cunning. 'From the identities they offered me so helpfully I came upon the name of Hugo Drax. What a coincidence! From Drache to Drax! Tentatively I thought it *might* be me. They were very proud. Yes, they said, *of course* it is you. The doctors triumphantly forced me into his shoes. I put them on and walked out of the hospital in them and I walked round London looking for someone to kill and rob. And one day, in a little office high above Piccadilly, a Jewish moneylender.' (Now Drax was talking faster. The words poured excitedly from his lips. Bond watched a fleck of foam gather at one corner of his mouth and grow.) 'Ha. It was easy. Crack on his bald skull. £15,000 in the safe. And then away and out of the country, Tangier – where you could do anything, buy anything, fix anything. Columbite. Rarer than platinum and everyone would want it. The Jet Age. I knew about these things. I had not forgotten my own profession. And then by God I worked. For five years I lived for money. And I was brave as a lion. I took terrible risks. And suddenly the first million was there. Then the second. Then the fifth. Then the twentieth. I came back to England. I spent a million of it and London was in my pocket. And then I went back to Germany. I found Krebs. I found fifty of them. Loyal Germans. Brilliant technicians. All living under false names like so many others of my old comrades. I gave them their orders and they waited, peacefully, innocently. And where was I?' Drax stared across at Bond, his eyes wide. 'I was in Moscow. Moscow! A man with Columbite to sell can go anywhere. I got to the right people. They listened to my plans. They gave me Walter, the new genius of their guided missile station at Peenemunde, and the good Russians started to build the atomic warhead,' he gestured up to the ceiling, 'that is now waiting up there. Then I came back to London.' A pause. 'The Coronation. My letter to the Palace. Triumph. Hooray for Drax,' he burst into a roar of laughter. 'England at my feet. Every bloody fool in the country! And then my men come over and we start. Under the very skirts of Britannia. On top of her famous cliffs. We work like devils. We built a jetty into your English Channel. For supplies! For supplies from my good friends the Russians that came in dead on time last Monday night. But then Tallon had to hear something. The old fool. He talks to the Ministry. But Krebs is listening. There were fifty volunteers to kill the man. Lots are drawn and Bartsch dies a hero's death.' Drax paused. 'He will not be forgotten.' Then he went on. 'The new warhead is hoisted into place.

It fits. A perfect piece of design. The same weight. Everything perfect, and the old one, the tin can full of the Ministry's cherished instruments, is now in Stettin – behind the Iron Curtain. And the faithful submarine is on her way back here and will soon,' he looked at his watch, 'be creeping under the waters of the English Channel to take us all off at one minute past midday tomorrow.'

Drax wiped his mouth with the back of his hand and lay back in his chair gazing up at the ceiling, his eyes full of visions. Suddenly he chuckled and squinted quizzically down his nose at Bond.

'And do you know what we shall do first when we go on board? We shall shave off those famous moustaches you were so interested in. You smelt a mouse, my dear Bond, where you ought to have smelt a rat. Those shaven heads and those moustaches we all cultivated so assiduously. Just a precaution, my dear fellow. Try shaving your own head and growing a big black moustache. Even your mother wouldn't recognize you. It's the combination that counts. Just a tiny refinement. Precision, my dear fellow. Precision in every detail. That has been my watchword.' He chuckled fatly and puffed away at his cigar.

Suddenly he looked sharply, suspiciously up at Bond. 'Well. Say something. Don't sit there like a dummy. What do you think of my story? Don't you think it's extraordinary, remarkable? For one man to have done all that? Come on, come on.' A hand came up to his mouth and he started tearing furiously at his nails. Then it was plunged back into his pocket and his eyes became cruel and cold. 'Or do you want me to have to send for Krebs,' he made a gesture towards the house telephone on his desk. 'The Persuader. Poor Krebs. He's like a child who's had his toys taken away from him. Or perhaps Walter. He would give you both something to remember. There's no softness in that one. Well?'

'Yes,' said Bond. He looked levelly at the great red face across the desk. 'It's a remarkable case-history. Galloping paranoia. Delusions of jealousy and persecution. Megalomaniac hatred and desire for revenge. Curiously enough,' he went on conversationally, 'it may have something to do with your teeth. Diastema, they call it. Comes from sucking your thumb when you're a child. Yes. I expect that's what the psychologists will say when they get you into the lunatic asylum. "Ogre's teeth." Being bullied at school and so on. Extraordinary the effect it has on a child. Then Nazism helped to fan the flames and then came the crack on your ugly head. The crack you engineered yourself. I expect that settled it. From then on you were really mad. Same sort of thing as people who think they're God. Extraordinary what tenacity they have. Absolute fanatics. You're almost a genius. Lombroso would have been delighted with you. As it is you're just a mad dog that'll have to be shot. Or else you'll commit suicide. Paranoiacs generally do. Too bad. Sad business.'

Bond paused and put all the scorn he could summon into his voice. 'And now let's get on with this farce, you great hairy-faced lunatic.'

It worked. With every word Drax's face had become more contorted with rage, his eyes were red with it, the sweat of fury was dripping off his jowls on to his shirt, the lips were drawn back from the gaping teeth and a string of saliva had crept out of his mouth and was hanging down from his chin. Now, at the last private-school insult that must have awoken God knows what stinging memories, he leapt up from his chair and lunged round the desk at Bond, his hairy fists flailing.

Bond gritted his teeth and took it.

When Drax had twice had to pick the chair up with Bond in it, the tornado of rage suddenly passed. He took out his silk handkerchief and wiped his face and hands. Then he walked quietly to the door and spoke across the lolling head of Bond to the girl.

'I don't think you two will give me any more trouble,' he said, and his voice was quite calm and certain. 'Krebs never makes a mistake with his knots.' He gesticulated towards the bloody figure in the other chair. 'When he wakes up,' he said, 'you can tell him that these doors will open once more, just before noon tomorrow. A few minutes later there will be nothing left of either of you. Not even,' he added as he wrenched open the inner door, 'the stoppings in your teeth.' The outer door slammed.

Bond slowly raised his head and grinned painfully at the girl with his bloodstained lips.

'Had to get him mad,' he said with difficulty. 'Didn't want to give him time to think. Had to work up a brainstorm.' Gala looked at him uncomprehendingly, her eyes wide at the terrible mask of his face.

''S'all right,' said Bond thickly. 'Don't worry. London's okay. Got a plan.'

Over on the desk the blowtorch gave a quiet 'plop' and went out.

Through half-closed eyes Bond looked intently at the torch while for a few precious seconds he sat and let life creep back into his body. His head felt as if it had been used as a football, but there was nothing broken. Drax had hit him unscientifically and with the welter of blows of a drunken man.

Gala watched him anxiously. The eyes in the bloody face were almost shut, but the line of the jaw was taut with concentration and she could feel the effort of will he was making.

He gave his head a shake and when he turned towards her she could see that his eyes were feverish with triumph.

He nodded towards the desk. 'The lighter,' he said urgently. 'I had to try and make him forget it. Follow me. I'll show you.' He started to rock the light steel chair inch by inch towards the desk. 'For God's sake don't tip over or we've had it. But make it fast or the blowlamp'll get cold.'

Uncomprehendingly, and feeling almost as if they were playing some ghastly children's game, Gala carefully rocked her way across the floor in his wake.

Seconds later Bond told her to stop beside the desk

while he went rocking on round to Drax's chair. Then he manoeuvred himself into position opposite his target and with a sudden lurch heaved himself and the chair forward so that his head came down.

There was a painful crack as the Ronson desk lighter connected with his teeth, but his lips held it and the top of it was in his mouth as he heaved the chair back with just enough force to prevent it spilling over. Then he started his patient journey back to where Gala was sitting at the corner of the desk on which Krebs had left the blowlamp.

He rested until his breath was steady again. 'Now we come to the difficult part,' he said grimly. 'While I try to get this torch going, you get your chair round so that your right arm is as close in front of me as possible.'

Obediently she edged herself round while Bond swayed his chair so that it leant against the edge of the desk and allowed his mouth to reach forward and grip the handle of the blowtorch between his teeth.

Then he eased the torch towards him and after minutes of patient work he had the torch and the lighter arranged to his liking at the edge of the desk.

After another rest he bent down, closed the valve of the torch with his teeth, and proceeded to get pressure back by slowly and repeatedly pulling up the plunger with his lips and pressing it back with his chin. His face could feel the warmth in the pre-heater and he could smell the remnants of gas in it. If only it hadn't cooled off too much.

He straightened up.

'Last lap, Gala,' he said, smiling crookedly at her. 'I may have to hurt you a bit. All right?'

'Of course,' said Gala.

'Then here goes,' said Bond, and he bent forward and released the safety valve on the left of the canister. Then he quickly bent forward over the Ronson, which was standing at right angles and just below the neck of the torch, and with his two front teeth pressed down sharply on the ignition lever.

It was a horrible manoeuvre and though he whipped back his head with the speed of a snake he let out a gasp of pain as the jet of blue fire from the torch seared across his bruised cheek and the bridge of his nose.

But the vaporized paraffin was hissing out its vital tongue of flame and he shook the water out of his streaming eyes and bent his head almost at right angles and again got his teeth to the handle of the blowtorch.

He thought his jaw would break with the weight of the thing and the nerves of his front teeth screamed at him, but he swayed his chair carefully upright away from the desk and then strained his bent neck forward until the tip of blue fire from the torch was biting into the flex that bound Gala's right wrist to the arm of her chair.

He tried desperately to keep the flame steady but the breath rasped through the girl's teeth as the handle shifted between his jaws and the flame of the torch brushed her forearm.

But then it was over. Melted by the fierce heat, the copper strands parted one by one and suddenly Gala's right arm was free and she was reaching to take the torch out of Bond's mouth.

Bond's head fell back on to his shoulders and he twisted his neck luxuriously to get the blood moving in the aching muscles.

Almost before he knew it, Gala was bending over his arms and legs and he too was free.

As he sat still for a moment, his eyes closed, waiting for the life to come back into his body, he suddenly, delightedly felt Gala's soft lips on his mouth.

He opened his eyes. She was standing in front of him, her eyes shining. 'That's for what you did,' she said seriously.

'You're a wonderful girl,' he said simply.

But then, knowing what he was going to have to do, knowing that while she might conceivably survive, he had only another few minutes to live, he closed his eyes so that she should not see the hopelessness in them.

Gala saw the expression on his face and she turned away. She thought it was only exhaustion and the cumulative effect of what his body had suffered, and she suddenly remembered the peroxide in the wash-room next to her office.

She went through the communicating door. How extraordinary it was to see her familiar things again. It must be someone else who had sat at that desk and typed letters and powdered her nose. She shrugged her shoulders and went into the little washroom. God what a sight and God how tired she felt! But first she took a wet towel and some peroxide and went back and spent ten minutes attending to the battlefield which was Bond's face.

He sat silent, a hand resting on her waist, and watched her gratefully. Then when she had gone back into her room and he heard her shut the door of the washroom behind her he got up, turned off the still hissing blowtorch, and walked into Drax's shower, stripped and stood for five minutes under the icy water. 'Preparing the corpse!' he reflected ruefully as he surveyed his battered face in the mirror.

He put on his clothes and went back to Drax's desk which he searched methodically. It yielded only one prize, the 'office bottle', a half-full bottle of Haig and Haig. He fetched two glasses and some water and called to Gala.

He heard the door of the washroom open. 'What is it?'

'Whisky.'

'You drink. I'll be ready in a minute.'

Bond looked at the bottle and poured himself three quarters of a toothglass and drank it straight down in two gulps. Then he gingerly lit a blessed cigarette and sat on the edge of the desk and felt the liquor burn down through his stomach into his legs.

He picked up the bottle again and looked at it. Plenty

for Gala and a whole full glass for himself before he walked out through the door. Better than nothing. It wouldn't be too bad with that inside him so long as he walked quickly out and shut the doors behind him. No looking back.

Gala came in, a transformed Gala, looking as beautiful as the night he had first seen her, except for the lines of exhaustion under the eyes that the powder could not quite conceal and the angry welts at her wrists and ankles.

Bond gave her a drink and took another one himself and their eyes smiled at each other over the rims of their glasses.

Then Bond stood up.

'Listen, Gala,' he said in a matter-of-fact voice. 'We've got to face it and get it over so I'll make it short and then we'll have another drink.' He heard her catch her breath, but he went on. 'In ten minutes or so I'm going to shut you into Drax's bathroom and put you under the shower and turn it full on.'

'James,' she cried. She stepped close to him. 'Don't go on. I know you're going to say something dreadful. Please stop, James.'

'Come on, Gala,' said Bond roughly. 'What the hell does it matter. It's a bloody miracle we have got the chance.' He moved away from her. He walked to the doors leading out into the shaft.

'And then,' he said, and he held up the precious lighter in his right hand, 'I shall walk out of here and shut the doors and go and light a last cigarette under the tail of the Moonraker.'

'God,' she whispered. 'What are you saying? You're mad.' She looked at him through eyes wide with horror.

'Don't be ridiculous,' said Bond impatiently. 'What the hell is there else to do? The explosion will be so terrific that one won't feel anything. And it's bound to work with all that fuel vapour hanging around. It's me or a million people in London. The warhead won't go off. Atom bombs don't explode like that. It'll be melted probably. There's just a chance you may get away. Most of the explosion will take the line of least resistance through the roof – and down the exhaust pit, if I can work the machinery that opens up the floor.' He smiled. 'Cheer up,' he said, walking over to her and taking one of her hands. 'The boy stood on the burning deck. I've wanted to copy him since I was five.'

Gala pulled her hand away. 'I don't care what you say,' said angrily. 'We've got to think of something else. You don't trust me to have any ideas. You just tell me what you think we've got to do.' She walked over to the wall map and pressed down the switch. 'Of course if we have to use the lighter we have to.' She gazed at the map of the false flight plan, barely seeing it. 'But the idea of you walking in there alone and standing in the middle of all those ghastly fumes from the fuel and calmly flicking that thing and then being blown to dust . . . And anyway, if we have to do it, we'll do it together. I'd rather that than be burnt to death in here. And anyway,' she paused, 'I'd like to go with you. We're in this together.'

Bond's eyes were tender as he walked towards her and put an arm round her waist and hugged her to him. 'Gala, you're a darling,' he said simply. 'And if there's any other way we'll take it. But,' he looked at his watch, 'it's past midnight and we've to decide quickly. At any moment it may occur to Drax to send guards down to see that we're all right, and God knows what time he'll be coming down to set the gyros.'

Gala twisted her body round like a cat. She gazed at him with her mouth open, her face taut with excitement. 'The gyros,' she whispered, 'to set the gyros.' She leant weakly back against the wall, her eyes searching Bond's face. 'Don't you *see*?' her voice was on the edge of hysteria. 'After he's gone, we could alter the gyros back, back to the old flight plan, then the rocket will simply fall into the North Sea where it's supposed to go.'

She stepped away from the wall and seized his shirt in both hands and looked imploringly at him. 'Can't we?' she said. 'Can't we?'

'Do you know the other settings?' asked Bond sharply.

'Of course I do,' she said urgently. 'I've been living with them for a year. We won't have a weather report but we'll just have to chance that. The forecast this morning said we would have the same conditions as today.'

'By God,' said Bond. 'We might do it. If only we can hide somewhere and make Drax think we've escaped. What about the exhaust pit? If I can work the machine to open the floor.'

'It's a straight hundred-foot drop,' said Gala, shaking her head. 'And the walls are polished steel. Just like glass. And there's no rope or anything down here. They cleared everything out of the workshop yesterday. And anyway there are guards on the beach.'

Bond reflected. Then his eyes brightened. 'I've got an idea,' he said. 'But first of all what about the radar, the homing device in London? Won't that pull the rocket off its course and back on to London?'

Gala shook her head. 'It's only got a range of about a hundred miles,' she said. 'The rocket won't even pick up its signal. If it's aimed into the North Sea it will get into the orbit of the transmitter on the raft. There's absolutely nothing wrong with my plans. But where can we hide?'

'One of the ventilator shafts,' said Bond. 'Come on.' He gave a last look round the room. The lighter was in his pocket. That would still be the last resort. There was nothing else they would want. He followed Gala out into the gleaming shaft and made for the instrument panel which controlled the steel cover to the exhaust pit.

After a quick examination he threw over a heavy lever from '*Zu*' to '*Auf*'. There was a soft hiss from the hydraulic machinery behind the wall and the two semicircles of steel opened beneath the tail of the rocket and slid back into their grooves. He walked over and looked down.

The arcs in the roof above glinted back at him from the polished walls of the wide steel funnel until they curved away out of sight towards the distant hollow boom of the sea.

Bond went back into Drax's office and pulled down the shower curtain in the bathroom. Then Gala and he tore it into strips and tied them together. He made a jagged rent at the end of the last strip so as to give an impression that the escape rope had broken. Then he tied the other end firmly round the pointed tip of one of the Moonraker's three fins and dropped the rest so that it hung down the shaft.

It was not much of a false scent, but it might gain some time.

The big round mouths of the ventilator shafts were spaced about ten yards apart and about four feet off the floor. Bond counted. There were fifty of them. He carefully opened the hinged grating that covered one of them and looked up. Forty feet away there was a faint glimmer from the moonlight outside. He decided that they were tunnelled straight up inside the wall of the site until they turned at right angles towards the gratings in the outside walls.

Bond reached up and ran his hand along the surface. It was unfinished roughcast concrete and he grunted with satisfaction as he felt first one sharp protuberance and then another. They were the jagged ends of the steel rods reinforcing the walls, cut off where the shafts had been bored.

It was going to be a painful business, but there was no doubt they could inch their way up one of these shafts, like mountaineers up a rock chimney, and, in the turn at the top, lie hidden from anything but the sort of painstaking search that would be difficult in the morning with all the officials from London round the site.

Bond knelt down and the girl climbed on to his back and started up.

An hour later, their feet and shoulders bruised and cut, they lay exhausted, squeezed tight in each other's arms, their heads inches away from the circular grating directly above the outside door, and listened to the guards restlessly shifting their feet in the darkness a hundred yards away.

Five o'clock, six, seven.

Slowly the sun came up behind the dome and the seagulls started to call in the cliffs and then suddenly there were the three figures walking towards them in the distance, passed by a fresh platoon of guards doubling, chins up, knees up, to relieve the night watch.

The figures came nearer and the squinting, exhausted eyes of the hidden couple could see every detail of Drax's blood-orange face, the lean, pale foxiness of Dr Walter, the suety, overslept puffiness of Krebs.

The three men walked like executioners, saying nothing. Drax took out his key and they silently filed through the door a few feet below the taut bodies of Bond and Gala.

Then for ten minutes there was silence except for the occasional boom of voices up the ventilator shaft as the three men moved about down on the steel floor round the exhaust pit. Bond smiled to himself at the thought of the rage and consternation on Drax's face; the miserable Krebs wilting under the lash of Drax's tongue; the bitter accusation in Walter's eyes. Then the door burst open beneath him and Krebs was calling urgently to the leader of the guards. A man detached himself from the semicircle and ran up.

'*Die Engländer,*' Kreb's voice was almost hysterical. 'Escaped. The *Herr Kapitän* thinks they may be in one of the ventilator shafts. We are going to take a chance. The dome will be opened again and we will clear out the fumes from the fuel. And then the *Herr Doktor* will put the steam hose up each shaft. If they're there it will finish them. Choose four men. The rubber gloves and firesuits are down there. We'll take the pressure off the heating. Tell the others to listen for the screams. *Verstanden?*'

'*Zu Befehl!*' The man doubled smartly back to his troop and Krebs, the sweat of anxiety on his face, turned and disappeared back through the door.

For a moment Bond lay motionless.

There was a heavy rumble above their heads as the dome divided and swung open.

The steam hose!

He had heard of mutinies in ships being fought with it. Rioters in factories. Would it reach forty feet? Would the pressure last? How many boilers fed the heating? Among the fifty ventilator shafts, where would they choose to begin? Had Bond or Gala left any clue to the one they had climbed?

He felt that Gala was waiting for him to explain. To do something. To protect them.

Five men came doubling from the semicircle of guards. They passed underneath and disappeared.

Bond put his mouth to Gala's ear. 'This may hurt,' he said. 'Can't say how much. Can't be helped. Just have to take it. No noise.' He felt the answering tentative pressure from her arms. 'Bring your knees up. Don't be shy. This is no time to be maidenly.'

'Shut up,' whispered Gala angrily. He felt one knee creep up until it was locked between his thighs. His own knee followed suit until it would go no further. She squirmed furiously. 'Don't be a bloody fool,' whispered Bond, pulling her head in close to his chest so that it was half covered by his open shirt.

He overlay her as much as possible. There was nothing to be done about their ankles or his hands. He pulled his shirt collar up as far over their heads as possible. They held tightly to each other.

Hot, cramped, breathless. Waiting, it suddenly

occurred to Bond, like two lovers in the undergrowth. Waiting for the footsteps to go by so that they could start again. He smiled grimly to himself and listened.

There was silence down the shaft. They must be in the engine room. Walter would be watching the hose being coupled to the outlet valve. Now there were distant noises. Where would they start?

Somewhere, not far away, there was a soft, long-drawn-out whisper, like the inefficient whistle of a distant train.

He drew his shirt collar back and stole a look out through the grating at the guards. Those he could see were looking straight at the launching-dome, somewhere to his left.

Again the long harsh whisper. And again.

It was getting louder. He could see the heads of the guards pivoting towards the grating in the wall which hid him and Gala. They must be watching, fascinated, as the thick white jets of steam shot out through the gratings high up in the cement wall, wondering if this one, or that one, or that one, would be accompanied by a double scream.

He could feel Gala's heart beating against his. She didn't know what was coming. She trusted him.

'It may hurt,' he whispered to her again. 'It may burn. It won't kill us. Be brave. Don't make a sound.'

'I'm all right,' she whispered angrily. But he could feel her body press closer in to his.

Whoosh. It was getting closer.

Whoosh! Two away.

WHOOSH!! Next door. A suspicion of the wet smell of steam came to him.

Hold tight, Bond said to himself. He smothered her in towards him and held his breath.

Now. Quick. Get it over, damn you.

And suddenly there was a great pressure and heat and a roaring in the ears and a moment of blazing pain.

Then dead silence, a mixture of sharp cold and fire on the ankles and hands, a feeling of soaking wet and a desperate, choking effort to get pure air into the lungs.

Their bodies automatically fought to withdraw from each other, to capture some inches of space and air for the areas of skin that were already blistering. The breath rattled in their throats and the water poured off the cement into their open mouths until they bent sideways and choked the water out to join the trickle that was oozing under their soaking bodies and along past their scalded ankles and then down the vertical walls of the shaft up which they had come.

And the howl of the steam pipe drew away from them until it became a whisper and finally stopped, and there was silence in their narrow cement prison except for their stubborn breathing and the ticking of Bond's watch.

And the two bodies lay and waited, nursing their pain.

Half an hour – half a year – later, Walter and Krebs and Drax filed out below them.

But, as a precaution, the guards had been left behind in the launching dome.

'Then we're all agreed?'

'Yes, Sir Hugo,' it was the Minister of Supply speaking. Bond recognized the dapper, assured figure. 'Those are the settings. My people have checked them independently with the Air Ministry this morning.'

'Then if you'll allow me the privilage,' Drax held up the slip of paper and made to turn towards the launching-dome.

'Hold it, Sir Hugo. Just like that, please. Arm in the air.' The bulbs flashed and the bank of cameras whirred and clicked for the last time and Drax turned and walked the few yards towards the dome, almost, it seemed to Bond, looking him straight in the eye through the grating above the door of the site.

The small crowd of reporters and cameramen dissolved and straggled off across the concrete apron, leaving only a nervously chatting group of officials to wait for Drax to emerge.

Bond looked at his watch. 11.45. Hurry up, damn you, he thought.

For the hundredth time he repeated to himself the figures Gala had taught him during the hours of cramped pain that had followed their ordeal by steam, and for the hundredth time he shifted his limbs to keep the circulation going.

'Get ready,' he whispered into Gala's ear. 'Are you all right?'

He could feel the girl smile. 'Fine.' She shut her mind to the thought of her blistered legs and the quick rasping descent back down the ventilator shaft.

The door clanged shut beneath them followed by the click of the lock and, preceded by the five guards, the figure of Drax appeared below striding masterfully towards the group of officials, the slip of lying figures in his hand.

Bond looked at his watch. 11.47. 'Now,' he whispered.

'Good luck,' she whispered back.

Slither, scrape, rip. His shoulders carefully expanding and contracting; blistered, bloodstained feet scrabbling for the sharp knobs of iron, Bond, his lacerated body tearing its way down the forty feet of shaft, prayed that the girl would have strength to stand it when she followed.

A last ten-foot drop that jarred his spine, a kick at the grating and he was out on the steel floor and running for the stairs, leaving a trail of red footprints and a spray of blood-drops from his raw shoulders.

The arcs had been extinguished, but the daylight streamed down through the open roof and the blue from the sky mingling with the fierce glitter of the sunshine gave Bond the impression that he was running up inside a huge sapphire.

The great deadly needle in the centre might have been made of glass. Looking above him as he sweated and panted up the endless sweep of the iron stairway, it was difficult for him to see where its tapering nose ended and the sky began.

Behind the crouching silence that enveloped the shimmering bullet, Bond could hear a quick, deadly ticking, the hasty tripping of tiny metal feet somewhere in the body of the Moonraker. It filled the great steel chamber like the beating heart in Poe's story and Bond knew that directly Drax at the firing point pressed the switch that sent the radio beam zinging over two hundred yards to the waiting rocket, the ticking would suddenly cease, there would be the soft whine of the lighted pinwheel, a wisp of steam from the turbines, and then the howling jet of flame on which the rocket would slowly rise and sweep majestically out on the start of its gigantic acceleration curve.

And then in front of him there was the spidery arm of the gantry folded back against the wall and Bond's hand was at the lever and the arm was slowly stretching down and out towards the square hairline on the glittering skin of the rocket that was the door of the gyro chamber.

Bond, on hands and knees, was along it even before the rubber pads came to rest against the polished chrome. There was the flush disc the size of a shilling, just as Gala had described. Press, click, and the tiny door had flicked open on its hard spring. Inside. Careful not to cut your head. The gleaming handles beneath the staring compass-roses. Turn. Twist. Steady. That's for the roll. Now the pitch and yaw. Turn. Twist. Ever so gently. And steady. A last look. A glance at his watch. Four minutes to go. Don't panic. Back out. Door click. A cat-like scurry. Don't look down. Gantry up. Clang against the wall. And now for the stairs.

Tick-tick-tick-tick.

As Bond shot down he caught a glimpse of Gala's tense, white face as she stood holding open the outer door of Drax's office. God, how his body hurt! A final leap and a clumsy swerve to the right. Clang as Gala slammed the outer door. Another clang and they were across the room and into the shower and the water was hissing down on their clinging, panting bodies.

Through the noise of it all, above the beating of his heart, Bond heard the sudden crackle of static and then the voice of the BBC announcer coming from the big set in Drax's room a few inches away through the thin wall of the bathroom. It had been Gala again who had remembered Drax's wireless and who had found time to throw the switches while Bond was working on the gyros.

'. . . be five minutes' delay,' said the breezy, excited voice. 'Sir Hugo has been persuaded to say a few words into the microphone.' Bond turned off the shower and the voice came to them more clearly. 'He looks very confident. Just saying something into the Minister's ear. They're both laughing. Wonder what it was? Ah, here's my colleague with the latest weather report from the Air Ministry. What's that? Perfect at all altitudes. Good show. It certainly is a wonderful day down below here. Haha. Those crowds in the distance by the coast-guard station will be getting quite a sunburn. There must be thousands. What's that you say? Twenty thousand? Well, it certainly looks like it. And Walmer Beach is black with them too. The whole of Kent seems to be out. Terrible crick in the neck we're all going to get, I'm afraid. Worse than Wimbledon. Haha. Hullo, what's going on down there by the jetty? By jove, there's a submarine just surfaced alongside. I say, what a sight. One of our biggest I should say. And Sir Hugo's team is down there too. Lined up on the jetty as if they were on parade. Magnificent body of men. Now they're filing on board. Perfect discipline. Must be an idea of the Admiralty's. Give them a special grandstand out in the Channel. Splendid show. Wish you could be here to see it. Now Sir Hugo is coming towards us. In a moment he'll be speaking to you. Fine figure of a man. Everyone in the firing point is giving him a cheer. I'm sure we all feel like cheering him today. He's coming into the firing point. I can see the sun glinting on the nose of the Moonraker way over there behind him. Just showing out of the top of the launching-dome. Hope somebody's got a camera. Now here he is,' a pause. 'Sir Hugo Drax.'

Bond looked into Gala's dripping face. Soaked and bleeding they stood in each other's arms, speechless and trembling slightly with the storm of their emotions. Their eyes were blank and fathomless as they met and held each other's gaze.

'Your majesty, men and women of England,' the voice was a velvet snarl. 'I am about to change the course of England's history.' A pause. 'In a few minutes' time the lives of all of you will be altered, in some cases, ahem, drastically, by the, er, impact of the Moonraker. I am very proud and pleased that fate has singled me out, from amongst all my fellow countrymen, to fire this great arrow of vengeance into the skies and thus to proclaim for all time, and for all the world to witness, the might of my fatherland. I hope that this occasion will be forever a warning that the fate of my country's enemies will be written in dust, in ashes, in tears, and,' a pause, 'in blood. And now thank you all for listening and I sincerely hope that those of you who are able will repeat my words to your children, if you have any, tonight.'

A rattle of rather hesitant applause sounded out of the machine and then came the breezy voice of the announcer. 'And that was Sir Hugo Drax saying a few words to you before he walks across the floor of the firing point to the switch on the wall which will fire the Moonraker. The first time he has spoken in public. Very, ahem, forthright. Doesn't mince his words. However, a lot of us will say there's no harm in that.

And now it's time for me to hand over to the expert, Group Captain Tandy of the Ministry of Supply, who will describe to you the actual firing of the Moonraker. After that you will hear Peter Trimble in one of the naval security patrol, HMS *Merganzer*, describe the scene in the target area. Group Captain Tandy.'

Bond glanced at his watch. 'Only a minute more,' he said to Gala. 'God, I'd like to get my hands on Drax. Here,' he reached for the cake of soap and gouged some pieces off it. 'Stuff this in your ears when the time comes. The noise is going to be terrific, I don't know about the heat. It won't last long and the steel walls may stand up to it.'

Gala looked at him. She smiled. 'If you hold me it won't be too bad,' she said.

'. . . and now Sir Hugo has his hand on the switch and he's watching the chronometer.'

'TEN,' broke in another voice, heavy and sonorous as the toll of a bell.

Bond turned on the shower and the water hissed down on their clinging bodies.

'NINE,' tolled the voice of the time-keeper.

'. . . the radar operators are watching the screens. Nothing but a mass of wavy lines . . .'

'EIGHT.'

'. . . all wearing ear-plugs. Blockhouse should be indestructible. Concrete walls are twelve feet thick. Pyramid roof, twenty-seven feet thick at the point . . .'

'SEVEN.'

'. . . first the radio beam will stop the time mechanism alongside the turbines. Set the pinwheel going. Flaming thing like a catherine wheel . . .'

'SIX.'

'. . . valves will open. Liquid fuel. Secret formula. Terrific stuff. Dynamite. Pours down from the fuel tanks . . .'

'FIVE.'

'. . . ignited by the pinwheel when the fuel gets to the rocket motor . . .'

'FOUR.'

'. . . meanwhile the peroxide and permanganate have mixed, made steam and the turbine pumps begin to turn . . .'

'THREE.'

'. . . pumping the flaming fuel through the motor out of the stern of the rocket into the exhaust pit. Gigantic heat . . . 3500 degrees . . .'

'TWO.'

'. . . Sir Hugo is about to press the switch. He's staring out through the slit. Perspiration on his forehead. Absolute silence in here. Terrific tension.'

'ONE.'

Nothing but the noise of the water, steadily pouring down on the two clinging bodies.

FIRE!

Bond's heart jumped into his throat at the shout. He felt Gala shudder. Silence. Nothing but the hissing of the water . . .

'. . . Sir Hugo's left the firing point. Walking calmly over to the edge of the cliff. So confident. He's stepped on to the hoist. He's going down. Of course. He must be going out to the submarine. Television screen shows a little steam coming out of the tail of the rocket. A few more seconds. Yes, he's out on the jetty. He looked back and raised his arm in the air. Good old Sir Hu . . .'

A soft thunder came to Bond and Gala. Louder. Louder. The tiled floor began to tremble under their feet. A hurricane scream. They were being pulverized by it. The walls were quaking, steaming. Their legs began going out of control under their teetering bodies. Hold her up. Hold her up. Stop it! Stop it!! STOP THAT NOISE!!!

Christ, he was going to faint. The water was boiling. Must turn it off. Got it. No. Pipe's burst. Steam, smell, iron, paint.

Get her out! Get her out!! Get her out!!!

And then there was silence. Silence you could feel, hold, squeeze. And they were on the floor of Drax's office. Only the light in the bathroom still shining out. And the smoke's clearing. And the filthy smell of burning iron and paint. Being sucked out by the air-conditioner. And the steel wall is bent towards them like a huge blister. Gala's eyes are open and she's smiling. But the rocket. What happened? London? North Sea? The radio. Looks all right. He shook his head and the deafness slowly cleared. He remembered the soap. Gouged it out.

'. . . through the sound barrier. Travelling perfectly right in the centre of the radar screen. A perfect launching. Afraid you couldn't hear anything because of the noise. Terrific. First of all the great sheet of flame coming out of the cliff from the exhaust pit and then you should have seen the nose slowly creep up out of the dome. And there she was like a great silver pencil. Standing upright on this huge column of flame and slowly climbing into the air and the flame splashing for hundreds of yards over the concrete. The howl of the thing must have nearly burst our microphones. Great bits have fallen off the cliff and the concrete looks like a spider's web. Terrible vibration. And then she was climbing faster and faster. A hundred miles an hour. A thousand. And,' he broke off, 'what's that you say? Really! And now she's travelling at over ten thousand miles an hour! She's three hundred miles up. Can't hear her any more, of course. We could only see her flame for a few seconds. Like a star. Sir Hugo must be a proud man. He's out there in the Channel now. The submarine went off like a rocket, haha, must be doing more than thirty knots. Throwing up a huge wake. Off the East Goodwins now. Travelling north. She'll soon be up with the patrol ships. They'll have a view of the launching and of the landing. Quite a surprise trip that. No one here had an inkling. Even the naval authorities seem a bit mystified. C-in-C Nore has been on the telephone. But now that's all I can tell you from here and I'll hand you over to Peter Trimble on board HMS *Merganzer* somewhere off the East Coast.'

Nothing but the pumping lungs showed that the two limp bodies in the creeping pool of water on the floor were still alive, but their battered ear-drums were desperately clinging to the crackle of static that came briefly from the blistered metal cabinet. Now for the verdict on their work.

'And this is Peter Trimble speaking. It's a beautiful morning, I mean – er – afternoon here. Just north of the Goodwin Sands. Calm as a millpond. No wind. Bright sunshine. And the target area is reported clear of shipping. Is that right, Commander Edwards? Yes, the Captain says it's quite clear. Nothing on the radar screens yet. I'm not allowed to tell you the range we shall pick her up at. Security and all that. But we shall only catch the rocket for a split second. Isn't that right, Captain? But the target's just showing on the screen. Out of sight from the bridge, of course. Must be seventy miles north of here. We could see the Moonraker going up. Terrific sight. Noise like thunder. Long flame coming out of the tail. Must have been ten miles away but you couldn't miss the light. Yes, Captain? Oh yes, I see. Well, that's very interesting. Big submarine coming up fast. Only about a mile away. Suppose it's the one they say Sir Hugo's aboard with his men. None of us here were told anything about her. Captain Edwards says she doesn't answer the Aldis lamp. Not flying colours. Very mysterious. I've got her now. Quite clear in my glasses. We've changed course to intercept her.

Captain says she isn't one of ours. Thinks she must be a foreigner. Hullo! She's broken out her colours. *What's* that? Good heavens. The Captain says she's a Russian. I say! And now she's hauled down her colours and she's submerging. Bang. Did you hear that? We fired a shot across her bows. But she's disappeared. What's that? The asdic operator says she's going even faster under water. Twenty-five knots. Terrific. Well, she can't see much under water. But she's right in the target area now. Twelve minutes past noon. The Moonraker must have turned and be on her way down. A thousand miles up. Coming down at ten thousand miles an hour. She'll be here any second now. Hope there's not going to be a tragedy. The Russian's well inside the danger zone. The radar operator's holding up his hand. That means she's due. She's coming. She's COMING . . . Whew! Not even a whisper. GOD! What's that? Look out! Look out! Terrific explosion. Black cloud going up into the air. There's a tidal wave coming at us. Great wall of water tearing down. There goes the submarine. God! Thrown out of the water upside down. It's coming. It's COMING . . .'

'. . . Two hundred dead so far and about the same number missing,' said M. 'Reports still coming in from the East Coast and there's bad news from Holland. Breached miles of their sea defences. Most of our losses were among the patrol craft. Two of them capsized, including the *Merganzer*. Commanding Officer missing. And that BBC chap. Goodwin Lightships broke their moorings. No news from Belgium or France yet. There are going to be some pretty heavy bills to pay when everything gets sorted out.'

It was the next afternoon and Bond, a rubber-tipped stick beside his chair, was back where he had started – across the desk from the quiet man with the cold grey eyes who had invited him to dinner and a game of cards a hundred years ago.

Under his clothes Bond was latticed with surgical tape. Pain burned up his legs whenever he moved his feet. There was a vivid red streak across his left cheek and the bridge of his nose, and the tannic ointment dressing glinted in the light from the window. He held a cigarette clumsily in one gloved hand. Incredibly M had invited him to smoke.

'Any news of the submarine, sir?' he asked.

'They've located her,' said M with satisfaction. 'Lying on her side in about thirty fathoms. The salvage ship that was to look after the remains of the rocket is over her now. The divers have been down and there's no answer to signals against her hull. The Soviet Ambassador has been round at the Foreign Office this morning. I gather he says a salvage ship is on her way down from the Baltic, but we've said that we can't wait as the wreck's a danger to navigation.' M chuckled. 'So she would be I dare say if anyone happened to be navigating at thirty fathoms in the Channel. But I'm glad I'm not a member of the Cabinet,' he added drily. 'They've been in session on and off since the end of the broadcast. Vallance got hold of those Edinburgh solicitors before they'd opened Drax's message to the world. I gather it's a terrific document. Reads as if it had been written by Jehovah. Vallance took it to the Cabinet last night and stayed at No. 10 to fill in the blanks.'

'I know,' said Bond. 'He kept on telephoning me at the hospital for details until after midnight. I could hardly think straight for all the dope they'd pushed into me. What's going to happen?'

'They're going to try the biggest cover-up job in history,' said M. 'A lot of scientific twaddle about the fuel having been only half used up. Unexpectedly powerful explosion on impact. Full compensation will be paid. Tragic loss of Sir Hugo Drax and his team. Great patriot. Tragic loss of one of HM submarines.

Latest experimental model. Orders misunderstood. Very sad. Fortunately only a skeleton crew. Next of kin will be informed. Tragic loss of BBC man. Unaccountable error in mistaking White Ensign for Soviet naval colours. Very similar design. White Ensign recovered from the wreck.'

'But what about the atomic explosion?' asked Bond. 'Radiation and atomic dust and all that. The famous mushroom-shaped cloud. Surely that's going to be a bit of a problem.'

'Apparently it's not worrying them too much,' said M. 'The cloud is going to be passed off as the normal formation after an explosion of that size. The Ministry of Supply know the whole story. Had to be told. Their men were down on the East Coast all last night with Geiger counters and there's not been a positive report yet.' M smiled coldly. 'The cloud's got to come down somewhere, of course, but by a happy chance such wind as there is is drifting it up north. Back home, as you might say.'

Bond smiled painfully. 'I see,' he said. 'How very appropriate.'

'Of course,' continued M, picking up his pipe and starting to fill it, 'there are going to be some nasty rumours. They've begun already. A lot of people saw you and Miss Brand being brought out of the site on stretchers. Then there's the Bowaters' case against Drax for the loss of all that newsprint. There'll be the inquest on the young man who was killed in the Alfa

Romeo. And somebody's got to explain away the remains of your car, amongst which,' he looked accusingly at Bond, 'a long-barrel Colt was found. And then there's the Ministry of Supply. Vallance had to call some of their men yesterday to help clean out that house in Ebury Street. But those people are trained to keep secrets. You won't get a leak there. Naturally it's going to be a risky business. The big lie always is. But what's the alternative? Trouble with Germany? War with Russia? Lots of people on both sides of the Atlantic would be only too glad of an excuse.'

M paused and put a match to his pipe. 'If the story holds,' he continued reflectively, 'we shan't come out of this too badly. We've wanted one of their high-speed U-boats and we'll be glad of the clues we can pick up about their atom bombs. The Russians know that we know that their gamble failed. Malenkov's none too firmly in the saddle and this may mean another Kremlin revolt. As for the Germans. Well, we all knew there was plenty of Nazism left and this will make the Cabinet go just a bit more carefully on German rearmament. And, as a very minor consequence,' he gave a wry smile, 'it will make Vallance's security job, and mine for the matter of that, just a little bit easier in the future. These politicians can't see that the atomic age has created the most deadly saboteur in the history of the world – the little man with the heavy suitcase.'

'Will the Press wear the story?' asked Bond dubiously.

M shrugged his shoulders. 'The Prime Minister saw the editors this morning,' he said, putting another match to his pipe, 'and I gather he's got away with it so far. If the rumours get bad later on, he'll probably have to see them again and tell them some of the truth. Then they'll play all right. They always do when it's important enough. The main thing is to gain time and stave off the firebrands. For the moment everyone's so proud of the Moonraker that they're not inquiring too closely into what went wrong.'

There was a soft burr from the intercom. on M's desk and a ruby light winked on and off. M picked up the single earphone and leant towards it. 'Yes?' he said. There was a pause. 'I'll take it on the Cabinet line.' He picked up the white receiver from the bank of four telephones.

'Yes,' said M. 'Speaking.' There was a pause. 'Yes, sir? Over.' M pressed down the button of his scrambler. He held the receiver close to his ear and not a sound from it reached Bond. There was a long pause during which M puffed occasionally at the pipe in his left hand. He took it out of his mouth. 'I agree, sir.' Another pause. 'I know my man would have been very proud, sir. But of course it's a rule here.' M frowned. 'If you will allow me to say so, sir, I think it would be very unwise.' A pause, then M's face cleared. 'Thank you, sir. And of course Vallance has not got the same problem. And it would be the least she deserves.' Another pause. 'I understand. That will be done.' Another pause. 'That's very kind of you, sir.'

M put the white receiver back on its cradle and the scrambler button clicked back to the *en clair* position.

For a moment M continued to look at the telephone as if in doubt about what had been said. Then he twisted his chair away from the desk and gazed thoughtfully out of the window.

There was silence in the room and Bond shifted in his chair to ease the pain that was creeping back into his body.

The same pigeon as on Monday, or perhaps another one, came to rest on the window-sill with the same clatter of wings. It walked up and down, nodding and cooing, and then planed off towards the trees in the park. The traffic murmured sleepily in the distance.

How nearly it had come, thought Bond, to being stilled. How nearly there might be nothing now but the distant clang of the ambulance bells beneath a lurid black and orange sky, the stench of burning, the screams of people still trapped in the buildings. The softly beating heart of London silenced for a generation. And a whole generation of her people dead in the streets amongst the ruins of a civilization that might not rise again for centuries.

All that would have come about but for a man who scornfully cheated at cards to feed the fires of his maniac ego; but for the stuffy chairman of Blades who detected him; but for M who agreed to help an old friend; but for Bond's half-remembered lessons from a card-sharper; but for Vallance's precautions; but for Gala's head for figures; but for a whole pattern of tiny circumstances, a whole pattern of chance.

Whose pattern?

There was a shrill squeak as M's chair swivelled round. Bond carefully focused again on the grey eyes across the desk.

'That was the Prime Minister,' M said gruffly. 'Says he wants you and Miss Brand out of the country.' M lowered his eyes and looked stolidly into the bowl of his pipe. 'You're both to be out by tomorrow afternoon. There are too many people in this case who know your faces. Might put two and two together, when they see the shape you're both in. Go anywhere you like. Unlimited expenses for both of you. Any currency you like. I'll tell the Paymaster. Stay away for a month. But keep out of circulation. You'd both be gone this afternoon only the girl's got an appointment at eleven tomorrow morning. At the Palace. Immediate award of the George Cross. Won't be gazetted until the New Year of course. Like to meet her one day. Must be a good girl. As a matter of fact,' M's expression as he looked up was unreadable, 'the Prime Minister had something in mind for you. Forgotten that we don't go in for those sort of things here. So he asked me to thank you for him. Said some nice things about the Service. Very kind of him.'

M gave one of the rare smiles that lit up his face

with quick brightness and warmth. Bond smiled back. They understood the things that had to be left unsaid.

Bond knew it was time to go. He got up. 'Thank you very much, sir,' he said. 'And I'm glad about the girl.'

'All right then,' said M on a note of dismissal. 'Well, that's the lot. See you in a month. Oh and by the way,' he added casually. 'Call in at your office. You'll find something there from me. Little memento.'

James Bond went down in the lift and limped along the familiar corridor to his office. When he walked through the inner door he found his secretary arranging some papers on the next desk to his.

'008 coming back?' he asked.

'Yes,' she smiled happily. 'He's being flown out tonight.'

'Well, I'm glad you'll have company,' said Bond. 'I'm going off again.'

'Oh,' she said. She looked quickly at his face and then away. 'You look as if you needed a bit of a rest.'

'I'm going to get one,' said Bond. 'A month's exile.' He thought of Gala. 'It's going to be pure holiday. Anything for me?'

'Your new car's downstairs. I've inspected it. The man said you'd ordered it on trial this morning. It looks lovely. Oh, and there's a parcel from M's office. Shall I unpack it?'

'Yes, do,' said Bond.

He sat down at his desk and looked at his watch. Five o'clock. He was feeling tired. He knew he was going to feel tired for several days. He always got these reactions at the end of an ugly assignment, the aftermath of days of taut nerves, tension, fear.

His secretary came back into the room with two heavy-looking cardboard boxes. She put them on his desk and he opened the top one. When he saw the grease-paper he knew what to expect.

There was a card in the box. He took it out and read it. In M's green ink it said: 'You may be needing these.' There was no signature.

Bond unwrapped the grease-paper and cradled the shining new Beretta in his hand. A memento. No. A reminder. He shrugged his shoulders and slipped the gun under his coat into the empty holster. He got clumsily to his feet.

'There'll be a long-barrel Colt in the other box,' he said to his secretary. 'Keep it until I get back. Then I'll take it down to the range and fire it in.'

He walked to the door. 'So long, Lil,' he said, 'regards to 008 and tell him to be careful of you. I'll be in France. Station F will have the address. But only in an emergency.'

She smiled at him. 'How much of an emergency?' she asked.

Bond gave a short laugh. 'Any invitation to a quiet game of bridge,' he said.

He limped out and shut the door behind him.

The 1953 Mark VI had an open touring body. It was battleship grey like the old 4½ litre that had gone to its grave in a Maidstone garage, and the dark blue leather upholstery gave a luxurious hiss as he climbed awkwardly in beside the test driver.

Half an hour later the driver helped him out at the corner of Birdcage Walk and Queen Anne's Gate. 'We could get more speed out of her if you want it, sir,' he said. 'If we could have her back for a fortnight we could tune her to do well over the hundred.'

'Later,' said Bond. 'She's sold. On one condition. That you get her over to the ferry terminal at Calais by tomorrow evening.'

The test driver grinned. 'Roger,' he said. 'I'll take her over myself. See you on the pier, sir.'

'Fine,' said Bond. 'Go easy on A20. The Dover road's a dangerous place these days.'

'Don't worry, sir,' said the driver, thinking that this man must be a bit of a cissy for all that he seemed to know plenty about motor-cars. 'Piece of cake.'

'Not every day,' said Bond with a smile. 'See you at Calais.'

Without waiting for a reply, he limped off with his stick through the dusty bars of evening sunlight that filtered down through the trees in the park.

Bond sat down on one of the seats opposite the island in the lake and took out his cigarette-case and lit a cigarette. He looked at his watch. Five minutes to six. He reminded himself that she was the sort of girl who would be punctual. He had reserved the corner table for dinner. And then? But first there would be the long luxurious planning. What would she like? Where would she like to go? Where had she ever been? Germany, of course. France? Miss out Paris. They could do that on their way back. Get as far as they could the first night, away from the Pas de Calais. There was that farmhouse with the wonderful food between Montreuil and Etaples. Then the fast sweep down to the Loire. The little places near the river for a few days. Not the château towns. Places like Beaugency, for instance. Then slowly south, always keeping to the western roads, avoiding the five-star life. Slowly exploring. Bond pulled himself up. Exploring what? Each other? Was he getting serious about this girl?

'James.'

It was a clear, high, rather nervous voice. Not the voice he had expected.

He looked up. She was standing a few feet away from him. He noticed that she was wearing a black beret at a rakish angle and that she looked exciting and mysterious like someone you see driving by abroad, alone in an open car, someone unattainable and more desirable than anyone you have ever known. Someone who is on her way to make love to somebody else. Someone who is not for you.

He got up and they took each other's hands.

It was she who released herself. She didn't sit down.

'I wish you were going to be there tomorrow, James.' Her eyes were soft as she looked at him. Soft, but, he thought, somehow evasive.

He smiled. 'Tomorrow morning or tomorrow night?'

'Don't be ridiculous,' she laughed, blushing. 'I meant at the Palace.'

'What are you going to do afterwards?' asked Bond. She looked at him carefully. What did the look remind him of? The Morphy look? The look he had given Drax on that last hand at Blades? No. Not quite. There was something else there. Tenderness? Regret?

She looked over his shoulder.

Bond turned round. A hundred yards away there was the tall figure of a young man with fair hair trimmed short. His back was towards them and he was idling along, killing time.

Bond turned back and Gala's eyes met his squarely.

'I'm going to marry that man,' she said quietly. 'Tomorrow afternoon.' And then, as if no other explanation was needed, 'His name's Detective-Inspector Vivian.'

'Oh,' said Bond. He smiled stiffly. 'I see.'

There was a moment of silence during which their eyes slid away from each other.

And yet why should he have expected anything else? A kiss. The contact of two frightened bodies clinging together in the midst of danger. There had been nothing more. And there had been the engagement ring to tell him. Why had he automatically assumed that it had only been worn to keep Drax at bay? Why had he imagined that she shared his desires, his plans?

And now what? wondered Bond. He shrugged his

shoulders to shift the pain of failure – the pain of failure that is so much greater than the pleasure of success. The exit line. He must get out of these two young lives and take his cold heart elsewhere. There must be no regrets. No false sentiment. He must play the role which she expected of him. The tough man of the world. The Secret Agent. The man who was only a silhouette.

She was looking at him rather nervously, waiting to be relieved of the stranger who had tried to get his foot in the door of her heart.

Bond smiled warmly at her. 'I'm jealous,' he said. 'I had other plans for you tomorrow night.'

She smiled back at him, grateful that the silence had been broken. 'What were they?' she asked.

'I was going to take you off to a farmhouse in France,' he said. 'And after a wonderful dinner I was going to see if it's true what they say about the scream of a rose.'

She laughed. 'I'm sorry I can't oblige. But there are plenty of others waiting to be picked.'

'Yes, I suppose so,' said Bond. 'Well, goodbye, Gala.' He held out his hand.

'Goodbye, James.'

He touched her for the last time and then they turned away from each other and walked off into their different lives.